Word to Death

A White House Dollhouse Mystery

Barbara Schlichting

Word to Death

Barbara Schlichting

Word to Death

Copyright © 2019 by Barbara Schlichting

Formatting by Rik – Wild Seas Formatting

ISBN: 978-1-7338897-9-7

First Lady Press

I dedicate this book to all the First Ladies.
Bless them for all they've done for our country.

Other titles by Barb

Single titles
THE BROKEN CIRCLE

White House Dollhouse Mystery Series
SPANGLED to Death
WORD to Death
Clued to Death
SUFFRAGETTE to DEATH

HISTORICAL FICTION
BODY ON THE TRACKS

POETRY
WHISPERS FROM THE WIND
Blood Red
Bike With Me

PICTURE BOOKS
Red Shoes by Barbie Marie
Martha Washington: HER FIRST FEW DAYS AS FIRST LADY

NON-FICTION
Immigrant Snap Chat

You may write to Barbara Schlichting at schlichtingbarb@gmail.com.

You may also contact her through her website. www.barbaraschlichting.com.

If you so choose, you may sign up for the newsletter on the website.

Chapter One

I expected Blanche at any moment, the Mary Lincoln impersonator from the Mary Todd Lincoln House in Lexington, Kentucky. Blanche needed a place to dress for the afternoon engagement at Inga's Antique Store, located at the end of the same block as my own shop. I own the White House Dollhouse Store in downtown Minneapolis, so it seemed fitting that she should dress here. Blanche's grand entrance for the tea party and diary reading would delight the audience.

Putting on my own period dress had taken all morning. The crinoline and hoop made me almost nuts from all the pulling, straightening, and latching. Fortunately, Inga had loaned me a shoe hook, which worked nicely.

The skirt swept across the floor as I walked around the showroom, circling my dollhouses carefully. "I'm busy this afternoon ladies, but Grandma will tend to things," I told the miniature dolls. Dolley Madison was my favorite, not only because of being distantly related, but because she had so much personality and character. Glancing at the nearest modern-day White House, I commanded, "Laura, stand straighter." I picked up First Lady Laura and set her closer to President Bush. "Much better." The overhead doorbell rang, and a short woman the size of Mary Lincoln walked in toting a very large hatbox.

"Hi! You must be Blanche. I'm Liv, and let me help you. I'll get Max to carry in your remaining boxes."

"Thank you," Blanche said. She glanced around the store. "What lovely miniature period White House dollhouses. I love them. You must show them to me before I leave tonight."

I thought her southern accent charming. "Thanks! I'd be glad to show you around after the shindig is over. I have Tad's play uniform and other Lincoln memorabilia left for unpacking later to share." I took the box out of her hands. "Follow me into the back room. That's where you'll dress."

"Max," I said, "how about running out and carrying in the other large box with her dress? She's right out front." I set the hatbox down on the counter. It was large enough to mail a large nest of baby chicks or a potted plant.

"Sure," Max said. "I think you should really park out back. It will be easier for you to return your costume to the car later."

"You're right," Blanche said. She handed him the keys then placed her briefcase and purse on the counter.

"It's a little dusty in here but not bad. Max carves the doll heads at those benches and lives upstairs. At the moment, he's carving Eleanor Roosevelt's head. He and Grandma will mind the store while we're at Inga's shop."

"You look magnificent, by the way," Blanche said.

"Thanks. I'm looking forward to the afternoon." I made a slight curtsey.

It wasn't long before Max had the remaining boxes stacked on the counter.

"I'm going upstairs but won't be gone long," Max said. He handed Blanche the car keys.

"Changing room?"

"Oh, right. Across, in here." I pointed to the restroom. "It's small, that's why you'll have to dress in this room. The back door is locked. You can leave your things here during the engagement. I'll be in the showroom if you need anything."

"Okay. I'll get started."

This short moment left me time to leave a note for Grandma.

> A.   Dust if time.
> B.   First Lady Wilson should be visible and out of the bedroom.
> C.   First Lady Nixon needs a hair tune-up.
> D.   Do you have time to:
>   A – Y or N?
>   B – Y or N?
>   C – Y or N?

I busied myself after that by reading through my latest emails until I heard Blanche call my name. I went to see how she was doing.

"Please help me hook the hoop before I break something!"

"Sure." I helped her adjust and latch things up. "Almost ready for the shoes." Together, we pulled the dress down over her shoulders and fanned it out over the hoop. "You're even wearing pantaloons! I'm impressed."

"This Victorian style dress is horrible."

"True. Thank heavens it's outdated."

"Anyway," Blanche said, "we can talk while I'll fix my hair."

I followed her across the hallway and stood outside of the bathroom as she swirled her hair into a bun.

"Ever heard of the Lost Speech?" Blanche asked. I shook my head and she explained. "The Lost Speech of Abraham Lincoln has never been found. I received an email from a close historian friend who believes it's still within reach, like it's ripe for discovery." She pushed in a hairpin. "There's also a newly found letter of Mary Lincoln's at the Presidential Library. They, of course, notified The Mary Todd Lincoln House. I'm going online to search for the speech once I return home."

"I've never heard of the Lost Speech." I cocked my head.

The letter piqued my interest also.

"I should show you the puzzle from her published diary. Mary Todd Lincoln's diary, that is. I brought a stack of copies and left them for sale at Inga's. The puzzle is made of letters arranged within circles. Most unusual."

"Do you have a picture of the puzzle?"

"Yes. I'm excited to show someone." Blanche opened her laptop and brought up an image. Rings of letters circled smaller rings, and in turn were circled by rings yet larger.

"Wow," I said. "This picture looks like the puzzles that Luke has at his coffee house, Brew Café, two doors down."

"Goodness. I should like to see them."

"I'm not sure if they're a perfect match, but close," I said. A thought came suddenly to me. "Wow, that speech would be worth a fortune, wouldn't it?"

"It certainly would be. People might even kill for it."

I shook my head. "I have to admit that I've never heard of it, and I have a doctorate in American History."

"What was your specialty?"

"The first ladies."

"Then your store certainly makes sense. I'm going over to that café now, and then head to Inga's. It's the only available spare time before my flight leaves, unless there's a few minutes after the tea."

"Sure, go right ahead. Don't forget to turn sideways as you enter and be ready for a few gawkers!"

"I'll tell them I'm Mary Lincoln's ghost!"

"Grandma should be walking in any minute. I'll meet you at Inga's."

The front bell rang.

"She's here. See you in a bit."

If anyone saw us embrace, they would've thought it hilarious. Two women wearing hoops! We must've looked like two question marks embracing with our butts sticking out.

I went out to the showroom. "Hi, Grandma," I said, bending over to give her a peck on the cheek and raising my hoops again. "Thanks. I left you a note of things to do." I grabbed a heavy shawl to wrap over my shoulders. "Max should be down shortly. He's right upstairs if you need anything."

"Don't worry. I know how to stay busy. Have fun," Grandma said. "It's getting slippery, so Grandpa may pick me up early."

"That's fine." I adored my grandparents, who raised me from the age of eleven when my parents were killed in a car accident. Last year, Grandpa walked me down the aisle when I married Aaron. Since then, Aaron and I moved to another location which was closer to my business. I could walk to it, weather permitting.

The weather was terribly cold, and I had to steady myself on the icy sidewalk to Inga's.

As I walked, men stepped sideways to allow more room to pass and nodded. Women smiled. One woman stopped me, and said I reminded her of Charlotte Bronte.

The warmth inside Inga's store greeted me as I entered.

Because of the hoop and crinoline, it was difficult to squeeze myself behind the counter. Holly, Inga's young employee, also wore a period dress, though my fingers itched to yank out her nose and hoop earrings. Meanwhile, Inga greeted her guests–mostly local historians and Civil War buffs. She had prepared a stylish offering of tea and scones as part of the festivities for the afternoon. I stood next to the counter where stacked copies of Mary Lincoln's diary were displayed and picked one up to ensure I got a copy before they were all purchased. I paid Holly, slid the receipt inside, and tucked it under the counter to take home later.

Inga swept up just then.

"You look great in that dress, Inga. You're the spitting image of Mrs. Lincoln." I looked around. "Where's Luke? I don't see him."

"He had to return to his café for a minute, but an employee is still here. She's that young Asian woman over there, helping to serve the refreshments. He said she's his cousin from Cambodia. Luke and his wife certainly seem to have a lot of cousins."

Someone waved to her from across the room. Inga waved back, and then confided in me. "It's a great crowd, but they're keeping me busy." A door slammed somewhere. "Oh, that's the back door." She looked around the corner. "Yes, Luke's back."

Mrs. Olson interrupted our privacy in her usual style. "Goodness, Inga, you look just like our famous First Lady." She picked up the china plate and silvered fork. "Is it true she was very short?"

"Only five feet, two inches tall," Inga agreed. She began pouring tea for guests. "Go ahead and mingle, Liv."

I began the process of turning around, not an easy thing to do when wearing a hoop.

"No, wait," said Inga. "Where is Blanche?" She glanced at the nearest clock. "She should have been here by now."

"That's true." I backed out from behind the counter to join the guests. "I'll text Max and Grandma. They might know." Within a few seconds Grandma's reply came:

> *Don't know. She never returned for her hat. Grandpa circled the block and came back for me. I have to leave. He's having a terrible time driving. Talk later.*

That made sense. She had her laptop and probably didn't want the bother of holding onto the hat in the wind. Still, she should've been here. Perplexed, I went to the window to look outside, but few people were stirring in such awful weather.

"I wonder where she's at?" Holly said. She'd joined me.

"Do you think something happened?" I asked her.

"I hope not. The weather's awful out there."

I walked over to Inga and whispered, "Grandma doesn't know where she is."

Inga looked at me and then turned away to finish pouring tea for a woman, then she beckoned me toward a quieter area.

"Something isn't right," Inga said. "I can feel it in my bones." Inga is one of Grandma's oldest friends, at least sixty years of friendship. I suspect she still regards me as a child to be commanded. "Go investigate."

"Plan to."

It was well after the event's starting time of two o'clock by the time I was finished dressing for going outside. I opened the door and the frigid air took my breath away. A crowd of people was gathered at the end of the block, which was odd, considering the bitter cold.

My full skirts swayed backwards against the powerful north wind. Sirens blared from a distance, becoming louder, propelling me to hurry. I slipped, barely catching myself. My hoops worked to my advantage and I easily pushed through the crowd. As soon as I saw the heavy, full skirt billowing from the wind, I knew who it was.

"Blanche!" I shouted, kneeling down. "Oh dear God! Did someone call an ambulance?" It seemed as if her neck was at an odd angle. I took off my mittens and took her hands in mine to warm them. "Blanche? Speak to me."

The crowd jostled me and made it hard to take care of her, plus my attire was in the way. Soon two police officers stood over me.

"Liv?"

"Aaron?" My husband, a police officer, was first on the scene. "Thank God, you're here."

"Let us take over. Go to the store and stay." Aaron held out his hand and helped me to stand. "Don't worry. An ambulance will soon be here."

"Okay." I nodded, turned, and fled to my store.

I quickly punched in the security code and entered. I made a beeline to the back room where I fumbled with the ties and tangled strings of my dress until at last I stepped out of it. I was thankful I hadn't tied anything into double knots. Though in a hurry, I took time to hang the dress properly. The dress had belonged to Mary Lincoln. I had purchased it recently when an assortment of her dresses were sold on an online auction. She wore it after she had served as First Lady, so the value was much lower than I'd expected. It seemed we were similar in height but not girth. She had to have weighed much more than me — otherwise I would never have been able to get into it.

I glanced down the street when dressed. People were coming and going. Holly walked past, and so did Luke. The sirens blared louder. Police car lights flashed along the blocked street, and rings of spectators huddled together to stare down the street.

Two detectives headed my way and I waited for them to enter.

"Liv Reynolds, Aaron's wife," I said.

"Detective Mergens. Remember me from the other case?" He showed his badge.

"Yes, of course. And Detective Erlandsen." "What can you tell me?"

"Her name is Blanche. She's a Mary Lincoln impersonator. Is she going to be all right?" I glanced toward the back room. "Come with me. Some of her stuff is in the back room."

They followed me to the room.

"What happened?" I asked. *Was it possible she might have a broken neck, since the angle of her head seemed odd? Something didn't seem right about the scene.* "She's a representative from the Mary Todd Lincoln House in Lexington, Kentucky. They could tell you more." Tears filled my eyes.

"Are you saying she's from out of state?"

"She was invited to an event here, to read from Mary Lincoln's diary at Inga's down the street..." I trailed off for a moment. "She's dead, isn't she?"

He continued to ignore my questions. "Inga from the antique store?"

"What? Oh, yes." I wiped my eyes. "Sure, that Inga. She gave a tea and had invited Blanche."

"Anything else?"

"Take a look. Her hat is still here. This is where she dressed. That's her purse, but she had her laptop with her."

"We'll have to look into that," Erlandsen said and made a note.

"Hate to bother you, but," Mergens said, "can we use your store for a base for a while?"

"Sure."

"We'll probably need to warm up. Got coffee?"

"Okay, I'll put on a pot."

"Leave everything of hers as it is while we're gone," Mergens said.

The two detectives left.

Naturally, curiosity got the best of me. I felt drawn to Blanche's hatbox. It was made of heavy cardboard that was gray with age. Peering closer, I noted that dirty smudges abounded, but were smoothed over. Inside the first box, I found jagged handwriting, reminiscent of an elderly person's script. The written name was Mrs. Tindall. The smeared ink was right beside a miniature drawing of a staircase, yet another thing to pique my interest. I grabbed for a blank sheet of paper from the printer on the counter and quickly made a sketch before replacing the lid. I slid the sheet inside of my cash drawer just as the police entered.

The name of Mrs. Tindall was familiar, but I couldn't place it. I pondered the question of who she was as the coffee brewed.

Chapter Two

The temperature continued to drop outside, bottoming out at twenty below zero when I left for home. The tires on my car squeaked as I drove into the garage stall. I stepped inside the house and shed my coat and other items. A nice hot shower was in order.

Aaron would be home shortly, so I made cups of hot chocolate for us, placing his on the counter before heading down the hall to the bedroom. I could hardly wait for the January thaw. No, skip that, July sounded even better.

By the time I'd toweled dry and pulled on my flannel snuggies, Aaron had brought his cup to the living room and was enjoying it. He set the cup beside him on the coffee table.

"You're beautiful. Did you know that?" His blue eyes glistened, and he looked so tired. "The police thanked me for the use of the store and fresh coffee. They wanted to make sure I told you."

"Sure. No trouble." I finished my cup of hot chocolate and set it down. "I'm beat." I smoothed down his messy brown hair. "How did she die?"

"That's the million dollar question," Aaron replied, pulling me closer. "But we don't think it was accidental."

"Why?" I stared into his eyes and yawned. "Tell me more."

"Head trauma," he said, yawning. "Ongoing

investigation, Miss Nosy."

"Give me a break. Blanche's death is frightening. She was a nice lady." I frowned. "This sounds like déjà vu."

"Let's hope not," Aaron said.

"Let's throw in a movie," I said. "It's too cold to be outside, and we can't do much of anything else."

"I'll find a comedy."

We spent the rest of the afternoon and into the evening watching television and waiting for a police call.

"I'm hitting the sack," Aaron finally said.

"I'll join you."

Taking my hand, we went down the hall to the bedroom. After jumping into bed, he kissed me goodnight, shut the light off, and pulled up the covers.

"Night, baby."

Aaron fell asleep immediately. I stared at him in the dark, wondering how he could do that after working a crime scene. I certainly couldn't sleep. At four in the morning, I got up to peer out the window. A white blanket of snow glistened under the streetlights — all was still and peaceful. But instead of enjoying the beauty in front of me, my thoughts went to Blanche and how fun she had been to talk with. I felt sick about her death.

I pictured her body, remembering the manner in which she lay. It appeared as if she'd fallen on the ice. If not for the recent snowfall, the sidewalks would have been empty of snow, with little ice underfoot. Slipping didn't fit the scenario, even though everything gets icier as the temperature drops. I figured she'd fallen and struck her head, and that caused her to black out. I had never heard of anyone slipping and falling, and then dying from it, but supposed it could happen. But, why didn't someone find her sooner? Unless it wasn't an accident, and there was someone nearby who did it. That notion didn't sit well with me. I wanted to think of my street as a safe area. Blanche was relatively young, forties maybe. If she had been in her seventies or eighties, then slipping and falling might have rung true. I shook my head and tried to make sense of it, but couldn't. Why would anyone want to kill her? It couldn't be for her laptop, could it? I'd have to mull it over later.

I thought about the concentric puzzle pages in the diary and about Abraham Lincoln and the Lost Speech. Where was it after all these years? I made a mental note to research it when given the first chance.

I crawled back to bed with two thoughts spinning through my head — where the Lost Speech might be and that Blanche had possibly been murdered. *Could Blanche have been killed because of what she knew about the Lost Speech??*

A frosty morning chilled me to the bone when I slipped out from under the bedcovers. I smelled bacon frying, and I heard Aaron preparing breakfast in the kitchen.

I went over the events from the day as I dressed. My curly red hair was especially unruly, and I finally gave up and tied it back into a ponytail. I hastened down the hall to the kitchen and reached for a hot cup of coffee.

"Morning. What time did you get up? I didn't sleep very well." Aaron stood a few inches taller, and I always felt like an imp beside him. I looked upward as he leaned over for a kiss, which gave me comfort and settled my anxiety about Blanche.

"Suspected as much." Aaron set the plate heaping with fried bacon on the table before cracking a couple of eggs. "I don't work until later today, so I'll take you to work. I want to make sure the security system works as it should."

"Thanks. I didn't want to be alone. Can you imagine? Another dead body, and I was just getting over the last one." I shook my head and reached for a tissue. "Blanche seemed like such a nice person." I blew my nose. "She wanted to see my houses, and I had those new toys to show her that are part of the display."

"Everyone likes the houses." Aaron dished up the eggs. "Want toast?" I went for the bread since I knew my way around a toaster.

"Sure. Let's just eat up. It may be a long day." He began to eat.

I dropped two slices down and buttered them when they popped up, setting them on the table. "You're probably right." I dug into my egg while pondering the situation. "What I don't understand is, why Blanche?"

"That's what the detectives aim to find out. They

took the dress and the hat. They'll be contacting Inga soon, if they haven't already, plus the people at the Mary Lincoln House. Possibly the Lexington police department also. Electronics are stolen all the time, so it depends on where the investigation leads. Her laptop could show up." Aaron cocked his head, and asked, "Do you know what was on the laptop?"

"A concentric puzzle similar to Luke's. That's why she went to the Brew Café, to see what his puzzles looked like. I wonder if she managed to talk with Luke? I meant to ask him, but Luke wasn't at Inga's when I arrived, something about having to fetch something from his café."

"Did you tell that to the detectives?"

I thought back. "Only about the laptop, I didn't mention Luke."

"You'll have to tell them. I don't hear much because it's their case."

"I didn't know much about her."

"True, neither you nor Inga knew her, except from e-mails and meeting yesterday," Aaron said as he helped himself to the other half my toast.

"I feel bad about the whole thing. I especially wanted her to see that uniform of Tad's." I checked the clock. "It's time to go." I finished my last bite and brought both plates to the sink. "I'm glad you're taking me to work and staying for awhile. I feel quite unsettled." I took a deep breath. "Ready to go?"

"Just a sec."

While he took care of a few matters, I dressed in my heavy coat and scarf, boots and mittens. With my bag over my shoulder, I was ready when he returned. It didn't take long for Aaron to slip into his outerwear.

"Set. Let's go," Aaron said.

The icy snow squeaked and scrunched under our tires as we drove up Main Street. Last night's three-inch accumulation of snow covered tree branches, making the scene picture perfect. Straight down from my store was the old Stone Arch Bridge, a Minneapolis landmark. Frost covered the bricks and beneath the bridge, the Mississippi River was iced over—unusual for a river of that magnitude. As Aaron parked in back of the store, I noticed Max's truck was gone.

"I wonder if Max knows what happened or if he saw anything?" I yawned.

"Good question, but there he is now." Aaron nodded toward the alley where Max's truck had appeared, coming from around the corner. "He must've had a hot date."

"We'll see." We climbed from the car and waited for him to park and get out of his truck. "Did you hear about Blanche?" I asked him, wrapping my arm within Aaron's for added warmth. "Nope... why?" Max looked haggard. "I left when Marie did."

"That's right. Grandma left early. Grandpa had circled the block and returned right away for her because of the roads."

"August ushered her out, and I locked up. I got a call and had to leave. Figured it'd be all right." His eyes were tired and his whiskers needed attention. If I didn't know better, I would think he hadn't shaved for two days, yet yesterday he looked fine. "Got caught up with something last night, so don't look at me like that." He stared back at me. "I had to take over an all-night gas station because Phil got sick."

"Sorry," I said. "It's freezing out here. Let's go inside, and we'll fill you in." We marched to the door where I punched in the code. "Didn't work. Must be the cold." I punched the numbers in once again, more slowly, and then finally we were allowed entrance. "Yikes! This cold weather affects everything."

Still shivering, we stomped the snow from our shoes and removed our jackets, hanging them up on the clothes tree inside the workroom door. Aaron flicked on the overhead light, and Max plunked onto one of several stools arranged around the work counter. It was Max's favorite spot. If not there carving doll's heads, he'd be in his apartment working on the dollhouses, doing such delicate tasks as assembling windows and frames or fencing.

"So, you didn't hear what happened?"

"Not really. I heard that the body of a woman was found at the end of the block but not much else." Max stared at me, raising his eyebrow. "Don't tell me. Not another? Oh, for crying out loud." He reached for his pack of smokes, and then slid them back in his pocket. He knew he couldn't light up due to so many wooden pieces and sawdust in the workroom. "Let's hear it."

"The victim was Blanche. She never made it to the tea."

"The 911 call is also being tracked. No clue yet about who made it," Aaron added. "The detectives are still questioning people. They talked with both Luke and Holly last night. Throw in a victim from out-of-state, and it gets tough to maneuver."

"It can't be as bad as the other murder." I looked around the room at the shelves filled with our inventory of dolls, dollhouses, and parts. "I plan to do a Google search on Blanche, just to see what I can learn about her, plus send a message to the House, to tell them I'm here if they need anything."

"The House?"

"Mary Todd Lincoln House."

"That would be nice, but don't interfere, Liv." Max drummed his fingers on the counter. "We don't want a repeat of the last time."

"Don't worry. Not gonna happen." I had narrowly escaped being murdered by someone who was searching for the Dolley Madison family secret. "I did find something interesting last night."

"Here it goes." Aaron looked at me and rolled his eyes. "Something from a long time ago?"

"The detectives left Blanche's hat because she wasn't wearing it. I looked inside the lid and found a drawing of a staircase. I copied the drawing and stuck the copy inside the cash register drawer last night. I'll get it in just a minute."

"Here... we... go," Max said.

"Staircase? That almost sounds like it could be a symbol for something. Hmm," Aaron said. "Don't go looking for trouble, dear."

"Glad we're on the same side." Max coursed his fingers through his thick, brown, wavy hair. "I hope it wasn't a murder."

"I noticed that her neck was at an odd angle." I sat down.

"That's how I knew there was something wrong."

"Drop it Liv. You're asking for trouble. Let the professionals do their stuff." Aaron waited a moment then continued, "It seems that right now it's considered a robbery gone sour."

"I'd rather skip this subject at the moment, at least until we hear the verdict—murder or an accident." The thought of another murder at my doorstep gave me the heebie-jeebies. "You two can keep talking if you want. I've got work to do. I'm going to get ready for today's opening." I got up and leaned over and gave Aaron a kiss. I grabbed the *Pennies for Our Troops* jar and headed into the showroom. "Who wants to shovel?" I hollered. "The sidewalks need it."

"Yep, got it," Aaron hollered back. He followed with the shovel in hand and headed right out the front door.

I flipped on the light switch and set the jar down before starting the computer. I saw from the checklist that Grandma had dusted. Then I circled the room, making sure the houses were as they should be. "Mrs. Kennedy, I certainly understand why you didn't want people in the White House. You must protect the children and your privacy." I straightened her pink pillbox hat. "Mrs. Roosevelt, Edith, however did you manage with Teddy's interest in hunting? The bearskin rug is huge." Finished, I headed for the computer. After logging into my accounts, I decided I should give Inga a call before it became busy.

"Inga? Liv here." I recited what was known about the investigation. After, she told me the police had called to arrange a time for an interview with her. We mutually agreed to keep the other informed on the matter and hung up.

The door opened and Aaron walked back inside. "That didn't take long," I said.

"Nope. Such a mess last night, the sidewalk only needed scraping." He walked toward the back. "I'm calling the station for an update on Blanche."

"Good."

I clicked on the House bookmark and went to their website. After finding a contact link, I sent a message letting them know what happened to Blanche, that the police were holding onto her period dress, and I had her hat. I also let them know if they needed any help with anything, I was available. After sending the message, I got up and unlocked the front door.

No sooner had I turned the sign to *Open* than my cell phone rang. It was Grandma, and I told her the whole sordid story. As soon as I had disconnected, with the same promise of keeping her informed, Aaron reentered the room. His grave expression sent goose pimples up and down my spine.

"It's definitely murder." He studied me. "Broken neck."

"Oh, my God. That's awful." I plunked down in my chair.

My heart began beating hard and fast. "Poor Blanche. She didn't deserve for this to happen. What an awfully terrible way to die."

"We'll get him. You are to stay out of it." Aaron placed his hand on my shoulder. "Right?"

"I know. It's just so awful." I sighed. "I need something hot to drink. That'll settle me, I think." I knew it wouldn't shove Blanche's image from my mind, but maybe it'd soothe my nerves. "So I was right about the neck angle."

"No comment," Aaron said. "The detectives will re-interview the most likely suspects, only this time the questions will be tougher to answer."

"I feel miserable," I said. "I want to know who they are. I have an idea."

"No Liv, you're not getting involved." He released his hold.

"I'll try not to." As I stood, I glanced at the time.

"Oops! I almost forgot. Let me call to see if the order of cookies for the First Lady birthday celebration is ready. Will you pick it up for me, if it is?" I quickly phoned the bakery and slipped the phone back into my pocket. "It's boxed — all twelve dozen cookies. The baker made an assortment of cutout houses and ladies."

"Okay. I'll return with the hot chocolate before going to get the cookies."

"Thank you." I sank into my chair once again, leaned my head into the palms of my hands and closed my eyes. I listened to the front door opening and closing.

My inbox tinged, and I opened the new message. It was from the House. The responder was Frances, and she thanked me for writing. We vowed to stay in touch. I looked up as Max entered and said, "I'm glad you're here. This is a terrible thing to have happened."

"At least it was outside the store—not inside this time. That's one thing going for us."

"I'm going to do a Google search on her—Blanche. She was certainly quite knowledgeable." I did a quick search on her. While the computer did its work, I mentioned, "Blanche spoke of a speech that Abraham Lincoln gave that was never completely transcribed by reporters. Ever hear of the Lost Speech before?"

"Nope." Max shook his head.

"Ah, here it is." A website came up. "It says she taught at the university and was an authority on Lincoln's speeches. She had recently focused her research on the Lost Speech. That's interesting."

"What are you getting at?" Aaron asked.

"Well, for one thing, why hasn't the speech ever been found?" I asked.

"Not this again," Max said.

"Her website features images of Tad's toys. One is of a very cute stuffed bear, identical to the one on display at the House." I switched back to the House website and clicked on the e-mail for Frances. "I'm going to ask if it's for sale. She also has a miniature dollhouse for sale that would fit my collection. I should purchase one, to put in our display."

"Whatever. I'm going back to work." Max left the show room.

I sent the message and glanced around the room. I wondered where a shelf would fit to display the three

First Lady miniature houses I owned. For Christmas, three years in a row, I had received one. Mary Lincoln's house would look spectacular beside the other three historical White Houses from the era of Madison, Adams and Jefferson. I sure would have liked that stuffed bear of Tad's, if it was for sale.

Blanche and I shared interests, hopefully, not the same fate.

Chapter Three

Grandma and Grandpa entered the store, and I fell into their arms. "There, there, now curly-top, tell us all about it," Grandpa said.

"It was horrible. Another murder and right outside my door!"

Disbelief filled my mind as I recounted the story.

"You'll be fine, sweetheart," Grandma said. "Let me see your beautiful eyes."

We broke apart for them to look at me.

"Where's Aaron?" Grandma asked.

"He went for the First Lady cookies."

"We'll talk at home." Grandpa steered Grandma toward the back hallway.

"Wait a sec, you old coot!" Grandma stopped to give me a kiss.

"Thank you."

My heart beat peacefully as customers walked through the doorway. "Hello. How may I help you?"

The lady's pink-tipped nose glistened from the heat. She wore a tightly fitted jacket, knit pants, and boots.

"Are you interested in the Teddy Roosevelt display?" I asked since we were standing next to the TR White House.

"Actually, I'm more interested in recent First Ladies. Barbara Bush, was my favorite," the young woman answered. Her eyes watered from the cold.

"She's such a great grandma, isn't she? Breaking bones while sliding with grandchildren. I want to be just like her someday."

"Only not break the bones," I said. My cellphone dinged, alerting me to a new message.

"Exactly." She grinned. "Mrs. Bush was always charming to everyone. She reminded me of Dolley Madison. I bet she baked cookies for her grandkids right there in the White House kitchen."

"That is entirely possible!" This customer made me feel warm all over. She reminded me of a well-liked grade school teacher that I once had. Mrs. Wheeler was full of that same energy and spunk. "Tell me more about Barbara Bush," she commanded with a smile.

"Well," I answered as I guided the customer toward the Bush White House. "Most everyone likes the First Ladies; it's the presidents that people have trouble with." I began telling her about the features that were the essence of Barbara. "She was so kind to everyone. She supported literacy, helped the homeless, the elderly, school volunteer programs, and people afflicted with the AIDS virus. She was refreshingly human."

"Oh, don't stop. I want to hear more."

"First Lady Barbara Bush went to classrooms and read to the children."

"Continue," the woman said.

"They had six children with one passing away at three years old from leukemia. Mrs. Bush watched as her daughter's spirit left her body. Her name was Robin."

"That is something I didn't know. Poor Barbara." She stooped and peered closely. "Tell me about the White House during her time there."

"During her years in office, the president signed legislation for the American Disability Act." This customer was making me work for the sale. I filled her with more tidbits about other administrations until my mind was taxed, and she made a purchase at last. I was pleased to notice she also dropped a ten into the *Pennies* jar. She left with the George H. W. Bush White House. Max helped load it into her van.

When the last box was carried out, Max came over to the counter. He pointed at the empty display where the dollhouse had been and grinned. "Makes it all worthwhile, doesn't it?"

"Yes. Selling one or two a day would allow me to pay my rent."

"It will come. Your name is getting out there. You've got a great website. You're honest, plus you know your stuff." He reached for his smokes. "People really like hearing little tidbits of info about the White House as well as the presidents who have lived in it. After all, it is sometimes referred to as the People's House."

"Exactly! But women like to hear about the First Ladies. They want to know what they stood for and how they helped the presidents or, like in Jackie Kennedy's case, how she restored the White House. The interest is there. People love the First Ladies."

"You can tell—by the gazillion questions you get." Max smiled. "I'm taking a break." I watched him go down the back hallway before turning to the computer.

I opened my messages to find a list from Grandma.

Is chicken soup still your favorite? Y or N If No, what is?
Pea Soup Vegetable

I typed *Y* and sent it.

Hearing a cough, I turned to see where it came from.

"Do you have a minute here, Liv?" Ronnie, a newspaper reporter, stood poised with his pen and paper, giving me a slight grin. In all the excitement about packing up the dollhouse, I hadn't noticed he had entered the store.

"Can you tell me about the woman who died? Where did she come from and exactly how did you know her? I promise to keep your name out of the paper, but I'm curious."

"Well, all right." Answering him would at least kill some time until my next customer arrived. "I don't really know much of anything about the case. I'm kept out of the loop because of Aaron being a cop. I really can't tell you anything, except that she's from Lexington, Kentucky, her name was Blanche, and she was a Mary Todd Lincoln impersonator." I walked to the front door and held it open for him. "Please, Ronnie, I really don't know anything else. I wish I did."

"I'll check in later. I need to advance my career. I would love a job with the *Tribune* instead of this rag. I think you know a few more things you aren't saying. As soon as the 'okay' is here, tell me." He snapped a few pictures before whisking out the door. "Reporters." I fumed. "Too bad, he's a grade school friend. I'd lock the door and throw away the key." I closed the door, crossed my arms, and stared up at the ceiling.

Inga breezed in the front door, along with a blast of frigid Arctic air just as I was about to sit down behind the front counter with plans to do more research.

"How's it going?" She looked like a cyclone had hit her, leading me to wonder if it was because of the wind or if she'd forgotten to comb her hair. It reminded me of a fluffy row of cotton balls. "The police questioned me. They asked every question imaginable about Blanche." She moved the penny jar aside and said, "Jar's almost filled. I hope they come soon for it. Better call Trisha." She leaned into the counter. "I'm puzzled over this and also saddened. Why did it happen?"

"I agree. I thought about it all night long and came to no conclusion at all. If the killer wanted her laptop, why kill her? What would be the point?" I hesitated before continuing, "The police won't confirm she had her laptop. You saw her leave with it, didn't you?"

"She carried in the two cartons of books. That's all I know."

"The laptop is nowhere to be found. It's all a big mess," I said.

"I agree. Why kill for it?" Inga shook her head.

"I've got something weird to tell you, and you won't like it." She massaged her chin.

I didn't like the sound of this. The back of my neck tingled.

"Go ahead." I started to bite a nail, and then folded my hands together as a preventative measure. Customers noticed them when I pointed out details and furnishings.

"The few copies of the diary she'd left behind are gone—disappeared." Inga's eyes opened wide. "Does that make sense? There were only six, but they've been stolen."

"Did you tell the police?"

"I didn't think of it at the time, but I will when I return to the store," Inga said.

"Why would anyone take them except to make a profit? But it wouldn't be enough money to even make it worth their trouble. Interesting, indeed." I raised a brow.

It reminded me of the staircase drawing. "I have something to show you." I pulled out the cash drawer to remove the staircase sketch. "Look at this. I copied this from a drawing that was inside of the hatbox, which had the name Mrs. Tindall written on it. I finally remembered why I knew that name. Mary Lincoln used it after the assassination, when she tried to sell her clothes for money in New York City. The poor thing was dead broke."

I pointed to the drawing and asked, "Why would she draw a staircase?"

"Good question." Inga shook her head. "Was she

really off her rocker, that much? What in the world does it mean?" She stared at it. "And why would Mary Lincoln draw it on the hatbox rim...? Why would she?" She looked up at me. "I don't get it."

"Me neither. The same questions are going around in my head." Still puzzled, I glanced up to her. "I'll do a search on this. I'd like to know how a staircase and Mrs. Lincoln, alias Mrs. Tindall, go together. There must be a common thread here, but what?" I shook my head. "Mrs. Lincoln was close friends with her maid, too. Can't remember her name, but I know that they traveled together. The woman's name should be easily found. You never know where any of this will lead."

"When you find out, let me know." Inga glanced out the window then back to me. "Maybe it has something to do with the assassination? She and Mr. Lincoln did have to climb up a stairway to the presidential suite. Not like they had elevators."

"I know. Look." I pointed. "The lines between the platforms aren't evenly spaced. Let's see, they're called risers, aren't they?" The drawing had piqued my curiosity.

"Maybe it's symbolic of something else?"

"No idea," I said. I put the sketch away and changed the subject. "Who do you think killed Blanche?"

"So it was murder?" Inga asked.

"Yes," I said. "I'm of the opinion that the Lost Speech aroused curiosity."

"And curious enough to kill for it." Inga glanced at her cell phone. "Yikes! I'd better hike to the store to open for the day. It's already later than I usually arrive." She headed to the door.

"Hold on a sec." I stepped around toward her. "Tomorrow is my First Lady birthday celebration. I'm having trouble trying to decide where to serve the cookies. What's your opinion?"

"I like the idea of setting up a table right inside the door. They can see it from the outside. Doing that might bring in more walkers."

"Do you have a small table I can borrow?"

"Sure—I used it for the tea yesterday. Send Max or Aaron for it." As she opened the door, she said, "Keep me updated."

"Will do."

Before going back to the computer, I rearranged the showroom so the table would fit nicely in front of the window. Inga was right. It was a good spot for it. Next, I went to get the tablecloth, napkins, and paper cups I had purchased and set them under the counter to have ready. Just then, Aaron walked in the back door with the cookies.

"Bring them up here," I called.

"I tasted two, and they passed the test." He grinned, setting the two big white bakery boxes down. "Hey, the police department is putting together a group to play pond hockey. I asked them to include me. My goalie equipment is still in the basement, right?"

"Yep. When will you start playing games?"

"Next week. We'll practice tomorrow night. Want to join us for burgers? There will be plenty of company. Most of the guys' wives or girlfriends plan to watch us make fools of ourselves. It's at the indoor arena in Columbia Heights."

"Love to. Right after closing?"

"Certainly," he said, smiling. "What's my next errand?"

"Table from Inga."

"On my way."

He left through the front door. I turned my attention to the computer and searched *Lincoln staircase* to see if there was some meaning behind the drawing. It came up blank, and so I quit browsing and sent an e-mail to Inga.

> *Inga, I searched staircase on the Web and came up with nothing of importance, except how to construct one. Why would Mary need to know how to make one? What does this have to do with anything?* ////Liv

I checked for further messages from Frances at the House or Blanche's contact address, but there weren't any. Researching Mary Lincoln's traveling companion, I found many sites had information. Her name was Elizabeth Keckley, a former slave and close friend and confidante to the First Lady. I bookmarked the page in case later scrutiny was needed.

When Aaron returned, we placed the small wood table in the chosen spot. It didn't take long to dress it with the tablecloth.

"I have only a couple more things to do before lunch," I told Aaron. Everything was in place for the celebration, which made me happy.

"I'll clear off the back entryway. It's a mess by the dumpster," Aaron said.

I went to get my recently purchased dress from the Mary Lincoln collection. My plan was to wear it on special occasions such as Abe Lincoln's or Mary Todd Lincoln's birthdays or dollhouse special sales events. I definitely planned to wear it that day, but I hoped to skip the tight-fitting crinoline and only wear the hoop. Back in the workroom, I flipped on a bright sewing light and took the Civil War-era dress from where it hung. Aaron entered the room as I was admiring the many pleats, meticulously measured, pinned, and sewn on the checked, cotton fabric. Hand-stitched lace along the collar and cuffs, inlaid pearls to spruce up the lace, all captured my attention. I thought of days of yore. "Look at the evenly spaced hand stitches. It's so lovely." I smiled up at him.

Aaron's stomach growled in return. I laughed. "Hungry? So am I."

"Let's get something down at the Brew Café. I love their wraps." Aaron locked the front door and we headed out the back. Bundled up and hand in hand we walked. I caught sight of something that glimmered on the walkway. I stopped and picked it up. It looked like a computer memory stick, so I slipped it into my pocket in case anyone mentioned missing one. The warmth of the Brew Café felt wonderful as we came in out of the cold. I found the pictures of concentric puzzles on a wall, and they kept my attention until it was time to order.

"Our regular order, please," I said to Luke, busy

behind the counter. "Luke, did Blanche seem nervous or anything like that when she came in yesterday?"

"No." Luke shook his head. "She stared at the puzzles and then at her laptop screen when she was in here."

"Did she say anything?" I asked.

"Not much. Something about these pictures not being quite the same, but similar. I had to hurry back to Inga's." We watched as Luke set the wraps on a plate and poured our drinks.

"You two shouldn't be talking. Leave it to the detectives," admonished Aaron.

"Here," Luke stated, setting our plates on the countertop. "Blanche told me about Lincoln's Lost Speech while she was dressing for Inga's. Did she say anything to you about it?"

"Now that you mention it, that was part of the conversation. I bet that Lost Speech would be a goldmine," Luke said.

"You betcha," Aaron replied, reaching for his meal. "Anything from that man would be worth a bundle."

"I bet it's in one of those historical documents that's hidden in someone's attic," I said, picking up my order. "Luke, I don't see that nice girl who helped you at Inga's yesterday."

"She's busy with school."

"Oh." I turned to Aaron. "Should we sit at that one?" I nodded toward the back table.

"Sure." Aaron headed for it and I followed. Just then, Luke's wife, Suni, came into the café. Suni didn't work at the shop, though she kept their account books. She was some kind of computer whiz and worked from home, spending her day on the Internet, or so people said about her. She beckoned to Luke, and he hurried outside with her. I frowned, wondering what prompted that.

When we sat, I noticed a concerned look in Aaron's eye. "What's bothering you?"

"I'm worried you'll start investigating the murder on your own. Leave it to the police. I don't want anything to happen to you." Aaron started eating. "Is it the speech you're looking for?"

"Of course. A perfect time-machine mystery." I couldn't quit thinking of Blanche and how she'd spent time researching it. The notion that it was hidden, after all these years, really tickled my interest. "I'm curious."

"I hope that's all it is," Aaron said. His brow furrowed. "I worry about you."

"I wrote to the House about the stuffed bear featured as Tad's toy there, and it's also on Blanche's website. I would like to have it, if it's for sale, plus purchase a miniature of the House. Both would be fun to own."

"I understand the house, but a bear? Whatever for?" Aaron's questions didn't keep him from devouring his food.

"It's a very cute bear, and it belonged to Tad Lincoln." I heard him groan, but I ignored him and finished my wrap.

After carting our trays to the waste container, we

strolled back to the store. Though it was quite brisk out, the sun sparkled, and it made me think of the coming spring.

"My shift starts in a few minutes," Aaron said. "I have to change, then report in."

"Okay," I said. We stopped in front of the door. I impishly picked up a mitt full of snow and threw it at him. "Gotch ya!"

"Your time is coming." Aaron brushed off the snow. "Your time is coming." Aaron brushed off the snow and opened the door and held it for me to enter. "Should I take anything home with me?"

"Yes. The crinoline, all that stuff, but leave my dress." I gathered all the necessary items and we carried them to the car. "You can leave them in the car, and I'll carry them in later. I'll be darned if I'll put that crinoline back on again. Yikes!"

"Nah. I'll set them on the bed. No problem. It'll give me a chance to figure out how to get you out of it." Aaron grinned. When we finished loading the costume undergarments, we stood by the car. "Love you."

"You, too."

Back in the store, I decided to unpack a box of miniature Tad toys purchased from a New Hampshire store that was going out of business. The owner had immediately taken my offer to buy some of his stock. The items would fit nicely inside the houses or on a display shelf.

I found a tiny kaleidoscope inside the box, along with a ball, sword, a Union cannon and balls, the stuffed bear, and jacks with the matching ball. I studied the pieces with my magnifier and found them to be very charming and also well made.

The bear especially caught my attention, because it had a pocket in the bottom, like it was wearing a pair of flannel pajamas with a drop-seat or "trap door." I chuckled and wondered if the stuffed bear on Blanche's website also had a pocket. Unlike our present-day teddy bears, these were made of plain, not furry, plush fabric and they were stuffed with cornhusks. I also knew that in Tad's day they were not called "Teddy Bears" because President Theodore "Teddy" Roosevelt inspired the first Teddy Bear in 1902. I carried the items out to the showroom and set them on the counter top. My Civil War Era houses were already filled with many items, but there were few family mementos. I started to rearrange the living quarters in the Lincoln White House. The President and Mrs. Lincoln were known to allow their children to do almost anything and everything, indulging all whims. I placed the jacks and ball on the floor and set the kaleidoscope on a small table.

The back door opened. I was happy to see my best friend Maggie stomping the snow from underfoot.

"Hey, you! Another one, eh?" Maggie asked. She had been the maid of honor at our wedding, and her fiancé was Aaron's patrol partner, Tim. "How are you taking it? Tim told me about the murder and thought I'd swing over."

I gave her a hug. Within the folds of her arms, I thought of cinnamon and spice and everything nice.

"Blanche was so nice." I gave her a full report about Blanche, and how I was planning to show her Tad's memorabilia before she left town. "Pretty incredible, isn't it? Let's get an extra chair. We can sit in the showroom. It's sunny and warmer in there." I picked up a chair and set it next to mine, behind the counter.

"Tim said it was a robbery gone sour. I figured you could fill me in, since he won't." She cocked her head. "You know how secretive cops are."

"It was murder. I always seem to be in the thick of things, don't I?" I rubbed my right eyebrow where a twitch had developed.

"The police don't know where to turn, that's my impression," Maggie said.

"Agreed." I frowned. "Too many unanswered questions concerning this." I shook my head and got up. I went over to hang the soldier uniform near the appropriate era's White House display. "This once belonged to Tad Lincoln. It's exactly what you see in the pictures."

"It's a miracle it's all been so carefully preserved, isn't it?" Maggie leaned back and looked at me with serious eyes. "But I don't like to hear about another murder."

"Well then, how about a hundred-year-old puzzle?" I gave her a rundown about the weird-looking pages in the diary and the staircase drawing in the hatbox.

"But, how does Blanche's missing laptop figure into this, if at all? For that matter, what strings them all together?" Maggie said.

"Mary Lincoln, but there's no cohesiveness to any of this."

"Think over what she read. Better yet, go get that diary," Maggie said.

"Hold on." I got up and went to the workroom and found it. I sat back down and opened the diary, riffling through several pages until coming to the pertinent ones. "See? Concentric writing. They look like big wheels made with letters."

"Interesting, but it's nutty, isn't it?" When I shrugged, she said, "Since the diary was sold on the open market, plenty of individuals have seen it, so it must not have much meaning."

"I'd like to decipher it."

"It'd be fun. I love a good puzzle." Maggie glanced outside. "The murder. Right outside, eh?"

"Sort of, closer to Luke's. Good thing it wasn't inside my store this time. I think I would have the place on the market right now if she'd been found in here."

"I would, too." We both shivered. "Who is top of your suspect list?"

"No clue."

"Has anyone been interviewed?" Maggie asked.

"I suspect the local store owners have been," I said. "Say, is Tim joining the pond hockey team?"

"Of course. It'll be fun to watch them skate."

"I'll see you tomorrow night for burgers, and we'll watch the practice," I said.

"Yep. Well, it's time for me to go to work." She

stood. "See you later."

There were two hours left until closing. I thought about displaying the houses inside a display case currently stored in the basement. I'd set the case right near the service counter.

Making my usual circuit around the room, I stopped once again at the Lincoln house. My thoughts unraveled over the trauma and drama that played a major role in their everyday lives. Back in the workroom, I laid out the fabric for sewing two inaugural gowns for Dolley Madison. Once the needle was threaded, I stitched and pulled, stitched and sewed. My thoughts relaxed from a jittery state as I settled into a more peaceful state. Just as I was fully content with my work, something surfaced from the dregs of my memory.

The letter from Springfield. Blanche mentioned it before tea. It must be important, especially if it only recently had been discovered. How could I have forgotten?

Was that what got Blanche killed?

Chapter Four

I glanced out through frosted windows and decided to call Inga rather than chase her down to her store to tell her about displaying the miniature houses.

Holly answered, and I asked, "Is Inga around?"

"Just stepped out. Not sure when she'll be back."

"Okay. Ever figure out what happened to the stolen books?"

"Nope. Not a word. Maybe they were sold?"

"Please tell her I called." I puzzled over the discrepancy of the books. Could they really have been stolen? I turned to the computer. It seemed to be running a little slow, but sometimes when more people were on the Internet, it took longer for the search engines to work.

I accessed my bookmark for Blanche's website — her research specialty and doctoral thesis had been on Abraham Lincoln's speeches from before his White House years. I found that to be interesting since she had done a remarkable job impersonating Mary Lincoln. My first impression was that she had focused on Mary Lincoln. Her blog site mentioned progress in her quest to locate the Lost Speech.

The phone rang. It was a prospective customer, inquiring about our store hours. I was about to go back to the web and research the speech when the front door tingled. I looked up and saw that Trisha, who worked for the Veteran's Administration, had come to

BARBARA SCHLICHTING

collect the cash from the *Pennies Jar*.

"It's cold out." Trisha stomped her boots inside the door, holding in one hand a cardboard tray with two steaming cups and an empty jar in the other. The chocolaty smell was heavenly. "Time to warm up." She strolled toward the counter, but I met her halfway and grabbed the cups. She replaced the full *Pennies Jar* with an empty one.

"Thanks." I sipped from my chosen cup.

"I figured you could use a warm treat. These old buildings leave a lot to be desired in the wintertime. It's not just cold. It's darn freezing." She shivered and drank from her cup. "Looks like you did pretty well with the collection. Or should I say, we did pretty well?" She held up the jar to peer at all the loose change and dollar bills inside of it.

"It seems like it." I opened one of the bakery boxes, offering her a cookie. "Spread the word that Monday we're having a special on the dollhouses plus goodies to celebrate the January First Lady birthdays."

"Thanks." She took a bite of a cookie before tossing her empty cup into the wastebasket. "Will do. Don't forget to tell people that all donations go directly to the Vets, if anyone asks." She headed for the door and stopped. "And thank you, again."

"You betcha!" I shivered as the cold air once again blasted into the room.

I finished my drink and checked for e-mail. Frances, from the House, had returned my message.

Liv, the stuffed bear is for sale. It's two hundred

dollars. The dollhouse is two-fifty. Both are high priced to help pay for maintenance and upkeep. We keep the house under glass and treat all stuffed animals with non-toxic solutions to prevent deterioration. Let me know. //Frances.

I replied:

Frances, I'll take both. The check's in the mail. //Liv.

As I wondered where the four-hundred and fifty dollars would come from, I glanced at the clock. It was finally closing time. I hoped for lots of sales on Monday, as well as plenty of prospective customers. I made sure the cookie boxes were sealed and readied the coffeepot for heating the cider.

"Good night, ladies," I called. I stopped near the Civil War White House. To the Mr. Lincoln doll, I said, "Mr. Prez, please take Mrs. Lincoln for a buggy ride tonight. She needs cheering up!" I winked at the doll. "You'll thank me in the morning."

I continued to the workroom where the garbage needed gathering and taken outside for disposal. I grabbed my jacket, went to the dumpster, and pulled out the little step stool I kept hidden behind there. The slippery foundation was worrisome, but I managed to empty the garbage without a hitch. It'd gotten so cold, that I wasn't looking forward to the walk home.

I noticed the neighboring house behind the store had a frozen rink in its backyard. One little boy was shooting hockey pucks into a small net. A charming, small snowman stood to the side. It seemed to be the size I would've constructed as a child. I went back inside.

After bundling up, I grabbed my bag before I stepped out into the frigid, cold night air. With the sun setting in late afternoon this time of the year, my walk home always seemed so desolate. I locked up, made sure the door was secure, and headed the short distance home.

Cars swished past me as I walked. I was relieved not to meet any outside lingerers as I went by the lone corner bar, still bedecked in holiday lights. The cold air felt good on my skin at first, but now it stung. My nose hurt and my eyes watered. The intake of air in my lungs hurt as I sucked in each breath. Underfoot, the snow squeaked and scrunched. I was happy when I turned the corner of my block and saw that the colored lights encircling the single pine tree in my front yard were lit. Aaron must have flipped the light switch before leaving for work. For some odd reason, Grandma insisted that the bulb string be left in place until the first day of March.

"Hi." I waved to the neighbor children playing, immediately ducking to avoid being hit by a flying snowball. I quickly made a snowball of my own and threw it, missing my target. I raced up to the door but was hit from behind by a snowball thrown by one of the kids. Laughing, I punched in the security code and it allowed me to enter the side door. I brushed snow from my back then stomped my boots. My feet and hands tingled from the cold. I went into the garage to check inside the car to see if Aaron had brought all the dress parts into the house. The hoop still sat in the backseat. I grabbed it and carried it in inside, setting it carefully on the table before locking up the garage and doors. I pulled off my boots and other outerwear. Then I took the hoop into the back bedroom where all my extra store items were stored.

After hanging up the crinoline and other dress pieces, I went out to the kitchen. I made myself a cup of hot chocolate and nuked a bag of popcorn. My phone rang and Aaron's number was displayed. "Hey, babe."

"Did those kids get you again with snowballs?" I admitted it with a smile, and he became serious. "Her laptop has been found. There were no fingerprints, and its hard drive is blank."

"That means?"

"Back to square one."

"Thanks for the update." I hesitated and asked, "Where was the laptop found? I presume her bag with her possessions were located, also."

"The pawnshop had the laptop."

"Thanks," I said. "Who are the main suspects?"

"Liv! No! You are to keep your nose out of police business."

"It's got to be either Luke or Holly."

"Why? Why those two?"

"They are the most needy. Holly for college tuition. Luke, I'm not sure, but he has a continual changeover of employees. It seems odd, to me. Also, his eyes lit up when he learned the value of Mister Lincoln's Lost Speech and that it's never been found."

"I'll tell the detectives, but you stay out of it."

"Okay."

"I'm meeting later with the guys to plan our hockey strategies. Tomorrow night is practice, don't forget."

"Okay. Enjoy yourself. You won't be too late, will you?"

"Probably will. None of us get off work until eleven."

"I forgot." We disconnected. I was not happy about the confirmed method of murder or the blank laptop. This meant the killer was on the loose, and the police weren't any closer to finding the murderer than they were last night. Blanche's website and all of her accounts were probably compromised, and all files copied, too. *What file could she have had that someone would murder for?* I grabbed my popped popcorn bag out of the microwave, headed into the living room and sank into my chair where I fell asleep watching an old TV movie. It was very late when I woke. I went down the hall to our bedroom and climbed into bed, covering myself up with heavy blankets.

The following morning was Sunday. I awoke with Aaron beside me. Hearing the west wind whistling through the trees, I pulled the blankets over my head.

The phone rang at the usual time, nine o'clock.

"Yes, Grandma," I said, yawning. "It's early." Grandma used to call at 8:30, but after a few lectures from me about calling so early, she now called at nine. I had scooted lower under the blankets and was just getting cozy with my husband. One of these days, I hoped to have enough courage to not answer the phone.

"We've ordered salads from Luke at the Brew Café, and Grandpa's going to grill salmon for dinner," Grandma announced. "We're having a few people from the neighborhood over. We decided that you and Aaron are invited." I could almost hear Grandma smiling, which made me believe Grandpa would be right next to her, sipping his coffee. "Can you and Aaron come? Yes, no, or are you undecided?"

"Oh yes, but Aaron has hockey later, so we won't be able to stay real late."

"It's just the afternoon, dear. Don't worry, you're not spending the night," Grandma said.

"All right. Do you want us to bring something, like maybe some Jell-O?" I asked to be polite, already knowing what the answer would be.

"That's quite all right, dear. We don't want indigestion." I heard the stifled giggle. "We'll eat at two. Come over when you're ready."

"Very funny," I said. "Bye," then hung up. My grandparents were in their eighties, but they still acted young and carefree. They'd been married for over sixty years, and you could tell they were still very much in love. They held hands—giggling in each other's presence at times. I found that remarkable. I hoped to be just like them at that age.

I rolled over to look at Aaron and said, "We're going to Grandma's for dinner at two today. They're also having some neighbors over. Grandpa's grilling. It will be like a winter patio party, I bet."

"What should we do until then?" Aaron pulled me

on top of him.

"Show me…"

A long while later my laptop hummed. We were in the kitchen, and Aaron was toasting a couple of bagels.

"This thing is so slow. I noticed that the store computer is slow, too. I thought it might be because of the weather and more people are online."

"It's hard to say, so we'd better take a look. Our router should be giving you good speed, since you're connected right to it." He replenished my coffee and set the toasted bagels and strawberry cream cheese spread on the table, along with knives for spreading. "Let me see." He turned the laptop toward himself. "Here it comes, but this worries me."

"The background is a stuffed toy bear. Isn't that cute?" I logged into the store's website. "Wait a second. Has my firewall been disabled?"

"That's impossible. Or at least I don't think it could happen. I'll talk to the police department's computer guy when I get a chance. We can run a virus scan later. Did anything strange show on the screen?"

"Just the image of a stuffed bear. I think it came from the Mary Todd Lincoln House." I reached for a bagel half, spread cream cheese on it, and took a bite. The wonderful taste brought a smile to my lips. I ate it right up.

"The detectives had me sign my life away but allowed me to bring Blanche's belongings home. Actually, there are a couple of things that disturb them, and they would like for you to inspect along the dress seams. Also, the hatbox rattles, like there's something inside. The detectives are afraid of ruining it because it once belonged to the first lady and its historical value. The Minnesota Historical Society was contacted, and they mentioned your name. Since you had spent many hours there researching your dissertation, they felt confident in your expertise." He smiled and winked. "Now you can inspect it."

"Oh wow! Where is it?" I glanced over toward the door and out into the living room but didn't see it. "Car?"

"Yep. I was too tired to carry it in." Aaron walked to the door and slipped into his boots. "Be right back." I quickly stood by the door so I could open it for him when he came back. When he did, I took the dress from his full arms. He was still holding the hatbox. "Yikes. It's cold out." He stomped his shoes.

"I'm dropping this on the couch for now. The hat and box are already in the back room." I carried the Civil War dress into the living room and set it down. "Where's the crinoline and pantaloons?"

"Still in the car. Be right back."

"I'm going to take a closer look at the dress and hat," I said.

I went to fetch the hat and box.

"How on earth could women wear these dad-blame-things?" Aaron asked when he returned again. "They should have been outlawed." He looked around. "If that's everything, I'm going to take a break and have my shower."

"I think they were outlawed. Think of the bra

burning in the sixties," I called after him as he headed to the bathroom.

I hadn't had much time to examine the two pieces. Opening the hatbox lid on the kitchen table, I stared again at the staircase drawing. I was convinced Mrs. Lincoln drew it, but for what purpose? Why would someone draw a staircase in a hatbox? Carefully, I ran my fingers around the inside of the lid. There were noticeable inconsistencies. The octagonal-shaped lid lip seemed right in measurement. But when studying the bottom, the depth of the platform seemed odd from the outside. I placed the hat inside the box. Next, I measured the approximate distance from the top to the bottom, inside and out. There was approximately a one-inch discrepancy, which meant that the box had a false bottom. I gently slid my fingers along the inner corners of the base. The corners seemed square and fit tight. I turned the box upside down and studied it. No particular marking caught my eye. However, the outside bottom platform fit flush across. That finding left me more than curious.

"Aaron!" I called but then remembered he was showering. I wasn't quite sure what to do, so I gave Inga a call. "Inga?"

"Oh! Liv!" I could hear the television blaring in the background. "Beautiful day, isn't it?"

"Yes, yes it is. I won't keep you, but I wanted you to know…" I told her about the hatbox and having the dress in my possession now. "What do you think about the hatbox bottom? What should I do?"

"Make sure it's the same coloring."

"Thanks." She gave me a couple of other suggestions, and we hung up. Just then, Aaron entered the room, fresh from the shower.

"What's up?"

"Look at this, will you?" I pointed out the inconsistencies in the box, and then turned it over. Sure enough, closer scrutiny revealed the bottom was a slightly different shade and there were glue marks around in a hodge-podge fashion. I shook the box. "Did you hear that?" I held my ear closer and said, "Hear it? Something rattled."

"That must be the noise they heard." Aaron massaged his chin. "Course, on the other hand..." He held up the box and shook it. "I wonder what it is?" He shook it again, keeping his ear right next to the bottom. "It's almost like a baby rattle."

"Look at this staircase." I pointed it out on the lid lip. "See? The name is Mrs. Tindall, which was Mary Lincoln's alias." I looked at him. "There's something here, but I'm not sure what. Don't you think so, too?"

"Oh, brother. We have to be really careful," he said and kissed my forehead. "I'm calling the detectives."

I listened to the one-sided conversation. When Aaron disconnected, I asked, "Well?"

"We have to wait until he contacts the Mary Lincoln House and also his superior."

"Oh," I said, frowning. I reached for a cookie. His phone rang almost immediately.

"Okay," Aaron said into his phone. Turning to me, he said, "Put some water on to boil. Big pot."

"We'll steam it, then?" I went over to the cabinet

and took out the largest pot we had. I filled it with water and placed it on the stovetop. I turned the dial to high, so it'd boil quicker. "Never thought of that."

"We don't want to ruin it. We can fold the paper back and settle this once and for all. The detectives and the spokesperson from the Lincoln House are willing to go along with it as long as it's restored to its original shape," Aaron said. "This might be tricky. If there is something inside, we don't want it dropping into boiling water, either. You'll have to be careful and kind of guide me as we steam it."

"I will. Don't worry. Another worry is this paper. It's older than the hills. Is it going to crumble from the moisture? Or will the design or top layer peel off?" I stood beside him. "I don't know what to think."

"Hopefully, it'll work out just right." We both noticed that the water was starting to steam. "Before we get started, let me call the detectives to keep them updated. This has to be done properly." Aaron found his phone and he didn't have to talk long. Looking at me, he said, "I'm to let them know what it is. It may or may not have anything to do with the investigation, so we can proceed."

"Good." I had been worried about the decision. "How should we do this?"

"Let's try loosening it together. It might be better than the hard, heavier steam. The glue may give way easily anyway, simply from the age."

"True."

Slowly, Aaron turned the hatbox around over the steam. After each complete turn, he moved to the counter and turned the hatbox upside down. I tried to loosen the glue as he held the hatbox. After two rounds, I hadn't been able to budge any of it. When the water was boiling harder and the steam became hotter, I began to notice a loosening of the glue, and soon I was able to ease the paper away from the side. Eventually, I curled it back far enough for us to decide if it was worth our while to continue.

Poking the tip of a knife along the side, I said, "There seems to be no resistance." I thought for a moment. "Should we give it a shake again, just to make sure?"

"Good idea." Aaron listened as he shook it. "It's louder."

"I agree."

I worked my fingers gradually around each of the angles. Eventually, I released the bottom platform, which turned out to be two layers thick of cardboard-like material. I heard a muffled clink as I shoved the knife farther under the platform. "I wonder?"

"Keep going. This has my curiosity now." Aaron went to get another knife and helped remove the platform. We each went in separate directions, so we could meet allowing us to lift the platform from its base without a hitch. "Almost ready."

"What do you think is hidden in here?" I asked, noting that his fingers were moving just as carefully as my own.

"No telling what we'll find."

Finally we lifted the platform, exposing a lump of wadded paper. I picked it up and questioned, "What in the world is this?" I set it aside. The small, yellowed bit of newspaper was dated, May 29, 1856.

"What the heck?" I gasped. "Look at the date of this." I held it up. "It's incredible. I wonder if the date means anything."

"No idea." Aaron shrugged. "What are the headlines?"

"They say, 'The Speech of Abraham Lincoln.' Then it reads: Among the 'appealing' details was the token Lincoln had from Rose's small brother and which he concealed in his pocket during the speech — a stiff little fish. With rare sense, the author wonders where it's disappeared?" Puzzled, I stared at Aaron. "What on earth does that mean?"

"No idea. You'll have to do research. Who was Rose? The way they wrote and talked back then leaves me confused sometimes, sweetheart."

I set the yellowed newspaper aside, not wanting to place it inside the box again. "I should fold up one of ours." I went after a newspaper, halving it until it became equal to the size of the latter one. I formed it to the right size then set it in. "All set."

"Let's hope the glue is still moist." Ever so gently, we placed the platform back and carefully folded the paper edging into place. "Hold on, a sec." Aaron smoothed his thumb across the seam. "Good as new."

"I wonder…" Sitting down by the table, I gently unwrapped the package. The brittle paper broke into small pieces at the corners, making me work at a slower pace. At last, the paper was off. We stared at the contents. "A necklace?" I held it up and said, "It looks like an acorn, doesn't it?"

"A silvered acorn necklace?"

"I'm calling the detectives." Aaron made the call. Disconnecting, he said, "It looks like I have to list it on the docket as evidence tomorrow. I'm to contact them later if there's more evidence."

"What's the point in having an acorn, if it is truly an acorn, silvered and strung to wear as a necklace?" And do we have a killer after an acorn?"

Chapter Five

It was time to get ready to go to my grandparents' house. They didn't live too far away, over by Lake of the Isles, one of several chain lakes in the heart of Minneapolis. They'd sold their house right after my wedding.

"I'm sending a message to Frances because she should know about the acorn," I said to Aaron. The message explained how we found the necklace and would like to investigate further. Also, I told Frances the police wanted me to examine the dress because the hem felt odd. "Done," I said after pressing the send button.

"I'm sure the police are in contact with her. Let's keep the necklace in an evidence bag and secure it in our lockbox," Aaron said.

"Grandma knows several university professors through the Garden Club, and one may be an expert in analyzing and dating historical pieces," I said. "We must discover what the necklace is about, such as, is it relevant and why?"

"I'll ask the detectives if we can have help in identifying it," Aaron said.

"Here." I handed it over. "It's time for me to get dressed."

After dressing into a pair of jeans, top, and pullover sweater, I asked, "How do I look?"

"Gorgeous." When he kissed me, I felt beautiful.

"Thank you," I said. "Not to belabor the subject, why would Mary, if it was she, have kept it hidden in the bottom of the hatbox?" The hair on the back of my neck seemed to twitch, which wasn't a good sign. "I'm going to find out if there's really a nut inside the silver or not."

"The detectives are eager to gain as much information as can be gleamed from it. Mergens is befuddled. All the clues are convoluted, and they don't have the time to figure out nuts. They have a strong idea who the killer was but without a motive, they're at a loss."

"Let's hope we'll be able to ask someone a few questions about silver-plated jewelry."

"It's possible. We have to keep the police and the Mary Todd Lincoln House updated." Aaron's phone dinged, and he read the message out loud: "*The hockey practice tonight has been moved to Longfellow Park. Burgers at Matt's afterwards. Five o'clock.*"

"It's time to load up the gear. We'll have to go right from Grandma's to practice."

"Right. How about you grab your outside clothes, and I'll run downstairs for my equipment?" Aaron suggested.

"Got it." I hurried to the bedroom, grabbed an extra heavy Norwegian knitted sweater — a Christmas gift — as well as leggings. The boots, extra mittens, and cap, I grabbed from the closet.

After Aaron used auto-start to warm up the car, we put on our outerwear and went out to the car. As we pulled out of the garage and out into the street, I noticed that the neighborhood children weren't outside. No flying snowballs for us to dodge.

"Now that it's colder, it's gotten more slippery, I see," Aaron stated, turning a corner.

Reaching Lake Calhoun, we made our way past the Calhoun Beach Manor and soon turned the corner of my grandparents' block in a newer development geared for senior living. The bushes in front of their townhouse were still lit up with lights, lingering remnants of the holidays that had just passed. Icicle lights cascaded from the rooftop, and the front lawn hosted lit reindeer and a family of snowmen, complete with a bulb lit up on the end of the carrot nose of one of them. It was unmistakably theirs, even if we hadn't seen it before. We parked in front of their house.

We walked up to the house, opened the front door, and marched inside.

"We're here!" I called, knowing full well they'd be busy getting things set up in the kitchen.

Aaron and I hung our coats on the coat tree in the hall. I hadn't been to their house in a couple weeks, not since the Christmas holiday and the weather becoming so incredibly cold. I did feel a little guilty but vowed to make it up to them. I stopped at the glass-door cabinet that showcased Grandma's First Lady dolls and peered closely at them. First in line, of course, was Martha Washington. Grandma had the entire set—including former First Lady, Mrs. Obama.

"Aren't they beautiful?" I smiled at Grandma.

"I'm going after a cigar," Aaron said, sidling off.

"August is in the back room, smoking, Aaron."

Grandma told him. To me, she said, "Luke just arrived with the salads I ordered. The guests will soon be here. Oh, dear. First time we are entertaining this bunch. How do I look?" Grandma stood back, smoothing down her skirt.

"Beautiful, Grandma. Dazzling." I smiled. She stood at about five feet, one or two inches tall, and her green, dancing eyes always seemed to twinkle. Her hair was always perfect and in the latest style. Boy did she have energy! Even at her age, she could run circles around me, plus multi-task! She was remarkable. I hoped to be half the woman she was when I got to that age—about ninety. Today, she was like a fireball as she waited for her guests. "You've met most of the neighbors, haven't you?"

"Yes! They all seem to dress so fancy, though." She narrowed her eyes at me and said, "I can tell by that smile of yours that you have something up your sleeve. What is it?"

"I must be grinning from ear to ear." I felt my cheeks burn. We found a trinket in the bottom of a hatbox that belonged to Mary Lincoln. I can't say much more because of the investigation. Aaron has it secured."

"Let's go into the kitchen and you can tell me about it. The food needs supervision. Luke has another new helper with him." She started heading to the kitchen but I grabbed her arm.

"Another helper?" I whispered, puzzled. "What happened to the one he had working for him?"

"No idea." She began walking. I was right beside

her. "He gave us the best deal on these salads."

"I love his food and coffee." I followed her. It bugged me that so many young female employees came and went from his café. Luke held knives and sliced veggies like a machine. A large platter, with a dipping bowl in the center, looked delicious. Plenty of full serving bowls and plates were set on the table.

After snatching a cold shrimp, I dipped it into cocktail sauce before eating it. "Everything looks delish." My eyes lit up when I gazed at the uncovered bowls of dip. I couldn't help myself, and I dipped a carrot into the vegetable dip. "Great. Spinach dip."

"I didn't realize these were your grandparents," Luke said, glancing at me. "Should've known because you've been in for coffee together, or she's come down and bought two cups." He went back to the food preparation.

I spent a moment watching Luke's new helper chop celery sticks. Like her predecessor, she looked Asian.

"You're new," I said to her. "How are you enjoying Minneapolis?"

She looked up at me for a moment but didn't appear to understand my words. I turned to Luke. "What happened to your other assistant, your cousin? Do you have enough help?"

"She moved back home. This girl is a big help, also my cousin. No need of another." He looked down at the dish he was preparing, dismissing further questions.

"Everyone needs family," Grandma stated,

coming in at the end of the conversation and lifting out silverware. "We're using paper plates since I don't want to put my chinaware in the dishwasher. It's too old. I'm not up to standing and washing dishes anymore. Enough of that nonsense."

"Great! About time." I nodded approval and sat down.

"Tell me quickly about your found trinket before the guests arrive." Grandma glanced at me. "I'm sure there's a story behind it."

"Remember the hat and period dress Blanche, the murdered woman, wore when she impersonated Mary Lincoln?" When she nodded, I continued, "Well, there was a rattle coming from inside her hatbox. The dress hem stitching is odd in places also." I watched while she counted out forks.

"Go on, I'm listening," Grandma said. "You shouldn't be messing with it, though."

"The historical society recommended me to study the dress for anything amiss plus to do the same with the hat."

"As long as the detectives know," Grandma said.

"They do. You see," I swallowed, "it seemed as if there was a false bottom to the hatbox. We used steam and peeled back the ends of the paper covering it, allowing us to lift out the bottom. I can't say what was inside the ball of paper."

"How strange," Luke said with a puzzled frown. "Are you saying that Mary Lincoln hid something in the box lid?"

"It appears like it." I popped a chunk of cantaloupe

into my mouth. "The newspaper lining the hatbox bottom dated from when Mr. Lincoln gave the Lost Speech."

"I wonder? Where would Mary have been comfortable hiding the speech, if she had?" Luke asked, setting some mixing bowls in the dishwasher. He then reached for the serving bowls. "Ever researched it? I don't have much time for stuff like that. Anyway, history wasn't one of my strong points."

"Never heard of it before Blanche mentioned it to me." I shook my head. "I'd like to know more about it myself. How can someone lose a manuscript of an important speech? That's what baffles me."

"You'll have to keep me informed, honey." Grandma smiled at me.

"Me too." Luke nodded and looked at his assistant. He placed a spoon in her hand and whispered something before going back to work.

I recalled Luke dressed as a butler that day at the diary reading, wearing just a modern day suit since they didn't have "tails" handy for his dress attire. His helper that day also seemed very quiet. I wondered if either of them spoke English. If they didn't understand what we were saying that would account for their not talking. Aaron and Grandpa's voices drew my attention. "You nearly ready to put the salmon steaks on the grill?" I asked as they came back into the kitchen.

"Yep. We're heading out to the garage to move the grill outside." Grandpa puffed on his cigar as he shrugged his arms into coat sleeves.

"Minnesota and all its natural cold. What better time to have a barbecue than wintertime to shed all the mid-winter blues?"

"You two are goofy," I said and watched them walk out, shutting the kitchen door behind them. The blast of cold air made me shiver. I decided to make sure there was plenty of open wine on the table and enough chairs for everyone.

"Liv, here's a short list of things for you to help me with before the guests arrive," Grandma said. She handed it to me.

"Okay." I read the list, crumpled it and stuffed it in my pocket.

Aaron found me straightening out the doilies over the furniture a short while later. "The grill is ready for firing. August made sure it's parked outside away from the garage and cars."

The doorbell rang. The guests had arrived.

We walked to the main door together and Aaron opened it, and we greeted the first of the guests, a man and woman.

"Hi. I'm Liv, and this is my husband, Aaron. Come in." We stepped aside to allow them to enter. Aaron hung the coats on hangers he found in the hall closet. The couple had no sooner entered than three more couples arrived. Soon the guests all mingled while we attended to their needs, directing them to drinks and munchies.

Grandma had joined us, and when everyone had a filled glass, I had a chance to sit down beside one of the ladies.

"I'm sorry, I've forgotten your name. I'm Liv, Marie's granddaughter." I took a slight sip of wine. The sunlight twinkled against the glass, revealing the tiny bubbles in the wine. The frost on the windows added to the room's atmosphere.

"I'm Mavis Hunter, dear." She swirled her glass. "We neighbors need to do more things of this nature. It's good to get out and meet people."

"Grandpa loves to grill."

"They all do." I took that to mean the men. She craned her head. "I see someone with whom I haven't spoken for awhile. Excuse me, Liv." She got up and walked away.

I went for the wine bottle and refilled everyone's glasses, chatting with each of the ladies along the way. It sounded like they each had a dog or a cat. They were all pulling photos from their purses or showing images from their cell phones.

While the ladies chatted, I went into the kitchen to see if Luke or Grandma needed any extra help.

"Please carry the salads out to the table, dear," Grandma instructed.

I obeyed by carrying out four large bowls, each filled with a different salad. Then I carried out the fruit and vegetable platters, as well as the dips. Everything looked delicious. Grandma had opted for a spring-like party menu, instead of a heavier meal.

"Here we are," Grandpa stated, carrying in a platter full of salmon. Aaron was right behind him. They set it in the middle of the table.

"Help yourself to the buffet. Sit wherever you would like." Grandma's eyes twinkled as she gazed around the room. "We have set out plenty of coffee tables. No room in these smaller townhouses for a proper dining room table."

"Quite all right, Marie," one of the gentlemen, a university professor, said as he pushed his glasses farther up his long nose. "Our homes are basically identical. You are doing a lovely job." He ran his fingers through his curly, unruly hair.

"Thank you." Grandma stood to the side and watched as everyone filled their plates and sat down. "Olivia, Aaron, go ahead."

We did as told and found two seats near the television, close to the professor and his wife.

"What is it that you teach, Mister...? I'm sorry, but I've forgotten your name," I asked, taking a bite of the salmon. "This is really good." I smiled.

"Doctor Bill Williams. My wife is Mary Ann." He nodded toward her.

"Nice meeting you," she said. Her red hair flowed to her shoulders, held back by an aqua-blue scarf, which matched her top perfectly. Even seated, she was almost as tall as her husband.

"I'm in the science department. Mostly biology, genetics... that type of thing." He took another bite. "This is good."

"I wonder..." I glanced at Aaron, who rolled his eyes, "about this idea of mine. I hate to impose, but could we speak alone after the meal about a certain matter?"

"Certainly," Dr. Williams said.

My nerves tingled with excitement. I couldn't wait for everyone to finish eating so I could tell him about the necklace. I had a gut feeling he'd be able to discover if it was a real acorn inside the necklace or not.

After the meal ended and people began milling about, I nodded at Aaron. To Dr. Williams, I said, "Do you have time now? Aaron and I will have to leave shortly."

"Perfect time."

Mary Ann stayed behind while the three of us headed for Grandpa's study where we closed the door for privacy.

"To make a long story short, we have a necklace that appears to be silvered and in the shape of an acorn. I believe it's very old. We'd like to have it looked at, and if it's an acorn, possibly have a genetic test run on it," Aaron said.

"Could you do that?" I asked.

"How very strange," Dr. Williams said, rubbing his chin. "If the silver looks old, but not too tarnished, then it's vintage most likely. Back in the Civil War era, and even after, women did that type of thing to preserve whatever little keepsakes they had. Or they had things silvered to make their family look not so downtrodden, like they had a little bit of money. Or maybe even just to hide their jewelry. Any number of reasons, really." He thought for a moment. "I suspect the tarnishing has been reduced because it had been wrapped and kept out of the elements."

"We found it today hidden inside of an old hatbox." Aaron touched my arm, warning me not to say too much.

"We do have a machine at the university that can do a scan, but why would you want to?" He glanced from one of us to the other. "It could destroy the outer layer, and would you want that to happen?"

"The method of the wrapping, plus the location of the find, only creates more questions and leaves me stymied." I took a deep breath. "I must know the answer."

"We're both just really curious," Aaron offered, raising his brow.

"Oh, sure," Dr. Williams said. "I'll do it."

"It must be kept a secret, and depending on the find, the police will be involved," Aaron said.

"It's for an investigation, I take it?" Dr. Williams asked. "Yes," Aaron answered.

"Here's my card." Bill fished his business cards from his wallet and handed one to each of us. "E-mail me. We'll arrange a time for testing."

"Thank you."

When the card went into my pocket, a shiver raced up and down my spine.

Chapter Six

We wound our way past Lakewood Cemetery as we drove down the boulevard that ran beside Lake-of-the-Isles and led to Lake Calhoun. It was one of the oldest cemeteries in Minneapolis. Most of the state's famous people were buried there, including Vice-president Hubert Humphrey. Minneapolis was once known as a milling town. The founders of Pillsbury flour were buried there as well veterans of the Civil War in a special memorial section. A small lake lay within the perimeter, and an old trolley car track, a major tourist attraction, ran along the cemetery edge. During the summertime, its clackety-clacks, announced its presence.

"We'll practice several times this week. I'll take off when I can from work. That's how we'll have to do it, but the team members will rotate shifts for the games next weekend. I have Saturday evening games," Aaron said, "and I want you to be with me."

"I love to watch you skate. How about Tim?"

"Don't worry, you'll be able to sit with Maggie. We requested our time off together."

"That's great," I said. "Maggie and I always find plenty to talk about."

"I know." Aaron chuckled.

It wasn't long before Aaron parked on the street near the Longfellow Park warming house. We gathered all our needed items and briskly walked toward the door.

Already filled with team members, the chatter was loud. We found a place near the back wall. It took Aaron a few minutes to dress, lace his skates, and tighten his goalie pads. He looked like a cartoon figure.

"I'll meet you out there," I said. "Good luck."

"Thanks, hon, I'll need it," he said.

Maggie entered just as Aaron hiked outside. The cold draft caused me to shiver. "Hi Maggie. Where's Tim?"

"On the rink. He's already dressed. He put his skates with blade guards on in the car," Maggie said, wrapping a scarf tightly around her neck.

"Are you ready to bear the cold?" I pulled an extra pair of mittens on over my gloves. "Why couldn't they like swimming?"

"Good question."

We spent most of the hour-long practice outside. Occasionally, we went inside to warm-up and regain feeling in our tingling toes. Both of us were happy when the men finished.

"You looked great out there," I said to Aaron. "Just like high school. Our lead goalie. You still have your moves."

"Thanks," he said, giving me a wink. "Always knew you were my biggest fan, prettiest too."

"Matt's for burgers?" I asked Aaron while he removed the equipment.

"Yep. The pitchers are being poured already."

"I'm sure of that," I said, knowing that Tim and

Maggie would probably arrive at the destination first.

"I can't wait to sink my teeth into a Juicy Lucy."

"Me neither," I said.

We hustled out the door, and boy, was I sure happy that the car was nearby. The temperature had dropped again. Aaron started the car and before long we turned onto Cedar Avenue. We parked, went inside, and sat beside our friends. As the room filled with teammates, the noise level grew louder. We got our burgers and had a great time, though after a while the crowd became smaller, and Aaron suggested we leave for home. Hockey, ice skating, going for food and refreshments after games, reminded me of how long we'd known each other and the all the fun we'd had together as friends.

I awoke the following morning to frosty windows and sunshine still on the horizon. It was already eight, and the sunbeams were barely reaching between the houses and trees. A very cold January day was dawning. Frost hung in the air while the tree branches were white with newly fallen snow.

"Brrr," I murmured, dressing in a heavy knit sweater and turtleneck and pulling on a pair of jeans.

My coat, scarf, and boots in the kitchen were handy to slip into.

The brisk walk to work left me half-frozen, and so, I hiked to the Brew Café first and got in line. Luke's absence was noticeable as I ordered two blueberry muffins, coffee, and a chicken salad wrap for lunch. I figured that with the first annual First Lady celebration, the store would overflow with customers, preventing me from taking a lunch. *Will Grandma brave the weather?* My phone buzzed with a message providing the answer. *"Don't worry, I'm coming."* I didn't give it another thought. My amazing Grandma even knew how to text, and I knew faithful Grandma would be right on time. Ten on the button.

As I shivered outside the back door of my store, I noticed Luke pulling into a parking spot behind the cafe. A woman, different than either of the other two helpers, climbed out of the passenger seat. She was too bundled up for me to catch a glimpse of her features, but I already suspected another cousin had arrived. I would have waved at them, but my hands were full. I barely managed to tap in the right code keys to enter. Brrr! I couldn't wait to get inside out of the cold. I figured my ancestors immigrated to Minnesota because they enjoyed ice fishing and freezing their you-know-whats-off in the wintertime.

I opened the back door and stepped inside, flicking on the hall light with my elbow. I stomped the snow from my boots and removed my outerwear. My Victorian style dress, similar to Blanche's, hung in the workroom so I slipped the dress on.

The stench hadn't caught my attention when I first came in, but it did once I stepped across the hallway into the bathroom. I went for my phone and placed a call to the building's maintenance office. The pipes were frozen by the extreme cold weather we'd been having. My next call went to the temporary cleaning service I had previously used. The service's secretary arranged for two ladies to clean up the mess.

My store's phone rang and I ran to pick it up. "White House Dollhouse Store, Liv speaking." The caller questioned the store hours. "Closing is five." I hung up the phone.

"Maybe a sale?" Max entered the room. "I need something to eat—I'll be right back."

"Okay. Warming up the cider is next on the agenda."

After smoothing the set tablecloth, I busied myself with arranging cookies, straightening the cups and paper plates. In the back corner, I set out the large electric crockpot for warming the cider. I stepped back and took a sip of my coffee, smiling to myself. I was ready. Once the door was unlocked and I had turned the cardboard *Open* sign in the window, and the lights came on and gave me a huge burst of pride and energy.

"Good morning, ladies! How was your night?" I asked the First Lady dolls.

I snapped up a tipped over table in the George H.W. Bush family living room and placed it upright. "Mrs. Bush, how are your granddaughters? Did you bake cookies with them?" Nancy Reagan looked more tired than usual. "Mrs. Reagan, did Ronnie chase you around the oval office last night?" I peered closely at the doll because I was sure that she winked, and then I turned my attention to other matters.

I made a mental note to find a shelf to place the miniature house collection. Next, I tweaked the First Lady portraits that hung on the back wall, making sure they were all straight. The shelved Penny dolls needed a bit of dusting and fixing, so I took care of that as well. Pretty soon the computer was humming. The phone rang. It was Mikal from next door, asking to come over for a visit. Within a minute, he entered the store.

"Mikal. I haven't seen you for a while. It's so cold out!" I looked him over. He hadn't aged a bit. His eyes still twinkled while his white hair and round head reminded me of a fluffy ball of fur.

"I'm grabbing a cookie. Is the coffee hot yet?"

"It's cider, and no." I hesitated a moment. "Grab what you want and let me bring a chair out here for you. I don't want anyone walking near the back hallway because there is sewer water seeping onto the floor." It didn't take long to fetch a folding chair from the workroom and open it. "There. Have a seat."

"Thanks. My pipes aren't right, either. Someone's coming out this afternoon to look at them." Mikal plunked down into the chair and sighed. "We haven't talked since the murder. We need to catch up." He shivered, so I turned up the thermostat.

"I don't know any more about the case, either." I leaned against the counter and told him all that I knew, including the concentric puzzle from Blanche and the picture likeness at Luke's café.

He rubbed his chin and ran his long fingers through his hair. "Did you know that a staircase is a Masonic symbol?"

"No! Really?" I gave him a puzzled look. "Masonic? Never gave it a thought."

"Sure is. Used to belong, but I don't anymore." He

crossed his legs and popped the last bite of his cookie into his mouth. "Go ahead. What else did you find out?"

"The hatbox had a false bottom." I placed my hands on my hips. "What was so funny is that we found a hidden newspaper. Why hide it? The newspaper was in the bottom but was from Bloomington, Illinois, on the exact date of the Lost Speech." I took a deep breath before continuing, "Isn't that just incredible? Or a little too coincidental?"

"Odd, that Luke's pictures are similar." He shook his head. "Doesn't make any sense at all, but neither did she." Mikal glanced around the room. "That woman, Mary Todd, was very smart, so I read. Abe's rival, really. If women could have run for office in those days, she would have bested the men. Mary pushed him into the presidency because she knew he was brilliant." He massaged his chin. "I dare say, this has me puzzled. If I knew how to operate one of those electronic gadgets, I'd search for the speech." He grinned. "I just don't get those things."

"Electronic gadgets? You mean computers?"

"Yes. Just plain old cell phones are enough electronics for me. It's too confusing to figure out the rest of those gadgets. Come by for a writing analysis. I might get some pearls of wisdom that will help you figure out the puzzle." Glancing out the window, he said, "I think my next customer just passed. I recognize her red cape and scarf. I'd better go. She wants both a palm reading and writing analysis."

"I'll do that later. Thanks for stopping over."

I watched him get up and leave. At the same time, I wondered about his age. He had to be in his mid-eighties. At least now he had someone to manage his little store when he was gone, which made me happy. I didn't like to see him work alone.

Finally, it was possible to give my attention to the computer and checked messages. There were several from friends. First I opened the one from Inga.

It read,

> *Liv, whatever became of the hatbox? Did you find anything? I'm so curious about this, write back asap.//Inga. PS. I'm home because of the broken water pipe.*

I responded,

> *Inga, Mikal was just in here asking about the murder and suggested the staircase may be a Masonic symbol. What's your thought? I'm also hoping for a flow of traffic and enough fresh air to keep the stink at bay. I've put in a request for cleaning ladies. Take care, Liv*

The next message was from the House. Frances wrote,

> *Liv, I dropped the two items you purchased in the registered mailbox this morning. You should get the package in a day or two. The police have notified me about the dress and hat. Don't worry about it. This dress isn't important nor is the hat. She had probably worn both when in NYC and trying to sell her belongings.*
>
> *Enjoy! Frances.*

Curator, The Mary Todd Lincoln House

I typed a simple "*thank you*" and sent it.

The back door opened, allowing Aaron to enter.

"I'm by the computer," I hollered to him. Turning toward the hallway, I saw him at the showroom entrance. "Going to stay awhile?" I went toward him.

"Only staying a minute. I'm basically just checking up on you." He grimaced. "The smell's not too bad in here. Thank heavens." "I know. I'm hoping for a lot of traffic. I've called for cleaning ladies."

"How about dinner tonight with Tim and Maggie?"

"You want to invite them over?" I cocked my head. "What could we fix instead of our usual pizza? We could throw some potatoes in the oven and you could grill a couple of steaks."

"That occurred to me." He took my hand and asked, "How are you doing? You're not frightened or worried anymore about being here alone, are you?"

"No. I've gotten over that. Inga asked about the hatbox. I only mentioned the newspaper. She's at home today because of the mess with the plumbing. Her floor arrangement is different, so it's understandable." I squeezed Aaron's hand tightly before releasing it. "By-the-way... The stuffed bear I ordered will be coming by registered mail in a day or two. I also just happened to order a miniature dollhouse to go with my collection. We can display them in the store, and guess who gets to put up a new shelf?"

Aaron gave a mock groan.

I continued babbling. "I can't wait to get the new purchases. It'll be so much fun to have them. I'm so lucky to have found them." I remembered something, and added, "Frances at the House said not to worry about the dress and hat. The police have been keeping her informed about the investigation. The dress and hat aren't considered important. Frances figures that they date from when she was trying to sell her clothes in New York City."

"That's a lot of news," Aaron said. "Now, about my new shelf?"

"I know who will have to put up a shelf." He grinned. "Should I mention tonight to Tim or not?"

"Sounds like a good idea. Get what you think we'll need at the grocery store."

"It's a deal. I have only a few hours left of work." He fluffed my hair. "See you in a few."

After Aaron left, I made out a check for the Mary Lincoln House. There were a few remaining e-mail messages that needed attention. Afterward, I made a new e-mail folder and titled it, *Lost Speech.* I clicked out of my e-mail account and logged into my website where I added a bit of information concerning President Lincoln and the Lost Speech. Since so little was known about it, I placed a message for the public, *Has anyone heard or seen a copy of Abraham Lincoln's lost speech?* and then logged out of the site. I hoped for a few positive responses.

"I'm here!" Grandma hollered.

"Great." I heard her drop her outerwear in the

workroom before entering the showroom. "You look great."

"Thanks." She was wearing a period dress similar to mine but with a shawl over her shoulders, a buttoned down front with long sleeves, and of course, it was of a different vintage than mine. My sleeves were puffy, but her silver hair matched the style better than my red head.

I glanced over at the door and smiled as five women entered. My heart pumped. "Good morning, ladies. Help yourself to cider and cookies while you take a look around at the dollhouses. Any questions, just ask."

Grandma meandered around the store, quietly murmuring tidbits about the various First Ladies whenever someone asked a question.

I stayed near the checkout counter and spoke to customers as they came and went. Occasionally, someone asked about a particular house, and I was pleased to be able to answer. By early afternoon, we had sold five houses, which was quite pleasing. Max helped pack and load them into the customers' cars. A few other women expressed interest in purchases but needed to confer with their spouses first.

"Grandpa's coming for me in a few minutes." Grandma gave me a kiss, and I thanked her as she went to get ready to leave.

I realized late that afternoon that only a dozen cookies were left. *Remember to order more the next time,* I told myself. I strolled around the houses and tweaked the placement of items before sitting by the computer. The *Pennies for Our Troops* jar was full again, so I placed a call to Trisha. She'd come for it in the morning.

I was about to check my e-mail one more time and think of closing, since it was already four, when two ladies entered the store.

They looked at me and asked, "We're not too late, are we?"

"Nope! Take your time!"

As they strolled around the showroom, I noted they seemed most interested in the Lincoln Civil War dollhouse, especially after examining the uniform from Tad Lincoln. It was too bad I wasn't a gambler because I would've bet the ladies would both purchase a house, and they did. After the ladies left, I changed back into my everyday clothes. I gathered the garbage and set the full bags near the door for Max to bring out. The last of the cider was dumped and the table cleared. The few remaining cookies were put in a plastic resealable bag, and then I refolded the uniform. With the chores completed, it was time to go home. Since I was relatively sure that the cleaning women would show up tomorrow, I left the floor cleaning to them. I carried the penny jar to the workroom and hid it in the usual place. I wondered if I should leave for home, or stay and research the meaning behind the quote in the June 8, 1925, issue of *Time* magazine by a Honore Willsie Morrow-Stokes from Bloomington, Illinois. Research won.

Lincoln had given his Lost Speech in Bloomington. I had run across the article about the Lost Speech, and since I had bookmarked the site, I easily found it again.

My eyes opened wider after the second reading of the article. The article referenced Ann Rutledge, another name that sounded familiar. A quick search online confirmed my hunch. Abraham Lincoln was deeply in love with her, but she died of typhoid fever before they could become engaged. A passionate poem dedicated to Ann was published in a local paper three years after her death. Though anonymous, it was widely believed to have been written by Lincoln. It was more than half a decade after Ann's death that Abe became smitten with Mary Todd, whom he had wanted to "dance with in the worst way."

I wondered if Mikal had time to give me the analysis so I gave him a phone call. He did, so I bundled up and went to his office.

"Hi Mikal," I said, entering.

"Brr! Shut the door quickly," Mikal said. "You know the routine. I'll be right back."

"Okay." I took the pad and pen in front of me and wrote:

> *Another crazy murder concerning a first lady. How can this happen to me once again? Oops! It's not me! I'm alive. It happened to Blanche. Poor Blanche. But the concentric puzzles? What of them? I hate puzzles. Always have. Haven't been able to put one together on my own since kindergarten and I'm in my thirties. Yikes! Help!*
>
> *Yours truly, Dolley Madison descendant Olivia Reynolds.*

No sooner had I finished writing, when Mikal entered the room.

"I'm ready."

"Let me read it," Mikal said. He used his overly large magnifying glass to study the writing. "Oh my goodness, Olivia. You're up to your eyeballs again, aren't you? When will you learn to keep out of the way of the First Ladies?" He winked at me. "Keep an eye out at all times. No one wants to see you get hurt."

"Hurt? Really? As in dead hurt or just plowed under?"

"Plowed into a cornrow."

"Can you tell me anything else?"

"You still have your humor. Look how you've made your 'o-s', they're great."

"That all?"

"One more thing. Stay warm so you don't get sick."

"I'll try to remember that since it's winter in Minnesota."

"Good night, Liv."

"Thanks, and you too."

I headed out the door and toward home.

Chapter Seven

True to form, Aaron had stuffed the refrigerator with four steaks, the same number of large russet potatoes for baking, fresh vegetables for salad and a bottle of wine. The wine bottle sat open on the counter along with two full glasses.

"Hi, honey!" I kissed him. "I would have been home sooner but got caught up on the computer. Guess what I found out? Actually, it's kind of spooky." I dropped my boots by the door and pulled off my warm jacket. "Hurry up and guess!"

"Not a clue." He chopped the green pepper and dribbled pieces into the lettuce-lined salad bowls. "Go ahead and tell me before you split."

"One of the reporters who was present when Lincoln gave the Lost Speech compared it to the Sermon on the Mount. One reason there's no transcript is because the reporters present quit writing as they were all so mesmerized by his words." I accepted a glass of wine from Aaron and took a sip. "Can you believe it?"

"Interesting but it still seems far-fetched. What was the speech about?"

"Well, it's my conclusion, based on what I've read of it, that it was about uniting the states and avoiding a civil war over the slavery issue."

"Wow. That's incredible." Aaron glanced at me. "Was it really that important a speech?"

"You bet it was. It really did make Lincoln a national figure." I reached for a carrot. "Here's the spooky part – another death comes into the story. Lincoln was in love with someone before he met Mary Todd, but she died."

"It is sort of creepy. Another death? They're stacking up like cordwood."

"Exactly." I took another bite. "When are Tim and Maggie arriving?"

With perfect timing, the doorbell rang.

"Come on in!" I called upon entering the front room. Tim and Maggie walked in. "Hey you!" I gave Maggie a hug. "You look wonderful!"

Maggie and I followed Tim to the kitchen where we found chef Aaron was seasoning the steaks.

When he was done he suggested we go to the living room before starting the grilling. Aaron poured two more glasses of wine for our guests, then topped off our glasses

Maggie and Tim sat cozily on the sofa while Aaron and I claimed our favorite chairs.

"The hat and dress Blanche wore when she impersonated Mary Lincoln actually had belonged to Mrs. Lincoln. They're in the back room. Tad Lincoln's uniform is in the store. My guess is that the folks at the Mary Todd Lincoln House will want them returned after the investigation." I sipped from my glass. "The detectives want me to inspect the seams, but any extra time has been hard to come by."

"Wow," Maggie said. "I'd like to see them."

"This way," I said. Maggie followed me to the back

bedroom. "The dress box is huge. So is the hat." I flipped on the light as we entered the room.

The dress box was perched on a large stool. I removed the lid and set it aside. I held up the satin carefully. It was a light blue dress with its many gathers and folds, and expertly embellished with fine lace.

"It's gorgeous!" Maggie's eyes were as large as saucers. "Can I touch it?"

"Gently." Carefully she reached out and smoothed her hand down the fabric. "Let's go into the other bedroom." I held the dress tight, and Maggie followed me down the hall. I laid it out on our bed while she turned on the overhead light. "There. Now we can inspect it closer. I've been waiting to do this." I lifted the hem and carefully ran my fingers across it. "The knots stand out from the even stitches. The detectives want me to inspect the seams before I return it. The hat needs returning, also."

"Let's see."

I turned the seam around to get a better look, and we both gazed down at a huge knot of white thread. "This doesn't seem right at all."

"Look. Here's blue and white, then about two inches of just white thread." Maggie touched the area, gently running her finger along the stitching. "Feel this."

"We need a pair of scissors," I said.

"Look at the hem. There are stitches in two different colors. Why? Those days, women knew how to sew and wouldn't mess it up like this."

"Exactly," Maggie agreed. "Nor would we be able to feel the knots."

"And, on top of that, you'd expect the stitches to be more evenly spaced." I smoothed the hem down. "It's time to open this up and see what the deal is."

"Chow time," Aaron called from the doorway.

"Later," Maggie said.

"Agreed."

I helped carry the salads and dinner plates over to the table while Tim filled our glasses once again. Aaron brought the steaks to the table and set the platter next to the bowl of baked potatoes I'd set there earlier.

"What do you suppose is hidden in the hem of the dress?" Maggie asked, taking a bite of steak.

"Hard to tell." I filled Tim in about finding the staircase drawing in the hatbox.

When we had finished eating, we each carried our plates to the sink. "It's my job to do the cleanup— that's how we do it around here." The dishes could wait. "Hold on a sec."

I found my little sewing kit in a cabinet drawer and told the others, "Follow me." All three followed me to the brightly lit bedroom. Holding my breath, I carefully snipped off bits of the odd thread and poked my baby finger inside the hemline. "Hmm, there might be something hidden, but I don't want to cut the thread any more than necessary." My finger wasn't long enough to reach it.

"Let me try," Maggie said, reaching out.

"Nope. Let her do it. The detectives will ask about

it later," Aaron stated and nodded at me. "Go ahead hon."

"Thanks for your support, sweetie." I bunched the fabric up while inching my finger farther inward. "Got it!" At last the small bit of paper between the fabric and my nail was maneuvered toward the opening. Gradually, I slid it out. Holding it between shaky fingers, I said, "It's just one letter, a capital G."

"Are you serious?" Tim asked.

"Serious as I'll ever be." I shrugged, holding it so they could see it. "What do you suppose this means?"

"Why on earth…?" Tim scratched his chin.

"I'm calling the detectives. Wait here," Aaron said. He left the room to make the call.

I studied the paper until Aaron returned.

"We need a copy," I said, removing my phone to snap a picture. "There."

"What did they say?" Tim asked.

"The dress needs to be returned with this note in the morning.

The other item," Aaron glanced at me, "we'll still research."

"What other item?" Maggie asked.

"It's part of the investigation. Can't say," Tim responded. "We still have the hat."

"I've already started a file on the store's website about the Lost Speech titled *Mary Lincoln*, and I've added one in my e-mail account. Every little tidbit that I drum up is going into it."

"I'd bet her pantaloons that Blanche was killed for this information," Maggie said.

"I agree. At least the images are stored. The dress, hat and note will go with Aaron in the morning. What we should do is try to compare this letter with the handwriting inside the hatbox." We peered down at the shaky scratches. "Let's go."

Maggie and I stepped into the other room and headed straight to the hatbox. Maggie held up the lid while I smoothed the newfound paper down right beside the drawing and handwriting.

"What do you think?" I asked. "Pretty shaky."

"Deranged?"

"Or elderly." I peered closer at the penmanship. "It appears to be the same—from the same person. I don't see anything to make me think otherwise. Do you?"

"Mmm, yeah pretty close."

I placed the message inside the box, and Maggie set the lid on top. "Let's go find the men."

We found them in the living room, finishing their beer. "I'm tired, hon. Shall we?" Maggie reached for her coat. "Does the handwriting look the same?" Aaron asked.

"Yes," I replied. "I'll ask Mikal to compare the writing on the lid and the message."

"Let me know what he says," Maggie said.

"Ready?" Tim stood up and held Maggie's coat as she slipped into it. He slid his arms into his own heavy coat and said, "See ya tomorrow."

Once they'd safely walked to their car, we locked the front door and shut off the outside light.

"Let's hit the sack." Aaron took my arm. "I forgot to tell you that I bought a shelf plus the hardware to put it up over the computer at the store."

"Wonderful. When can you install it?"

"Asap tomorrow." He kissed me. "How'd the day go? You never did say."

"Great. Grandma was perfect. In her soft manner, she managed to sell five houses while I stayed at the counter and rang up sales. Then in the afternoon, we sold two more." I grinned. "Can't believe it!"

"Now you can pay for the miniature house and stuffed bear you ordered." He placed his arm over my shoulder.

"It's been a good day."

Together we walked down the hallway to our bedroom. Within minutes, we had fallen asleep.

In the morning, our blankets were strewn around from tossing and turning. I dressed for work quickly in heavy warm clothes. The bathroom mirror image of my hair was reminiscent of a hurricane. I splashed water on myself, applied makeup, and then struggled to capture my hair in a clasp.

My outerwear was handy to slip into and soon I was on my way to work. The air was brisk, hurrying me along.

The hair on the back of my neck bristled as I stepped inside the slightly opened back door of the store. I still smelled the sewage and hoped the cleaning ladies would soon arrive. A light shone from the workroom, and I called, "Max!" When he didn't answer, I figured he'd forgotten to shut off the light.

I walked into the workroom and gasped. It took a few seconds for me to find my voice. "Help!" The workbench and tabletop were filled with a conglomeration of miniature items. Boxes were upended. The sewing machine table was covered in a hodgepodge of my miniature inventory. "Help!"

I heard footsteps overhead and knew Max was on his way. I slumped into the nearest chair, placing my head in my hands.

"For the love of…" Max groaned. "Did you call it in yet?"

"No." I shook my head, removed my phone from my pocket, and called it in to the precinct to report it.

"I came downstairs in a hurry." Max studied me. "Been any farther into the store?"

"No." I held my head between my palms. "I can't bring myself to look."

"Want me to?"

"You can come along, but it's my store, I'll go too." We walked into the showroom together.

"Looks okay."

"Thank heavens the houses weren't touched." I wiped my eyes. "This makes me so sick."

"Anything stand out?"

I opened the cabinet with the *Pennies for Our Troops* jar and shook my head. "This is still here. They weren't after cash." I couldn't help sniffling.

"I know. It brings back memories." With concerned eyes, Max asked, "Should I call to see about the cleaning crew?"

"Better wait." I found I was still holding my cell phone and slid it into my jacket pocket. I felt something weird in the pocket and realized it was the computer memory stick. "Oh. Forgot about that."

"What?" Max asked.

"This." I held it up. "Found it outside." I put it back in my pocket. "I should remember to give it to the police, it could be a clue to Blanche's death."

Max leaned against the workbench. "What on earth were the intruders looking for?"

"No idea." I shook my head. "Nothing's here except the dollhouses and furnishings." I ran my fingers through my hair. "I need a cup of java."

"Let me go and get us both a cup, plus a muffin or something for you. I'm sure you didn't eat breakfast." He smiled at me. "The police will be here any minute. Do you want me to wait? Are you okay?"

"I'm fine. Go. Coffee's just what I need."

I watched him leave. Within a couple minutes, I heard pounding on the front door. I went out to let two patrol officers enter. Just as I opened the door, two cars slid into each other on the icy street in front of the store, narrowly missing the squad car parked out front. The crunch was jarring in the cold winter air.

One of the patrol officers shook his head. "We'll be right back as soon as another squad arrives."

"Got it." I closed the door and turned toward the showroom. My heart pumped as I leaned into the door. After a few moments, I went to sit in my usual place behind the counter. It wasn't long before the officers came back.

"Sorry about that," one of the officers said, brushing the snow from his pant legs and stomping his shoes on the mat.

"'Tis the season of snow and car wrecks," his partner added. "People don't take the necessary time to slow down."

"Right. Everyone's in a hurry." I took a deep breath and said, "The mess is back here." He followed me toward the workroom. The detectives soon arrived as well and began asking what seemed like a million questions. Something didn't seem quite right, but what was it? When I finally had a moment, I went out the back door, stood across the alleyway and stared at the store. The snow was trampled near the dumpster, which led me to take a closer look.

Opening the door, I called the officers out, and said, "Take a look at all the footprints. Something's odd about them."

"I don't see what you mean," the uniformed officer stated as he stared downward.

"A set of prints looks more square than shaped like typical boot or shoe prints." Scrunching down, I aimed my cell phone and snapped a few pictures while the officer followed my example. "It needs to be done before the snow here either melts or gets more trampled upon."

When finished shooting photos, he went back inside, but I continued to search the area, trying to figure out where the prints were leading but with no success. I dragged the stepstool out from behind the dumpster, then went back inside for the garbage. The officers were busy, and both ignored me for the moment, so I brought the bags outside. I stepped up onto the stool, heaving the bags over the edge. A thump and low groan startled me.

"Liv, that bag looks heavy. Let me do it for you," Ronnie called from around the corner. "Wait!" He started toward me.

"Help!" I yelled. It took a moment for me to realize that my bag had landed right on top of a partially covered body. "Ronnie! Come quick!" I heard that low, mournful groan once again. I pulled myself as high as possible and bent over the edge. "Hello," I asked, and bent farther over the edge. I lost my balance and fell in a second later.

"Help!"

Chapter Eight

"Good grief! Why didn't you wait? I had to set my camera in the car," Ronnie stated, staring down at me. "What next?" He grinned.

"Get me out of here! I'm on top of someone," I growled. He reached his arms down and lifted me up. "Why are you here?"

"Because of the call-in about your break-in." Ronnie brushed off his hands and coat.

"I've got to get the police out here." I opened the back door and shouted, "Someone get out here! There's someone in the dumpster." I slammed the door shut and ran back to the dumpster. I hollered down to the woman, "Help is on the way. You'll be fine."

The door opened with the two uniformed officers rushing at me. Ronnie brushed me aside and was getting ready to jump into it.

"Move it, mister," one officer ordered. "Okay." Ronnie reluctantly moved to the side.

"Let's get her out! She must be near death!" I said.

An officer used my stool and leaned over in an attempt to reach the woman. I watched as an officer called it in to the dispatcher, certain that an ambulance would arrive soon.

"Shoot! I'll climb down. Get ready to take her," the first officer ordered.

"We'll take it from here," the second officer

reassured me. "Go back inside but don't touch anything," ordered the first officer.

"I'm staying right here." I clamped my jaw tight and crossed my arms. Two unmarked squad cars parked in the alleyway.

The officers lifted the woman out and laid her on a blanket. They covered her with a warmed blanket, pulling it over her face. Her hair, all I could see of her, was long and shiny black. The officers also took the garbage bags I'd just thrown in. Max returned while the detectives were busy conferring and taking pictures.

I moved toward the medics and noticed an officer walking the breadth of the alley with his eyes focused downward, searching for evidence.

Aaron parked his squad car farther down the alley as I went to go back inside. It was such a relief to see it.

It seemed to take a very long time until an officer entered and asked me a few more questions. He politely told me to stay put until the detectives were able to make their inquiries. I stood just inside the workroom door, gazing at the mess. Who would do something like this and why? My legs felt like lead. I couldn't move. At last Detective Mergens entered.

"Mrs. Reynolds?" Mergens said.

"Liv. Yes?"

"What can you tell me about the woman?" Mergens asked. "And how the heck did you end up inside the dumpster? Start from when you first walked out the door." He had his pad and pencil ready when I began with the story.

After I finished, he said, "Thank you," and slid his notepad back into his breast pocket.

"Is she all right?"

"I can't tell you. She is in need of medical care, barely alive because of the cold temps, probably hypothermia. It's up to the doctors to save her."

"Having the dumpster cover down must've helped to keep her body heat inside." I played with my hair. "Do you know if I can go back into my workroom yet?"

"Hold on." He held up a finger while he radioed an officer. He looked up at me. "Go ahead. They've finished fingerprinting."

"I took pictures earlier of the prints in the snow surrounding the dumpster. Do you want them?"

"Yes, please. I'll add them to the photos the officer took." Mergens handed me his card and said, "Forward them to this number, that's my cell."

"Would you prefer e-mail instead?"

"Doesn't matter."

When he left, I entered the workroom and turned the heat up. I wanted a hot cup of coffee or hot chocolate, to give me strength for the job that lay ahead. I decided to go into the showroom.

"Ladies!" I said to the dolls. "Don't worry, the police will leave soon. Dolley? Do you have a shot of that whiskey you kept hidden up your sleeve? No? Shoot!"

I glanced outside, just in time to see a tow truck raising one of the wrecked cars from the earlier accident. The owner of one, presumably, stood slumped on the curb, his hands in his pockets, looking as if he'd lost his best friend. I sighed and went to sit by the computer and fired it up for the day.

"Honey." Aaron surprised me from behind and kissed me. "This must've been a nightmare to walk in on, eh?"

"What a day." I looked up at him. "What can you tell me about the person who was pulled out of the dumpster?"

"I'm not sure about her condition. I'm surprised you even heard her groan, to tell you the truth."

"There were no cars out back. I wonder how she got there." I shrugged. "I have to refocus now. I can't dwell on it. Something is happening around here, but what?" I shook my head. "Women in dumpsters? Blanche murdered near our doorstep? It's all pretty horrific."

"Don't do anything rash. Please talk to me first before you do anything. Promise?"

"Promise."

"Think everything through, and logically." Aaron massaged my shoulders. "What's next on the day's agenda?"

"I don't know," I replied. "I want to see if anyone has responded to my question about the Lost Speech. The computer is acting slow again."

I logged into the website and found three messages and read them for Aaron. "One guy says, 'It's lost. Give it up.' Another said, 'Look up the word *lost* in the dictionary.' The other message said, 'Don't you have something better to do with your time?'" I logged out. "These guys are so rude. What's with people nowadays?"

I let the computer screen go into sleep mode. "It's time to tackle the workroom. Wonder when the cleaners will get here?"

Aaron slid his arm around me as we strolled into the workroom.

I glanced at the sewing machine and cringed.

"Mrs. Nixon's dress is unsalvageable." The tiny cut pieces of chiffon were torn. "I'll have to reorder furniture, also. Several chairs and tables are broken."

"At least the doll heads aren't broken," Aaron said.

The detectives came in to let us know they were finished. "We'll be in touch if we have any more questions," Mergens said.

"Whatever criminal activity is happening to you, or around you, you can be sure we'll get to the bottom of it. We're keeping tabs on it," said Erlandsen.

"I hope so because I'm scared to death," I said, shivering.

Aaron tightened his arm around me. "Both of us are. Keep me in the loop."

"Will do."

With the door closing behind the detectives as they left, I sank into Aaron. "I'm going to dust the showroom and straighten up the houses. I can't face this workroom mess right now."

The cleaning ladies arrived, and I had to stifle a chuckle. It was Suzy and Ruth again. I noticed that they both wore heavy shirts, most likely so they could better hide their flasks. A while back, there had been a murder in my store and these two women did a superb job at cleaning up.

"Remember us?" Suzy asked, her grin lighting up her wrinkled face. White curls peeked out from under her knit cap and reminded me of a small poodle. When she removed her cap, two forgotten hairpins revealed themselves, holding down a very tightly wrapped curl. Now my gut hurt from holding back laughter.

"I think I'll leave you, Liv, and head back to work." Aaron said. "Don't forget there's hockey practice tonight."

"Okay. Have fun and don't freeze half to death," I said and then winced, remembering the girl I found in the dumpster.

"See you later." He marched out the door. I noticed that the women stared after him.

"Mighty good looking." Suzy grinned.

"I think so, too. Thanks."

"The showroom floor will need a quick once-over with mild soap and tepid water," I said. "The bathroom needs a good cleaning, especially the floor."

"What does 'tepid' mean?"

Suzy winked as she leaned in closer to me. She whispered, "Sometimes ya have to spell tings out for da old girl." She touched her forehead and glanced at Ruth.

"Barely warm." I thought I'd bust a kidney from holding back my laughter. These ladies' Scandinavian twang was quite comical. "The sooner you get this cleaning finished, the better. It's stunk in here now for a few days. This is the third day, I guess."

"We can do it, can't we, Ruth?" Suzy's toothless grin was almost my undoing.

"I'm not a total idjut!"

"Ladies, you can get started. The cleaning detergent and mops and so forth are right inside the back door. I'll either be in the workroom or out in the showroom. I don't plan to go anywhere."

"How come that room's such a mess?" Suzy asked. "Someone broke in." I walked into the room. I had wanted to shut the door to drown them out but decided against it.

"What if we get murdered like that woman did outside?" Ruth asked.

"No one's getting murdered here," I said.

"I seen that ambulance pulling away. We was scared," Suzy said. "Don't worry."

"They're droppin' like flies around here," Ruth said.

From the corner of my eye I saw Suzy hand Ruth her flask. Ruth nudged it away, pulling out her own flask. The two ladies each took a couple swallows, then set to work.

Aaron was right—it was a big mess, and one that only I could clean up. I began by picking up all the small pieces of chinaware and placing them inside one of the larger boxes. Instead of sorting, I carefully stacked the few remaining Lincoln dinner plates. The real Lincoln chinaware for the White House was exceptional. The previous set hadn't been replaced since ten years before the Pierce administration, and

Mrs. Lincoln wanted the President's House to be the finest in the land. She was addicted to buying. She'd be seeing a psychiatrist if she were alive today.

The Lincoln White House was indeed spectacular.

Mary Lincoln chose a set with royal purple and double gilt edges. Each piece had the arms of the United States on it, and the gold border was entwined with two lines signifying the union of the North and South. After ordering the china, Mary was criticized, of course. Pieces of it are displayed, not only in the White House, but admired by visitors in the Smithsonian Museum in Washington, D.C.

The royal purple color in the dishes stood out, and the American bald eagle was regal as it carried the national motto, *E Pluribus Unum*, through clouds. Mrs. Lincoln was the first of the First Ladies to choose an entire set of chinaware. I continued stacking the tiny plates, cups and saucers, relieved to see that the collection had only a few broken items.

Next, I spread out the miniature furniture. These pieces would take up most of my sorting time. Mary loved flower sprays and bouquets on hand for the designated tables. Tables and chairs varied with each first family, or at least the arrangement of the furnishings did. Of course, there were also the lavatories to furnish with soaps and towels.

I'd become enamored with the First Ladies when my parents brought me to Washington D.C. as a child and have been so ever since. I learned that I was a distant relative of Dolley Madison. I later fought off a killer in search of the "family secret," which only added to my fascination. A sudden knock on the doorframe broke my concentration, and I jumped.

"Yes?" I asked, turning around. Ruth stood wringing her hands like a little girl in trouble. "What's the matter?"

"Well. You see?" When Ruth crinkled her reddened nose, it reminded me of a dried carrot. I wondered if she had a snoot full before the day even began?

"Yes?"

"It stinks!" She held her nose.

"I didn't think it was that bad. Maybe I've grown used to it?" I raised a brow. "The bathroom should be about done, eh?"

"Don't mind her, she's a little dazed this morning." Suzy did another wink, only this time I counted three winks. "Let's get this part finished, then we'll take ten. Okay?"

"Fine." I winked back at her and then sat down again by the workbench. I wondered if they'd wash the showroom floor today or tomorrow?

I had started sorting the couches and desks when the bell over the front door dinged.

"Coming," I called. I headed into the showroom.

"Liv, I've wondered about you." Mikal strolled around the dollhouses and studied some of the furnishings.

"So, what brings you here on such a warm, sunny day in January?"

"You always see right through me." Mikal stopped in front of Lincoln's Civil War house. "I was wondering about you. What happened out back this morning? Couldn't miss noticing the police, you know. I am right next door." He looked at the Lincoln bed, and said, "Hmm… I wonder if this room is really still haunted?"

"Good question." I steered him to the counter, then I went behind and sat. "I'm glad you're here, actually." I loved bouncing ideas off him. "A few things trouble me."

"Why's that?" Mikal cocked his head. "Wait. First explain the early morning police thing." He crossed his arms as I told him about finding the workroom a big mess. "What on earth were they after?"

"No idea." I said. "You knew I'd fallen into the dumpster?"

"Yes. Fill me in." He pinched his nose and giggled. "Don't hardly smell it."

"I heard a noise like a groan and looked in. Everyone tells me to butt-out. It's a good thing I didn't listen this morning." I crossed my arms. "Don't know anything except the person who was in there is lucky to be alive. I'm glad I found her. Actually, Ronnie deserves credit also."

"This is all mystifying."

"I know. I was throwing the garbage out from the break-in and shouldn't have been. I should have known better, and the police took the bags as evidence." I blew my nose. "I'm jinxed." I leaned closer. "Guess what? Last night, my friend Maggie and I found a small snippet of paper inside the hem of a dress that once belonged to Mary Lincoln."

"Really? The dress worn by the woman who was killed?" When I nodded, he asked, "What did it say?"

"That's what's so odd. It just had the letter, 'G' written on it. Then, there's the hatbox with a drawing of a staircase on the inside of the lid, along with the name, Mrs. Tindall, and that was Mary Lincoln's alias."

"How interesting." Mikal furrowed his brow. "I don't know what to say. What on earth is this all about?"

"We're wondering if they are written by the same hand. Maybe we can find samples of letters written by her online somewhere."

"First off, we don't even know if the messages are from her." Mikal started to tap his cheek in thought. "Can you bring the hatbox lid in tomorrow along with the paper? I'll be able to tell you if the lettering is of an old style from then nineteenth century."

"Sure. I can do that." I gazed up at the clock. It was already four, and the two cleaning ladies hadn't returned from their ten-minute break. "How about if I get here a little earlier tomorrow, like nine? Then we can sit without worry of interruptions?"

"Sounds like a solid plan." He looked up at the Penny Doll collection. "My mother used to have a few of those. I wonder what happened to them? Probably my sister took them." He headed for the door and stopped. "Nine tomorrow morning. I'll bring the coffee, since you'll have the goods." He stepped out, closing the door behind him.

I got up and went toward the back, just in time to

see the back door fly open. The two cleaning women staggered inside.

"You two look three sheets to the wind. Is it really that cold out?" I placed my hands on my hips. "I'm not paying for a two-hour break, you know?" I eyed them closely. "What's up? Show me what's done for today."

"It's like this…" Suzy narrowed her eyes at me. "Ruth got sick but is better now."

"Show me what you've done," I repeated and stepped aside. Suzy opened the bathroom door, revealing a sparkling clean room. Looking downward, I noticed the shine on the floor. "It looks great. Really, it does." I'd forgotten how thoroughly the two could clean. Everything glistened and smelled good. "It's lovely."

"Can we come back in the morning to mop the showroom floor?" Suzy asked. "We're tired. You can bill the temp service for just the two hours today."

"Oh, all right." These two women befuddled me. "Tomorrow at ten. Okay?" I looked Suzy squarely in the eye. "No flask."

"What about me?"

"You, too." I shook my head at Ruth. "It makes you sick. It wasn't the smell, Ruth. It was the flask. Got it?"

"You betcha."

Watching them sway to the door, I called out, "Ten o'clock! No flasks!"

Suzy raised her hand as they stepped outside.

I went back out to the computer and sat down. After rebooting, I logged into the Mary Todd Lincoln House website and sent a message.

Frances// Have you heard any news concerning the murder? The detectives had me check the dress hem because it didn't seem right. I found a snippet of paper inside it. I will slip-stitch it together tonight. It'll be like it had been. Aaron gave the paper to the police.//Liv

Next, I searched for the Presidential Lincoln Library in Springfield, Illinois. Eventually, I came to the contact page and clicked on it. I wrote:

Dear Sir,

I'm the owner of the White House Dollhouse Store in Minneapolis, Minnesota. Recently, a Mary Lincoln impersonator was scheduled to read from some of her diaries at a nearby antique shop. From her, I've learned that there is a newly found letter on display. I wondered if I may have a copy of that letter, if I pay for the copying and postage?

Also, she mentioned the Lost Speech during the reading time. I had never heard of it until then. Can you tell me more about it? I'd love to know. I'll give you my address upon your reply to my inquiry. Thank you very much.

Sincerely, Olivia Reynolds

Owner and proprietor of the White House Dollhouse Store

After clicking out of the site, I decided to research the stores where I purchased many of my items for the dollhouses. Were there rose bouquets available that might fit the bedroom decor? Sure enough, there were vases of pink, white, and red roses. I went ahead and ordered a dozen.

Once logged out, I shut the computer down and prepared to leave for the night.

"Good night, ladies!" I called.

After making sure the front door was locked, I grabbed my bag and bundled up. I took one last look in the bathroom and marveled at the cleanliness. I knew the cleaning ladies would be in at ten, and the wood floor would shine like the sun when they finished the job—provided they left their flasks at home.

After locking the door and stepping out into the back alley, I heard a car engine start. I glanced toward it. Two men sat in the front seat, and I recognized the two women working for Luke in the back seat as they drove past me. The men looked as though they might be from Cambodia as well. *Who were they?* Shivering, I headed out into the cold. The setting sun made me frown, and I dreaded the long evening without Aaron home. The sun set early this time of year. I couldn't wait for those nice, easy, lazy days of spring and summer.

I set off at a brisk pace and wondered what to fix for supper. When the string of lights and large, pudgy snowmen came into view, I knew I was almost home. Within a few minutes, I was in my warm house.

I removed my outerwear. The doorbell rang as I emptied my jacket pocket into the catchall drawer. No one was at the door when I opened it, but a shipping box was on the step. The delivery truck driver waved as he drove from the curb.

Excited, I brought the box in, ripped it open, and removed the stuffed bear and set it aside. Left inside the box was a spectacular dollhouse. All of the little pieces were wrapped up, so I decided to wait and unwrap the entire piece once the shelf was in place at the store. After inspecting the house and bear, everything went back into the packing box.

I spent the evening in front of the TV, eating junk food. With pen in hand, I started a list. Item number one was Holly, for no particular reason except she was young and probably in need of money to pay college loans. However, no one had touched my cashbox drawer. That didn't seem right, so I crossed her from my list.

Mikal was in his eighties. He'd never do such a thing.

Inga had her store, and she was an old friend of Grandma's.

Luke? He seemed to do fine with his restaurant, though it was unusual to have so many young Cambodian women coming and going. Surely they couldn't all be his cousins or his wife's cousins. Then again, I didn't know much about Cambodian families or how large they might be.

And who was the woman in the bottom of my dumpster, and why was she there?

And what did my store have to do with it?

My mind spun in circles, but eventually I fell asleep.

"Hey you, you little monkey," Aaron said. He flipped back the blankets. "You're taking up the bed."

Aaron had returned late from practice.

"You're the monkey!" I threw a pillow at him. "Teach you a thing or two."

"Well, baby girl," Aaron said. He slipped under the blankets. "Monkey's don't wear clothes."

Chapter Nine

Frost hung on the trees that lined the streets on my way to work, and my car trunk was loaded with the box with the stuffed bear and the Lincoln House, as well as the hatbox lid. The snippet of paper was tucked into my bag. Children were climbing into school buses, and I had to stop for a few of them. The stuffed bear had spiked my interest in the Lost Speech again. As I drove up the alleyway and parked, I began to think of it as Mary Lincoln's puzzle.

With my hands full, I stepped out of the car. No sooner had I greeted the ladies and carried an extra chair into the showroom, then Mikal came in with two coffees in hand.

"Thanks." I took my cup from him and locked the door behind him. "Would you like to sit here or would you rather sit in the workroom?"

"I like it better here." Mikal sat down, placing a large hand on his knee as he took a sip of his steaming coffee. "I'm anxious to see all of this."

"Yes. Hold on a sec." I set my cup down, and then went to get the items. "I have Tad's stuffed toy bear. There's something on it that I want you to see."

"Another mystery?" Mikal's eyebrows arched. "What is it?"

"Look at this." I removed the bear from its box before flipping the bear up to its bottom. Pulling down on a small, attached trapdoor, I said, "See? It looks as if a family tree was embroidered into it. The fabric was cut down, to be sewn so that only this part could be viewed. Does this make any sense? I'm clueless, once again. That woman is an enigma."

"She was to just about everyone, even to herself, I believe." Mikal reached out and said, "May I?" I handed the bear to him. He brought up it to his nose where he drew in a deep breath. "Smells old."

"The fabric is, that's for sure. It's almost worn thin in spots, also the seams are frazzled. I think it's preserved only because it was forgotten about. It's probably been shelved for several years," I said. "Let's see here, now." When Mikal studied the embroidered tree, his eyes glazed over. "Why would a family tree be embroidered on a bear's butt?"

"Good question." I took it from him and set it back inside the box, wrapping paper around it before placing the lid back on it. "Why didn't Frances say anything about it?"

"The person you purchased it from?"

"Yes."

"She probably just chalked it up to Mrs. Lincoln's craziness."

"Which may explain everything. Who knows?" I took out the small paper from an envelope and handed it over. "Here's the message. The staircase is right here." I turned the lid so he would have a better vantage for study.

"The upper-case 'G' of course isn't shown on the staircase, but by looking at the flow of the lines, the way the corners and curves of the stairs were made, it seems as if it's done by the same person, certainly with a similar pen nib and ink. The stopping, starting, lifting of the pen, it all constitutes the seemingly natural flow and rhythm of the one person's hand." Mikal looked at me. He always had good advice. Since I was prone to bodies dropping around me, I figured he was good for several more cups of hot chocolate. "I am almost ninety-nine percent positive they are both by the same person. This is all from Mary Lincoln, as far as your knowledge allows you to know?"

"Yes, most certainly." I nodded. Setting my coffee cup down, I picked up the message and placed it back inside the envelope before carrying all three items to the workroom. Returning, I asked, "What do you make of it? I can't tell you too much because of the ongoing investigation, and you have to promise not to tell anyone about it, at least for now."

"It certainly is intriguing." Mikal sighed. "Mum's the word." He pinched his fingers together and drew a line across his lips as if to zip them shut.

"Good." I finished my coffee and tossed the cup into the garbage bin. "I'm calling it the Mary Lincoln puzzle."

"Well…she was a puzzle." He shook his head. Glancing at the clock, he said, "Time for me to go. I've got a client due at any time."

After Mikal left, I gave Inga a call, but she didn't answer. I left a phone message, and then turned on the computer only to get that humming noise again. I was logging into my files when the back door opened.

"Hello," I called.

"Only me." Max clopped inside the hallway, stopping at the doorway. "I will be gone all day for personal business."

"Anything I need to know about?"

"Nope. The security folks have been here and gone. The back door should be better secured now."

"I hadn't noticed. What did they do?"

"They put in a more advanced electronic strip around the frame. The other one wasn't made for such extreme temperatures. It was a little outdated."

"Oh. Okay. Thanks. The cleaning ladies will soon be here. Let's leave it open for them."

"Sure. Have a good one." After he walked to the door, I heard him holler, "Stay out of the dumpster. Any garbage, let me take care of it." He opened and closed the door.

"Thanks for the advice." I called to the empty room. I didn't like being alone. Winter days such as this made me wonder if hiring another employee might be worthwhile just to keep me company. However, Max always seemed to do fine in here without me, and so did Grandma. Between the two, they managed to run the store when Aaron and I were on our honeymoon and occasional overnight trips since then.

The e-mail file from my website popped up as the back door opened once again. When Suzy loudly said, "Ja, ja," I got up and went out to meet the cleaning ladies.

"All set." Suzy stood holding a dust mop and grinning. Her gold tooth sparkled as the overhead lighting hit it just right.

"This here's a wet mop. It'll use just a little bit of water with a little bit of wax." Ruth stood straight, but she suddenly began to sway. I had to look away. *Had they been drinking already?*

"Let me take your flasks." I held out my hand. "Now. Or else you won't get paid." Fortunately, they did as told. "Get the wood floor done right away, so it'll dry."

"Right."

"You betcha."

They both "huffed" when I turned my back. I could almost feel their eyes shoot glances like daggers into me. *Should they be reported?* After double-checking the front door, I logged out from my computer file and went to the back workroom. No sooner were the items sorted than Inga called. I'm sure she did a couple of jumping jacks after I told her the news about the antique bear. The store was quiet and still, so I walked to the showroom entrance to check on the two cleaning ladies. No one was in the room, but it looked absolutely gorgeous. Standing with my mouth hanging open and my eyes opened wider, I gushed, "Wow," and jumped as the door behind me closed.

"You betcha," Suzy said.

"Ja, ya know." Ruth nodded.

Both stood grinning without pails or mops. They could've cleaned from the front of the store toward the back, but instead they must have gone out the front only to return through the back door.

"Why come through the back door?"

"We didn't want to track snow all over the beautiful floor, now did we?" Suzy said with her hands on hips.

"We don't want to make a mess, you know?" Ruth shook her head.

"Guess not." I had all I could do not to curl up from laughter. "Thank you for being so conscientious."

"Whatever that means." Ruth held out her hand. "Now, may I have my flask?"

"Ja, me too."

"Sure. Wait a minute." I went into the workroom, returning with both flasks. "Here." I gave them back. "I still pay the temp service, don't I?" I wondered if their boss should know about the ladies' drinking. They did such a nice job, but I could tell that the alcohol abuse was starting to become a problem.

"Ja. They pay us." Suzy nodded and turned toward the door. "Ruth?"

"You betcha."

I shook my head in disbelief as they walked out the door. *How could two women drink so much and still be recommended?* I heaved a sigh, then picked up the phone to call the temporary agency that sent them. A woman answered. I proceeded to explain the situation, but I also gave the two five stars for their excellent cleaning.

Before disconnecting, she said, "Everyone says the same, which is why they've been kept on. No one cleans as well. So, what do you want? A clean shop or a semi-clean shop? Those are your choices."

I slumped down into the chair and thought about

that. "Clean shop." I disconnected, hoping that I said the right thing.

I logged back into my website and checked messages. There were two more pertaining to the Lost Speech.

The first read:

Lost?? Hmm…look up the word in the dictionary.//

John

I responded:

John, Thank you. I think I'll look it up.//Liv The second read: Did he stuff it in his stove pipe hat?//Beth I responded: Beth, Didn't think of that, but a great idea.//Liv

Just as I was about to log out of the site, a third message popped up.

It read:

What was lost will be found.

I responded:

Let's hope.//Liv

The return address looked different from the final message, which was perplexing. It was unrecognizable. Was it from a foreign country? I forwarded the three messages to my personal e-mail account before logging from the site. In my personal account there were several messages, mostly from Maggie. She was asking about the message we found in the hem of the dress and also wanted to know what I had planned for the evening, since Aaron would be working late.

I messaged a return:

> *Maggie//Mikal studied and compared the message from the dress and the staircase, deeming them to be written by the same hand. Another interesting item is the bear. Tad's stuffed toy bear. It has a trapdoor, like in long underwear, but there is an embroidered family tree under the fabric flap. It's deeply puzzling, don't you think? How about a movie tonight? Meet you at the Riverview for first showing.//Liv*

After sending the message, I opened the Lincoln file and filed Maggie's sent message plus the forwarded messages in it. The next e-mail of interest was from the Lincoln Library, in reply to my recent message requesting a copy or a scanned attachment of the newly found Mary Lincoln letter. The message read:

> *Dear Mrs. Reynolds,*
>
> *The requested letter is unavailable at this time as we are still testing its authenticity. Please accept my sincerest apologies, but it will be posted soon on our website.*
>
> *Dr. James Wordsworth.*

Not wanting to sound ungracious, I replied:

> *Dear Dr. Wordsworth, Thank you for the response. Mrs. Reynolds*

I hit "send," leaving the file open for further reading. It was already past lunchtime. I thought about dashing to the Brew Café. "Ladies, it's lunchtime," I said to the dolls. At the same moment, the front door opened, sending in a gust of cold air into the room.

"Had lunch?" Inga burst in, carrying two bags. "Got us each a bowl of chili. Sounds good, doesn't it?" Shivering, she said, "Yikes. When will summer come?"

"Not soon enough. I'll fetch you a chair." I hurried to the workroom to get the chair Mikal had used. "Have a seat." I set the chair down beside the checkout counter. *Why was she reading my messages?*

"Oh. Sorry. Caught in the act," Inga said, blushing. "I noticed that the letters mentioned a stuffed bear. Was it Tad's? Don't worry. I didn't read anything personal." She opened the lunch bags after scooting around to the other side of the counter and shoved one of the bowls over toward me. "Here."

"Thanks. It sure smells good." My mouth watered when I took a whiff of the chili. "I didn't know I was this hungry until right now." I took a bite. "How do you like the floor?"

"The 'ladies,' I use the term loosely, did a superb job." Inga began eating. "They work hard. My store is now in good working order, too. If only we'd get more customers. It's been really slow, but I keep Holly on, only I can't give her many hours."

"You can't, really. It's barely worthwhile for me to open my doors." I continued enjoying the chili. "The First Lady celebration brought out a number of women and plenty of sales, though. Did you hear about my dumpster dive yesterday?"

"Who hasn't? That was going to be my next question after the stuffed bear." She cocked her head and said, "Well?"

"I heard a moan coming from the dumpster when I went to empty the trash, and then I ended up falling in. Yuck!" I shuddered. "If we had not found her, she might have died." I folded my arms. "Don't know anything except the woman is in a bad way. They have no suspects about the break-in, either." I shrugged. "Would you like to see the bear?"

"Of course. I was just telling Luke about it, too. What an amazing find!" Inga twitched her nose. "Bet my nose is red from the hot chili, isn't it?"

"Yep." I grinned. "What did Luke think about it?"

"He didn't say much, but he sure seemed interested."

"I wonder why." I finished eating and grabbed the garbage bin. "Here." We tossed our empty bowls and rubbish into it. After setting the bin down, I said, "Be right back." I went to the workroom and returned with the bear.

"Oh, my. You can sure tell that it's old, can't you?" She took it from my hands. "It's lovely. Really lovely." She held it to her nose and said, "It even smells old, doesn't it?"

"That's the same thing Mikal said." Turning it over, I revealed the mystery. "What do you think?"

"My goodness!" Inga peered closely at it. "It does look like a family tree. Why on earth would she embroider one? Why in that location? Mary had to have really lost it by that time, don't you think?"

"Don't you think the bear's rear end might mean something?"

"Yes, it sags and is in need of a lift."

Chapter Ten

On the way home from the movie, I crossed the Hennepin Avenue Bridge and followed the road onto Main Street and headed north. After passing the old Grain Belt Brewery, now a library, I had only a few more blocks to go. It comforted me to know that the old building still looked as good as ever.

Turning onto the block and approaching my house, I could see our snowman lights lighting the yard. *Wait, did our living room lights flicker?* It must have been fatigue that made me see things. I pressed the remote to open the garage door and pulled inside.

An eerie, creepy feeling crept over me as I entered the kitchen. I pulled off my coat, hung it up, and removed my boots. The hair on the back of my neck bristled as I looked around the room. The silverware, knives, and utensil drawers were tipped upside down on the counter, their contents strewn across the kitchen floor.

I picked up a long knife and dug out my cellphone. *Did I really hear the living room floor squeak?* The closet door was ajar, so I crept behind it. Somehow, I pressed the right buttons on my phone and whispered, "Help. There's someone in my house." My teeth chattered loudly, and I wondered if I heard the front door squeak open and close. Was it safe? My eyes were wide as I snuck out from behind the door and tiptoed to the living room. A draft of cold air could be felt in the living room. I closed and locked the front door, and then slumped against it. I called Aaron and left him a voice mail message.

It took me a few minutes before I was ready to go to the bathroom in search of a box of tissues. Outside the spare bedroom door I stopped right in my tracks. Mary Lincoln's hat was ripped to shreds. Tad's uniform was in a heap on the floor.

After snatching a tissue, I went back to the living room and sank into the sofa. In the background, I heard sirens. Aaron found me staring out the window with the television sound soft in the background.

"Why did this happen? Why?"

"Don't worry, baby, I'm right here." He sat beside me and placed his arm around me. "The police will soon be here."

"I… thought I… saw a light…"

"Wait for the patrol officers, honey." He smoothed the hair back from my face. "Don't worry, this will soon be over."

"Yes." I furrowed my brow. "I…had this weird feeling…" The sirens blared. "… come over me. I saw the kitchen mess."

"They're here," Aaron said. We both heard the sirens stop and the slamming of car doors. "I'll go and open the garage door."

The officers entered the room, and I turned down the sound on the TV. A news bulletin about the hunt for two missing girls caused me to remember the girl in the dumpster and shudder. I looked up at the officers.

"Mrs. Reynolds?" The first officer held open his badge. "Officer Olson."

"Officer Johnson," the second officer chimed in as he showed his badge.

"Call me Liv, please."

"Can you tell us what happened?"

"Sure." I proceeded to tell the two men what had happened from the time of entering the house until Aaron returned home. "Have you looked around at anything at all? Know if anything is missing?"

I shook my head.

"Ready to come and have a quick look without touching?" Officer Olson asked.

"Sure."

"You two show us the way," Officer Olson said.

"Let's go." I clutched Aaron's hand as we entered the spare bedroom to survey the mess. The flowers were ripped off the hat and scattered across the bed, along with the green leaves and attached netting. Very little was left on the hat. It looked like an old bushel basket. It hurt to look at it. I reached out to touch it but was prevented from doing so.

"Remember?"

"Sorry." I looked at the hatbox and said, "It's pulled apart. The lid, message, and stuffed bear are still in the trunk, but look what they did to Tad's uniform."

"You don't suppose they were after that, do you?"

"No idea." That made me think of the necklace. "Just a minute." I scooted out to the security box in our bedroom. When I opened it, my eyes lit up because the necklace was still in place. I shut it up again and went back to the spare room. "It's still here." "Why would someone do this to an old ladies' hat?" Officer Johnson asked, hands on his hips. "Was it your grandma's or what?"

"Believe it or not, it belonged to Mary Lincoln." I took out my phone to make a call to the detectives. No one answered, so I left a voice mail stating exactly what had happened.

"That might shed a whole new light on the investigation," Officer Olson said. "Does this pertain to an ongoing investigation?"

"I believe that it does," Aaron answered.

"It needed reporting." My phone buzzed, and I answered. It was a short call. "They're coming over." To Aaron, I asked, "Why would someone go through our kitchen drawers?"

"Remember, Liv. We're leaving it to the detectives."

Officer Olson closed his notebook after making a note of everything. "They'll be here asap."

"See anything missing from the kitchen?"

"Nah," Aaron shook his head. "I know how many knives there are."

"We'll wait in the living room."

Aaron stayed out of the officers' way while we settled in on the couch. Through half-closed eyes, I saw the flashes of photographs being taken.

The detectives arrived in a matter of a few minutes and knocked on the door.

Officer Olson cleared his throat. "There's a mess in

two rooms as far as we all know."

"You two go knock on doors. We'll take it from here," Erlandsen directed.

"The hat and dress are destroyed," I told him. "The hat, especially. The Mary Todd Lincoln Home must be contacted. I wonder if they're insured. Oh, and I've been meaning to ask you, did Blanche have family?"

"No. No other family," Erlandsen informed us. "Concerning the clothing, we've already contacted the Mary Lincoln House. They understand why it was in your possession as well as the necklace."

"That's the next piece of the equation. They want Blanche's laptop back, asap. However, it's blank," Mergens said. "Can you give us a clue as to why?"

"Not really," I said, perplexed, "but she was researching a speech that Mr. Lincoln gave."

"That speech is ancient history. It shouldn't pertain to today," Mergens said.

"But, you don't have a clear motive, do you?" I asked.

"Let them do their job," Aaron said, squeezing my hand.

"We're on it," Erlandsen said.

The rest of the evening was spent watching the detectives go from room to room. They looked things over while we listened to their muffled voices. Every so often, I would ask a question. Aaron and I gave each other a secret squeeze under a blanket while Mergens asked us yet one more question. The little guy reminded me of *Columbo*. After the officers had left, both detectives stood before us. I got a niggling feeling they were going to ask something weird.

"What?" I asked, studying both. "You've got something spinning around."

"May we?" Mergens nodded toward the spare chairs. "Go ahead."

They sat down. Mergens pushed his glasses up on his forehead and rubbed his eyes. I thought he was going to explain, but his partner jumped in.

"It's like this—something's up and we haven't a clue. It's just like the last time, only then we didn't listen to you," Erlandsen said. "We're open to listening this time since it's centered around you." I knew that he meant the Dolley Madison case. The clues were unclear then too, just like this puzzle surrounding Mary Lincoln.

"Thank you. I don't know what to say." I swallowed hard and looked at Aaron. "First, tell me what you've found out about the dumpster woman. Then I'll know how to answer."

"Wherever that leads, it doesn't concern whatever is happening here and now. Another investigator is working on that, and it involves Immigration and the local FBI bureau." Erlandsen shrugged. "We've got to concentrate on the murder."

"Look you two, in particular, you, Liv. This is no game," Mergens spoke emphatically. Frowning, he said, "Burglary? Twice? That doesn't make sense. The guy's after something and you have it. Any idea what it might be?" He looked first at me and then turned his gaze to Aaron. "You must have some theory or an idea?"

I gulped. "Well…yeah…kind of do…but am completely unsure of it." I grimaced, knowing how disjointed I sounded.

"Let's have it. Start again with what you said previously." Both detectives sat poised with pads and pencils at the ready. "Well…give me a sec to organize my thoughts." I looked around the room before beginning. "It's all centered around President Lincoln. You've probably already sensed that. Why? I'm not sure, but he gave a speech that has been referred to as 'the Lost Speech,' as there are no known copies." I waited for both detectives to finish writing and look up at me. "By the way, are there any suspects in Blanche's death?" When they both shook their heads, I said, "I wish you had the case solved."

"No clues. Nothing to link anyone to the murder. The woman's neck was broken before the fall."

"Hmm…" I barely swallowed because of the lump in my throat. "So that means that the person who broke in here could be the same one who murdered Blanche. How comforting." I squirmed.

"Let's get back to the matter at hand," Erlandsen suggested.

"The necklace that we discovered belonged to Mary Lincoln. We told you about that. A university professor who studies historical items has made arrangements to test it." They nodded and scribbled notes. "The necklace charm is in the shape of an acorn and was hidden inside a hat box that also belonged to Mary Lincoln."

"Very puzzling. We want to see it before we grant

permission for testing," Mergens said. "Continue."

"See if this works for you. The hem of the dress Blanche wore, one of Mary Lincoln's, was odd as you know. We found a curled snippet of paper with the letter 'G' written on it. We also noted a staircase drawn on the inside of the hatbox lid." I sat up and moved the blanket away. "It's all a mystery whether that all adds up to something." I stood and told them I would get the necklace. "I'll let you decide if we should follow through with the professor."

"I'll get it," Aaron said. "It's in an evidence bag, and given the way it was found, I doubt there will be any significant prints." While Aaron went upstairs, the detectives continued with me.

"No theories?"

"It's all connected to Mary Lincoln. That, I'm positive of," I repeated. "I had Mikal, the handwriting analyst who runs the shop next to mine, look at the letter 'G' and the drawing of the staircase. He deemed that they were written by the same hand. Or at least that's his best guess." I massaged my forehead. "I also have a stuffed bear that belonged to Tad Lincoln. It's very odd. There is an embroidered family tree on a flap of fabric on its rear, sort of a trapdoor, like long john underwear has."

"You're kidding?"

"The hatbox lid, 'G' paper and stuffed bear are in the trunk of our car," I said.

Aaron came back. "Here's the necklace." He held it out for them to see.

"Tell you what, let's go ahead with testing," said

Erlandsen. "This investigation is getting weirder and weirder. We'll contact the Mary Todd Lincoln House and apprise them of the continued situation. These are the only clues we have that may point toward a motive. Talk about perplexing."

"Why would someone do this to an acorn?" Mergens asked. "Our superiors will have to be kept abreast of the situation." He took out his phone and went to another room.

"Aaron? How about getting the items from the trunk?" Erlandsen asked.

"It should only take a minute. And while he's doing that, I'm taking a bathroom break. Be right back."

On my return, I noticed the detectives were holding the paper with the staircase up against the light, which caused me to cringe. "You must be careful with that. It's very, very old," I admonished them and glared at Aaron.

"Sorry," Mergens said. "Just looking for ourselves." He put the paper down. "From what I can tell, they do appear to be written by the same person. Very old paper…unlined…brittle…yellowed. The writing is shaky in a few spots, just like on the stairs." Frowning, he crinkled his brow. "The bear smells old, too."

"Everyone who has seen this bear mentioned that." I rolled my eyes.

"The necklace does have a 'nut' appearance, doesn't it?" Mergens picked it up and studied it. "Interesting." He set it on the table next to the other items. "The lieutenant gave us permission to continue with the investigation as we see fit. It's a go with the professor."

"Good. I think Dr. Williams was excited about doing the test."

"Well, this is sure a hodgepodge of things with nothing concrete to tie them together," Erlandsen said, fingering the items.

"Just like the last time with the Madison stuff."

I crossed my arms. "Together, it has to mean something. There's a newly found letter at the Lincoln library, which I haven't seen yet. There's one more thing. In Mary Lincoln's published diary, there are a few pages were she drew concentric word puzzles."

"Well, they say she was a bit off, you know." Erlandsen scratched his hair. "But, a First Lady doing all this stuff... and with the Civil War going on... maybe she did hide something of his."

"The bear with embroidery on its butt. Now what could that signify?" Aaron wondered.

"Actually, just about anything. But she must have embroidered it for a reason," I said.

"Right, there must be a motive behind all this." Aaron glanced at me. "The hat's a shredded mess now. The person who broke in must've believed there was something hidden in it, don't you think?"

"Who knows about all of this?" Erlandsen asked.

"Inga, the owner of the antique shop near my store, knows, so I assume Holly, her employee, does too." I watched as the detectives wrote the names down. "Luke does, thanks to his catering job at Grandma's, and also Inga mentioned the speech to him. Mikal also knows about it. Luckily the hatbox lid and bear were still in the car—nothing happened to them. The little piece of paper, also." After a moment, I said, "But the necklace. It's really only us that know it's a necklace that we found. They may have suspicions, but that's all it is."

"And, the professor," Aaron said.

"But, how does trashing your kitchen play into this?" Mergens asked.

"That's the part that doesn't make any sense," I said.

"Tell you what, you two," Mergens said as he adjusted his glasses, "take some time in the next few days and go through each drawer. If you find anything missing or unknown, let us know."

"Good idea. Kitchen drawers are great places to drop things that are soon forgotten." Erlandsen glanced at us. "I think you spooked the intruder, and he or she didn't get what they wanted." He hesitated, and then asked, "Anything unusual around this block—or over near your store? Any suspicious neighbors?"

"One thing, which does seem odd—Luke."

"Brew Café owner?"

"Yes." I agreed. "His helpers come and go. He seems to always have new employees. I saw a couple of men drive away with two of Luke's helpers the other day."

"That doesn't seem right. Why would there be such a turnover of employees? We'll check into it."

Finally the detectives left and we were alone. "What do you think about Luke?" Aaron asked.

"The employees really could be family members. I know he comes from a large family, and most of them live in Cambodia where he grew up. I frowned.

"The two men could've been brothers," Aaron said. "The woman in the dumpster didn't speak English." Aaron raised a brow. "Do you have any idea what is happening all around us?"

"I haven't a clue."

Chapter Eleven

Aaron and I stared vacantly at the television screen. I realized I had no idea what program it was. "Are you watching this show?" I snuggled into his shoulder.

"No, I'm thinking."

"How is this all connected? It's weird. I think this mystery is about Lincoln and Tad because of the stuffed bear."

"We're spinning our wheels." Aaron flipped the station to another one. "I'm worried about you." He riffled my hair.

"I'm worried too. I don't like all of this bad stuff happening around me." I felt confused. "You're right, we are going in circles, but it all has to lead somewhere. I just wish I could figure out where."

"Give it time. You'll figure it out... Keep the faith, hon." Aaron pressed the remote button, shutting off the television. "The detectives will look into everything, that's for sure. Including this thing with Luke and the girls."

"Maybe they're foreign exchange students." Shivering, I gazed out at the new fallen snow. "That poor girl in the dumpster...half-frozen."

"We have to think clearly now and be extra careful." Aaron kissed me. "Let's put these items in the lock box, including the necklace."

"I can just wear that under my blouse where it won't be seen."

Aaron smiled at my gesture and where I was pointing.

I blushed. "I'll go get my iPad and send Dr. Williams, the professor, a message right now. Maybe we'll hear back in the morning." I reached around to the shelf where I kept my iPad. My e-mail account seemed to open slower than usual when I turned it on. "This is weird. My business computer at the shop is really slow, too. Also, that bear is showing up on the screen saver here, too. Hmm. I think it needs an expert to check it out." I pressed the new message button and typed in:

Hi Dr. Williams,

I am Marie Ott's granddaughter and I hope that you remember me. I have the silvered acorn necklace and am still wondering if you could do me a favor? Would you be able to take a few scans of it? I'd like to know, as would the investigators, if indeed there is a real acorn inside of it – and if there is – is it possible to date it? I could bring it in to your office at your convenience.

Thank you, Liv Reynolds

I hit "send."

"We should give Grandma and Grandpa a call now, don't you think?"

"I'll take care of the kitchen mess. We'll pick up the hat mess together." Aaron got up and left the room.

Grandma answered on the third ring. "Grandma." I sniffled and blew my nose a couple of times while she waited.

"Olivia, what is it?" I could almost hear as she looked up at the ceiling or placed her hand on her right hip. She had an earpiece for her phone, so at least she didn't have to hold the phone tight against her ear like I had to. "Olivia?"

"I found someone in the dumpster behind the store this morning. I fell in, too, but the woman… she's alive and in the hospital." I rambled on until Grandma quacked, "What?" I went ahead with my explanation about finding the woman. Also, the mess of dumped miniature pieces in the store, and the crazy cleaning ladies.

"You fell into the dumpster!" Grandma said. She was more concerned with me falling into the dumpster than if the person was alive. "I don't want you to be there alone, Olivia. That's final."

"She did what?" Grandpa hollered in the background.

"I'm okay. There's more news. Someone broke in here, too, our house," I said. "But other than that and those other things, we're doing fine, really we are. Don't worry."

"Give it to me straight," Grandpa shouted in the background. "The Mary Lincoln hat has been destroyed." I continued telling her about it, plus how the house was found. I then brought her up to date about the rest of the Mary Lincoln puzzle. When finished, I asked, "What do you think it all means?"

"Is the dress that you wore at the birthday celebration also one of Mary Lincoln's?" Grandma always got to the point.

"Yes."

"Then check out the hem. I'll wait for you to call me back."

"All right." She had already disconnected before I clicked out of the call. I went out to Aaron. "Checking my Mary Lincoln dress hem is next on the agenda." I noticed that he'd already picked up two of the tipped-over drawers, but there were several more left to straighten out.

"Good idea. When I'm done here, I'll join you."

He glanced at me. "We'll get through all of this together, babe." "Right." I blew him a kiss before heading down the hallway to the back bedroom.

Seeing the shredded flowers that had once adorned the old hat, and remembering the beauty of it, saddened me. I picked up bits of grasses and feathers and piled them on the bedspread. That attempt at cleaning complete, I opened the closet and removed the worn dress from the hanger. I had some investigating to do.

As I carried the dress into the living room, I wondered if there would be anything at all inserted in the hem of this one. *Maybe doing some in-depth research on Mary Lincoln after the assassination might give me insight into her mental state.*

I sat down on the couch, clicked the television on, drew my legs up underneath me to get comfortable, and began to search the hemline. Since the colored thread was dark and hard to see, I switched on the reading lamp for a more direct light. The multi-yard hem seemed to go on forever as I slowly smoothed my fingers over the stitches. But I found nothing.

I studied the inside of the hemline. Mary Lincoln *had* hid something... I could feel it in my bones. I decided it would have been hidden either for Tad or out of dire necessity. I had read they were always short of cash. Every cent that Abraham made, she spent. It was easy to see why Congress would get mad at her for spending, especially with a war raging.

Realizing I wasn't paying close enough attention to my work, I glanced back down at the hem, noting that the job was almost complete. Right before the final seam, I caught a change in thread color—just like in the other dress. I stared at it. With small scissors in hand, I snipped the knot. I carefully slid the thread out from each stitch until enough open space allowed me to insert my finger inside the opening and I touched the paper. Holding my breath, I gently slid it out into the open. The small slip of paper had a pillar drawn on it. I studied it closer and shook my head, murmuring, "a pillar?" I held it closer to the light and shouted, "Aaron!"

I jumped up and brought the small piece of paper out to the kitchen. "Guess what? Look at this."

Aaron was fitting the last drawer in place. "This is crazy."

I held the paper out for him to see. "I'm at a loss. What does all this mean?"

"It's almost like the ones at the U.S. Capitol building or the White House." He shook his head. "Geez. Call Marie back."

"I'm right on it," I said. I returned to the living room and called Grandma. She answered before the end of the first ring, which didn't surprise me. "What does a pillar symbolize?" I went on to explain our latest discovery.

"Hmm…a 'G,' a pillar, and a staircase are all symbols. Here, I'll put Grandpa on; you get Aaron on the phone, too. They might be able to figure it out," Grandma said.

"Oh, sure. And we can't?" I said, running my fingers through my unruly red hair. "We didn't just fall from the turnip truck, ya know."

"I'll give you five minutes, then Grandpa's calling," Grandma said.

"You're impossible." I disconnected and picked up my iPad. After typing in three words, the search brought me to symbols. I clicked on the Masonic site and found that all three were Masonic symbols. The "G" stood for The Grand Master staircase. The search exposed the meaning of the pillar as, The Temple of Solomon, rooted deeply in Masonic teachings.

"Oh my," I muttered. "Talk about perplexing." I picked up the phone and once again speed-dialed Grandma. "It's all embedded with Masonic symbolism."

"You'll have to keep investigating." I could hear Grandma yawning. "We're going to bed. If you find out more, call me in the morning."

"Will do." I placed the phone down on the table and held up the iPad and read about the symbols until Aaron entered. "Hold on a sec." I bookmarked the site, got up, grabbed the dress, carried it to the bedroom and rehung it.

"They are all Masonic symbols." I sat down on the couch with him beside me. "Interesting, eh?" I said, showing it to him.

"I don't want to think about another mystery that happened well over a century ago. It's too much." He nudged me. "Do you?"

"I think we're locked into it."

"But, what is it?"

"No idea." I held up the iPad. "Read through this, will you?"

"Sure." He took it from me as I leaned into him. "We don't have anything to go on, though." He passed it back. "Here, fluffy."

"I wonder if it does have anything to do with the Lost Speech? It makes me wonder about Mary's diary pages." I covered my mouth and yawned. "Let's get the hat mess picked up. Those Victorian hats are so beautiful. Why rip one apart?"

"More clues, maybe? Let's take the dresses and hat downstairs. We'll hide them in the basement."

"Good idea."

We walked back to the bedroom together. The hat mess took a while to pick up. We placed all of the remnants in the box, along with the hat, and placed the lid back on. We both had our hands full, me with the dress, and he with the hatbox.

I followed Aaron into the kitchen and down the basement stairs. We stopped at the bottom to flick the light switch.

"We should fix this basement up, it's nothing but cement blocks," I said.

"Let's get this over with. I can think of better things to do than hold onto a dress of Mary Lincoln." Aaron glanced around the room.

"Keep your shirt on." I handed him the hanger and he set the hatbox down. Near the laundry there were a few shelves. I found two garment bags and brought them over to Aaron. "Hold this open so I can put the dresses and hat inside."

"Anything to get back upstairs where it's warm." I opened the bag, Aaron hung the hanger hook on the wire, and I slid the dress inside. "Are we finished?"

"Nope. Let's go and get the rest of the stuff and keep it all down here," I said. "I'll try carrying both crinolines and the pantaloons, but what about the hoops?" I followed him up the stairs.

"I'm not touching them."

As we headed down the hallway, I took his hand and squeezed it, smiling up at him. We gathered up the items in the back bedroom until our arms were full, and then we hurried back downstairs and hung them all up. I made two more trips for the hoop skirts. They barely fit down the narrow stairs. "Thank heavens these hoops aren't in style anymore," I said to Aaron when we'd finished. It was amazing how our accumulation of Lincoln artifacts had grown.

As I made ready for bed, I wondered if I would be able to get a decent night's sleep. Aaron turned on the electric blanket and I curled into him and closed my eyes. I still got up several times during the night. Once

I called the hospital for an update on the girl in the dumpster but wasn't told anything more than I already knew. She was under close supervision, no visitors were allowed, and she hadn't regained consciousness. At one point, I fixed myself a cup of hot chocolate and another time it was chocolate ice cream. Now, finally, just when I was ready for sleep, the sky was beginning to brighten.

It was hard to get up. I yawned and rolled over, pulling the blankets up over my head. It wasn't until Aaron came and yanked them down that I got up.

"Brr." I placed a foot down on the pale blue carpeting. "It must be too cold for you to run to work. What's the temp?" Aaron had brought a steaming cup of coffee to the bedroom for me, and I sipped it carefully. Setting the cup down, I reached for my robe and pulled it on.

"Forty below." Aaron frowned. "But, it's going to warm up—all the way to twenty below."

"Did you really have to tell me the temp?" I shivered. "Let's go to work together. I hate the idea going in alone. I'm chicken now that all of this has happened."

"All right. Can't say as I blame you." He grinned. "Don't concern yourself with the garbage from now on."

"Thanks. It's off my to-do list," I groused. I didn't want a reminder of the day before, with my mind stuck on the image of that poor girl in the bottom of the dumpster. When I breathed in deeply, the remembered stench permeated my nostrils. "Can you hang that shelf for me today? Please?"

"Oh sure, Liv."

I followed him out to the kitchen where we ate a small breakfast before getting dressed. I wore a turtleneck under a Scottish highland green knit sweater and jeans. Aaron wore a tan shirt and jeans. Once we'd bundled up into our heavy outerwear, we jumped into the car.

"Did you make sure the house was locked?" I asked.

"Yes. I checked every door, twice. Even the one between the house and garage is locked. I don't usually check it because it's never locked, until today." Aaron backed from the garage after the door had lifted. He turned and headed for the street. "Don't worry, honey."

"I won't." I clenched my jaw tightly as we waited for a traffic light to turn.

"Yeah, right." He glanced at me, winking. "I have a couple more practices before the tourney. Do you want to come tonight?"

"Not on your life! I'm going to stay home. I don't care to become a popsicle."

I was comforted knowing I wouldn't have to enter the store alone. After last night, and the other store break-in, I was frightened. When these types of things happened back when we were involved in the Dolley Madison search, Grandpa made sure someone was with me all the time.

It didn't take long before we were at the store, and Aaron parked in the lot out back.

"I hope no one broke in here last night," I said, standing beside Aaron as he pressed in the door code.

"Think positive, but let me go in first." He grinned.

"Yeah, as if *you* are." I stepped aside as he entered. I really wanted to peek inside but hoped for the best.

"All clear," he said, coming back out to get me.

"Good." Taking my hand, Aaron led me inside the back door, shutting it behind us. I held my breath as I poked my nose into the workroom. "Looks fine."

"So does the showroom."

We both removed our coats and hung them on the clothes tree. "I'm starting the computer and will check for a return message from Bill."

"I'll go for a hot cup of coffee for each of us." Aaron stood, blowing on his fingertips to warm them.

"Wait, honey. I want you to see how long it takes for this computer to boot up."

Together we walked over to it, and I pressed the start button. Once it started humming, I looked up at him. "Who do you think broke into the house?"

"Not a clue." He shook his head. "I'll call the detectives after a while. They have to have time to study all the information before they know anything.

"You know who strikes me as odd?" He massaged his chin. "Mikal."

"Mikal?" I raised a brow and stared at him. "That makes no sense. No sense whatsoever. He's ancient, anyway."

"True. But remember how he broke into the store the last time? There wasn't any reason for him to do that, was there?"

"He had a hunch and ran with it." I frowned. "But why would he break into my house? That person could run fast. Mikal is too old." I shook my head. "You're not making any sense."

"Listen to me." Aaron took in a deep breath. "What do we really know about him? Besides, old people aren't that old anymore. Not like when we were kids."

"There's truth to that. Health care is exceptional nowadays." I glanced at the computer screen and pressed the button to open my file. "See? Look at how slow this thing is. It's a snail."

"Also, Mikal seems too interested. Look at how he insisted on doing the handwriting analysis? He's too nosy, in my opinion." Aaron looked over my shoulder at the computer. "Let's see your e-mail."

I pressed the button and my messages popped up on the screen. As I opened the reply from Dr. Williams, the page began jumping up and down.

"Your computer has been hacked."

"First, Blanche, then breaking into our house, and now the computer hacked," I said. "Are they connected?"

"Good question."

Chapter Twelve

Aaron finished hanging the shelf above the counter as a tech geek worked on the computer. The detectives arrived and parked outside the front door. Before they entered, I took a moment to greet the ladies. First Lady Edith Wilson beckoned me over by the wink in her eye. As I picked up the doll, I whispered, "It's okay. The stranger will soon leave. He's trying to figure out what's wrong with the computer." I set the doll back and began to circle the room. Mrs. Lincoln looked quite sad, so I leaned over to whisper in her ear. "Can you tell me where you hid the speech, that is, if you did? Now is a great time to come forward to tell me."

Since a computer geek monopolized my computer, I joined Aaron in the workroom to speak with the detectives again about last night's break-in. I wanted to see if they knew anything more about the girl.

"How is she doing? I worried so about her last night that I called the hospital."

"That was you? We were told someone called. I'll relay the message," Mergens stated. "Mustn't call, Liv. It ruffles their feathers. These G-Men, you know?" He shook his head.

"Does that mean she was a foreigner?"

"Yes. Cambodian, we believe." Mergens looked at me square in the eye. "We'll keep you updated. Keep your nose out of it."

I glanced at Erlandsen who was frowning.

"He's right." Looking down at his pad, he said, "Start from the top. Tell it to us again."

Once again the events of the previous evening were repeated, even though they had asked me a million questions last night. I then told them about the computer hack. When finished, I went toward the counter as the computer geek stared intensely at my computer screen. "Figure out anything yet?"

His eyebrows pointed upward like an arrow and his round glasses were thick like glass bottles. "It's obscure. The mailbox comes and goes. I've quarantined and gotten rid of the virus." He pressed a couple more buttons. "Now I'm running a search to try and figure out where this came from, but I doubt we can really trace him."

"It's so mean the way hackers mess things up nowadays." Puzzled, I rubbed my chin. "Can you tell if they were after anything in general?"

"Not really, but it seems a file named *Mary Lincoln* was modified." He looked at me with a frown. "Why do you suppose that would be?"

"Interesting. Is there anything else you can tell me?"

"Nothing for sure. The person who hacked your computer would have to be caught in the act. That's near impossible since they usually work in the middle of the night." He clicked back to the malware site. "I'm going to run a diagnostic test. It'll take a long time. Mind if I leave it running and return later?"

"How long?" "About an hour." "Sure, go ahead."

He no sooner left than the front door opened and

a couple entered.

"How may I help you?" I smiled at both, realizing that they must be daughter and father. Both were tall and slim along with the same smile. She was a beautiful young woman, probably high-school age. He was dressed in an expensive suit and carried himself with an air of authority.

"We'll just look around for the moment."

"Interested in any first lady in particular?" I stayed by the counter, not wanting them to feel as if I was invading their space as they looked around the room.

"What about the Kennedys and Camelot?" the man asked. "That's right over here." I steered them toward the 1960-era White Houses. "First Lady Jackie Kennedy had the garden redesigned by Rachel Lambert Mellon. She planted flowerbeds in a French style but used mostly all American specimens. 'Katherine' crabapples line the edges with little leaf lindens and diamond-shaped hedges of thyme. It's all very beautiful, isn't it?"

"Jackie was beautiful and very feminine. She spoke fluent French, too. I loved her as a First Lady." The man smiled. "Frankly, we were thinking about purchasing a dollhouse for her mother, my wife, Pat, for Valentine's Day."

"Mom's always talked about her dollhouse from when she was a kid," the young woman stated. "Dad thought this would be a good idea."

"Don't you like dollhouses, too?" I raised a brow. *Really, what girl didn't?*

"I think Mom's a little too old for dollhouses, but

Dad tells me she's not." She rolled her eyes up toward the ceiling, in the way all teenagers did.

"A woman is never too old for a dollhouse. A White House reflecting the era of your favorite First Lady? What more could a woman ask for?" I cocked my head.

"Agreed." The father nodded at me. "Also, Jackie's voice was dreamy. I remember watching that news special when she gave a tour of the White House at Christmas. I was just a little boy then." He thought for a moment and said, "Let us roam around a bit and look at all the houses."

"Sure. Go ahead." I backed away and went to sit by the computer. As I did, Aaron entered with a worried look in his eyes. "What?"

"They don't know anything. There's nothing to connect the break-in here with the one at our house last night. Nor can they connect the two break-ins with Blanche's murder, and they have nothing more to say about the dumpster girl. They're stymied."

"This is ridiculous." I kept my voice low so the customers couldn't hear. "What about Luke's parade of helpers? Did they look into that?"

He shook his head. "Can't see how that would be connected with anything happening to us. I agree, this *is* ridiculous."

"They must be connected, and we have to find out how." I glanced over at the computer, which had started humming again. "It all makes me wonder...that maybe it is all somehow connected to that speech," he said.

"I'm hesitant to believe that it stems from a speech made over a hundred and fifty years ago." I ran my fingers through my hair. "I really don't want to chase down ghosts, especially since there's no known copy of the speech, nor did the reporters transcribe it," I said.

"Me, neither. We don't need to chase down ghosts."

Just then the customer cleared his throat, and I glanced past Aaron to where he stood. "Sorry. How may I help you?"

"We've decided to order a Kennedy White House." He beamed, as did his daughter. "She's come around to my way of thinking."

"Daddy!" She turned beet red, and I stifled a chuckle.

"You chose one of the most beautiful houses. They were such an elegant couple. I'm sure your wife will love it." I began putting together the bill. "My computer is down right now, I'll have to give you a handwritten receipt."

"I'll write a check instead of using my credit card. That should help."

"Yes, very much." I took the check and completed writing the tab. "We can load the dollhouse up for you now, if you're ready?"

"I'll go and get a box." Aaron headed toward the workroom. "Valentine's Day is only a week away. For once, I'll be early."

He chuckled as he dropped a couple of coins into the *Pennies* jar.

Aaron set the large packing box down on the counter. I picked up one of the brochures describing the house. "Here." I handed it to the girl. "Let me pack up all the furnishings." We carried all the items over to the counter where I began wrapping them individually. "There are markings on the backs too, telling where the piece belongs." As I busied myself with the packing, the men carried the house over and set it inside the box.

"Let's carry it out to the car."

"I'll get the doors." The girl followed, opening them as the men carried the large package out to the car.

"You'll have to let us know how your wife liked this. I'm anxious to hear. I bet she'll fall in love with it. If she prefers a different house, give us a call and we'll make an exchange." I handed over the receipt. "Enjoy it."

"We will." He turned toward his daughter and said, "Trish, let's go."

We watched them drive away.

"That made for a good day," Aaron said.

"Made opening the store worthwhile." I smiled and glanced up at the clock. "Time for lunch."

"Let's run down to Luke's."

"Good idea."

We locked the back door, zipped into our coats, and headed out the front door. Two joggers swept past us heading down the cleared sidewalk, which made me feel guilty for not doing the same.

"When on earth will it warm up for good?"

In just a few minutes, we were inside the warm and cozy Brew Café where we placed our orders of squash and bean soup. A hint of cinnamon gave it a distinctive taste. We brought the bowls to a table and sat down. I glanced toward the back room where Luke caught my eye and nodded. I watched him enter the larger room, and soon he was walking toward us.

Luke wore a white apron filled with splatters. His hands looked as if they had been covered in flour. "Rolling out dough for buns. Decided to bake cinnamon buns in the morning. Thought I'd try something new to bring in more customers…it's been too slow lately." Concerned, he asked, "Heard any news on how that girl is faring? Finding her in the dumpster must have been horrific for you, Liv."

"It was. Don't know a thing, except that she's alive." I scratched my head and asked, "Wasn't she one of your helpers?"

"No. I've been questioned backward and forward, but no…she wasn't one of my employees. Immigration has been here constantly, asking questions." He placed his hands on his hips. "Have you been busy?"

"Sorry to hear my shop's not the only business that's been slow. If not for my First Lady celebration the other day, I'd really be in a bind. I did sell a house this morning, though." I finished my soup. "Delicious."

"Thanks," Luke said.

"I don't see yesterday's helper? Did you hire a new girl?"

"Excuse me," He turned at the sound of his name. "Have to get back to work."

We watched him go behind the counter.

"Why didn't he answer the question about his helper?" I asked. "I don't see any young girl working here today. Maybe he's hard up for cash."

"No idea."

"Me neither. I won't feel at ease until that case is solved." I frowned and said, "Let's get back to the store. The computer guy should return soon. In fact, he's probably standing out front wondering where we are."

We finished our meal and bussed our dishes before walking out the door.

As we neared the store, we saw the computer man coming from the other direction. We unlocked the door and he followed us inside.

"Darn weather." He shivered. "Okay, let's see what we have now." He walked over to the computer chair and sat down.

"Be right back." Aaron and I hung our coats before going back out to the showroom. "What did you find?"

"A few nasty things, but it's okay now. I'll get your system back on track, then take off." He pressed a few buttons. "Want your e-mail or website?"

"Website. Nothing happened to it, right?"

"Let's see." He clicked on the bookmark, and the website flashed onto the screen. "Let's run through each page." After he had done precisely that, we found it was in good working order. "I'll log in to your e-mail, since that's where the most damage happened."

"How can someone do that?" Aaron leaned into the counter. "They must know their stuff."

"Most definitely." He checked a few other sites. "It's all good now." He stood up to zip his jacket.

"How much do I owe you?" I asked. "A hundred bucks."

"Okay. Hold on and let me get back there." I opened the cash drawer, removed five twenties, and handed them over. "I appreciate this."

"Anytime. Day or night. If this happens again, call right away." He headed to the door. "You've got my number?"

"Yes." As soon as he had walked out the door, I opened my account and took a look at my files. "Look, Aaron, every message in the *Mary Lincoln* file has been either modified or deleted. Why?"

"That's the question of the hour. I'm starting to think that I should contact the police geek squad," Aaron replied. "Have you heard back from Dr. Williams?"

"Let's see." With more than fifty messages to weed through, it took me a few minutes to determine that he had not replied. "Not yet, which seems odd." Just then my cell phone rang. "Grandma," I answered and proceeded to tell her about the computer hacking, before disconnecting.

I glanced over at Aaron. "Grandma thinks the hacking is connected to the break-ins."

"I'm starting to think that woman loves a good

conspiracy."

"Maybe." I zipped through the older letters and found what I was searching for. "Look at this message from the Lincoln Library?" I turned the monitor so he could read it.

"That's odd. They won't put the new letter on display for public viewing."

"I know. There's got to be something weird about it, don't you think? I'll just wait. Maybe the Mary Todd Lincoln House will get a copy and share it with me."

"That's a possibility."

"I'm going to see Inga for a minute. See if she can shed some light on what happened last night. Who knows, maybe she can tell me why the hat was torn to bits?"

"How would she know?"

"She has a great imagination." I went for my coat and hollered, "Be right back!"

The short jaunt in the nippy air took my breath away. I was happy to get inside the store.

"Liv! Good to see you. Good to see anyone," Holly stated. "Brr! Shut the door fast."

"Pretty quiet, eh?" I looked around the room. "Where's Inga?

The back room?"

"She just stepped out. She went to see Luke." I watched as Holly quickly clicked out of the Internet site she had been viewing. "What were you looking up?" I leaned closer, pushing Inga's *Pennies Jar*.

"Nothing much." I noticed that her smile looked a little sheepish.

"I've tried to get a copy of a newly found letter of Mary Lincoln's, but the library won't put it on display or send a copy. I find it very upsetting."

"The Lincoln Library in Springfield?" Her eyes looked sort of mysterious.

"Yeah. But, really, it's no big deal." I shrugged. "When do you expect Inga to return?"

"Five minutes."

"I'll look around for awhile then."

I began my little tour around the store, starting with the antique writing desks in the back corner of the store. Abraham Lincoln's legs were long, how could he write at such a small desk?

"Is this desk new? I haven't seen it here before." I glanced over at Holly. "Come here for a moment, would you?"

"Sure."

I heard her footsteps clopping across the hardwood floor. "Look at this. Did Inga just get this one?"

"Yes," she said. "I believe so."

"This says, 'Lincoln law desk.'" Perplexed, I held up the label. "This can't be right. Why isn't it in a museum? It should be." The small oak desk was intriguing with its many slots and the one drawer. I tried opening it, but it wouldn't budge. "It's stuck."

Just then the back door swung open and I heard Inga call, "I'm back!"

"We're over here by the desks." I stood up. My back was starting to feel as if it might break in two from leaning over it.

"That desk just came in yesterday. Isn't it beautiful? Hardly a scratch," Inga noted. Her pink cheeks and nose made me smile. "I should have called or e-mailed but haven't had time." She touched the wood. "The oak has held up on this piece after all these years. It's precious."

"I'm having trouble picturing Abe sitting at it, he was so tall." I ran my palm across the flat top, feeling the warmth of the ancient wood.

"I wonder why the drawer is stuck, when the rest of it looks in such good condition."

Holly called out, "I'm leaving now. I have to get to class." Inga called back. "Okay. Tomorrow at ten?"

"I have classes all day. I'll text you." She turned and walked from the room.

"How many hours does she put in?" I looked Inga in the eye. "Only about fifteen. Business is really slow." Inga tried to pull out the drawer.

"Mind if I try opening it?"

"No, go ahead."

I jammed my fingers into the drawer as far as possible and felt a small instrument. The drawer opened after jimmying it, a letter opener dropped down. "Here's the culprit." I ran my fingers across the bottom of the slots — only to find a small, hidden shelf. "He must have hidden things in here, away from his partner."

"That's possible." Inga stepped back. "This is a wonderful collection, don't you think? A desk from FDR, and one from Teddy Roosevelt, too. I have an ashtray and cigarette holder right on FDR's desk. It's cute, isn't it?"

"Yes, also two stuffed animals on top of TR's. Very nice."

"Got time to sit?" Inga began walking over to the counter where she had her chair and computer. I followed right behind her.

"For only a couple minutes. Someone broke into our house last night and tore apart Blanche's Mary Lincoln hat. Fortunately, the hatbox lid, note from the dress hem, and toy bear weren't found."

I rubbed my chin. "Do you have any idea why this happened? The detectives can't seem to find a common thread."

"Nope. Holly and I were questioned again this morning, including about the dumpster girl."

"The threads of this mystery are either tightening or unraveling — and I have no idea which!"

Chapter Thirteen

I raised a questioning brow. "Why? What are they after?"

"Let's each think on this for a day or two, just to see what we come up with." Inga changed the subject. "Do you like this desk? It's for sale, you know. It'd fit nicely by the Lincoln dollhouse." She gave me a huge, enticing smile.

"Consider it sold, but I'm not sure about ready cash." I crossed over toward the door. "Do you think Mr. Lincoln would hide something inside one of his desks? Like that Lost Speech?" I studied her. "To hide it from his wife or law partner? Who would benefit from it?"

"Interesting question. There's his hat. Wouldn't he have put it there? They say he did use it like a briefcase." She grinned. "That man always had some kind of trick up his sleeve, it seems — or under his hat."

"Yes, I wouldn't be surprised. It makes me wonder, too, about Tad's uniform. Why was it so nicely preserved?" I hurried out the door, shutting it behind me. On the way back to my store, I thought about the desk. It was in much too good shape and too small to have been his law desk. *Had he used it at home?*

I rushed inside my store, stomping my feet upon entering. Aaron was perched behind the computer monitor with Max behind him, peering over his shoulder. "What are you two looking at?"

"The bear image has been taken out of the screen saver."

"That must have been part of the virus." I went over to them and leaned against the counter. I rubbed my hands up and down my arms to try to warm up.

"My computer upstairs seems to be fine. It must only affect the store computer," Max said. "You don't have one at home, do you?"

"We use my iPad or a laptop."

"Hey, you'll find this article interesting." Max held out the newspaper and pointed. "Read this."

"Sure." I grabbed the paper and began reading. The article told about several recent burglaries. "This is unreal." My eyes grew wider as I read further. "Listen to this: Only Lincoln memorabilia were stolen. All other items, including those of presidents, FDR, Teddy Roosevelt, Reagan, and Clinton were untouched." I scrunched the paper and said, "I wonder why they smashed up my business instead of stealing my Lincoln memorabilia. It's like they want me to notice what they're doing." Perplexed, I cocked my head. "Are these crimes committed by the same person? It can't be, can it?"

"It sure seems like it." Aaron glanced at me. "I'm shutting the computer down and rebooting it, to make sure that it starts faster."

"The computer geek has gone through all this, so you shouldn't be worried." Max stepped out from behind Aaron.

"Too many weird things are happening," Aaron said, getting up. "Liv, what's next on your agenda today?"

"I have to take a closer look at that little uniform, and those concentric puzzle pages need deciphering." I folded up the paper and set it aside for further reading.

"I haven't seen her diary yet," Max said.

"Me, neither," said Aaron.

"I'll get it." I went to the workroom and found the book on one of the shelves. With diary in hand, I returned. "Here." Just as I placed it on the counter top, Max's cell phone rang.

"It's Anna," Max said and turned away to take the call.

Max was talking about his sister. I opened the book to search for the pages with the puzzles. I found them as Max disconnected.

"Gotta run."

"Do you want to take a look at these, or not?"

"Yep, but later. Have to pick Anna up from class." He headed toward the back door. "Later!"

I shrugged, turning the book around for Aaron to see. "How on earth do you figure this out? What does it all mean?"

"Let's make extra copies."

"Good idea." I picked up the book, and Aaron followed me into the workroom where I copied and printed them out.

"I should check my e-mail, since I haven't today. After that, let's close up and go home. Are you scheduled to go in to work later?"

"Nope. Remember? A practice session is

scheduled." Aaron said.

I went to turn the computer back on and was pleased to find that it started just fine. "It's humming. Good. It takes only a minute to log into my files." It was going to take me some time to repair the damage the hacker did to my Lincoln file. A few of the file names still looked garbled. "At least now it's safe to use, plus we have updated software to guard against another hack and viruses. I'm going to send Inga a message."

"Be right back after I get some meat for supper." The back door slammed as I wrote:

> *Inga, I'll talk to Aaron tonight about paying for the Lincoln desk. Any other Lincoln items? The paper has an article about a thief taking only Lincoln items. Better be safe and lock everything up, including the desk in the back room.*

Before sending the e-mail, I added a sentence:

> *This really isn't a joke. Be careful! //Liv*

Next, I e-mailed Maggie:

> *Hi Maggie, someone hacked my account. The computer geek was here all morning scanning files. Inga purchased a Lincoln desk. It's really cute. I'm going to buy it. Catcha later //Me*

I sent the message and then looked for the message which had been sent to me that morning when the computer virus acted up. It wasn't anywhere on my computer. I sat back for a moment before constructing yet another message. Then I wrote:

Dr. Williams,

You sent me an email earlier, but my computer was hacked, and I lost it.

I'm excited to learn more about this acorn necklace. When it fits your schedule, I will bring it to your office.

Please let me know. Sincerely,

Liv Reynolds

Owner and operator of White House Dollhouse Store.

My website displayed two more responses to the question about the Lost Speech. They both read:

He's dead. RIP. THREE BLIND MICE.

I deleted both.

I posted more pictures of the dollhouses and several First Ladies. My e-mail showed that another new message was received. Inga had sent:

Bring the stuffed bear in tomorrow. I have an interested buyer, if you want to sell it. //Inga

I replied: *Sure*

By the time I logged out and shut the computer down, Aaron had returned.

"Ready to go?" Aaron asked.

"Of course!"

I grabbed my coat and followed Aaron out the back door, locking it behind.

The drive home didn't take long, and I was happy to get inside our warm house. I helped Aaron carry in the groceries and put them away.

"Why am I so cold, and why is the cold bothering me so much?"

"It's because of what's been happening. Nothing's right."

"Guess you're right." I sighed. I poured two full glasses of soda, setting one in front of Aaron, and then grabbed my iPad and typed in:

Maggie//House broken into last night at home. Ripped apart the hat.

That's it. We're fine. //Me.

I hit send, and then set the iPad aside. "Done." I took a sip.

"I've got spaghetti cooking. Let's get a salad going."

I put together a lettuce salad and set the kitchen table.

While we ate, I told him that I had sent another message to Dr. Williams. I also explained about the desk and wondered about financing it.

"How much?"

"She hasn't said. My guess is a couple thousand," I said. "At least. Don't worry, we should get our income tax return soon, and you can use that to pay for it. You could put it between the dollhouses and display Mary Lincoln dolls or something like that on it."

"Thank you. You're terrific."

I got up, carried the dirty dishes to the sink, and began filling the dishwasher. After putting the food away and finishing with the cleanup, I grabbed my iPad and joined Aaron in the living room. The iPad dinged, signaling the arrival of a new message, actually there were two. One was from Maggie. I opened that one first. She had written:

Liv//I'd tried to do something and punched the wrong button. Sorry about that. Good grief! Another break-in? Keep me posted. I heard about your dumpster dive. You must tell all.//M

The other e-mail was from an unknown sender. I opened it, only to be surprised. "Oh my God! Aaron! Look at this!" It was the newly found Mary Lincoln letter. "They weren't allowing the public access to this letter. How on earth?" My brows furrowed. "Someone hacked into their site and sent me this." My mouth dropped open, and my heart pumped hard. "Why?"

"Let me see it." I held my iPad so we could both read:

Dearest Taddie,

Father's Lost Speech will be found. Follow the Star of Bethlehem.

Your loving mother

"But look, Aaron," I said, pointing to the drawing at the bottom of the page. "It's a pentacle. What in the world?"

"This makes no sense. None whatsoever." Aaron nodded at it. "How can you make heads or tails of this?"

"I know, where is this leading us?" I set the iPad aside. "Who sent this? Is this why they didn't post it on their website?"

"Let me look." He picked it up and pressed a couple of buttons. "We should either bring this in to the station tomorrow, or at least have a police techie come out to the store and take a look at your computer."

"When's your shift?"

"I'll take you to work, then bring it in. I don't work until three, but the tech guy only works in the morning."

"I don't like this, Aaron. It's creepy."

"There are plenty of people who are looking out for you." He slid out his cell phone and dialed the station. I listened as he spoke to the on-duty detective, telling him about the latest incidents with the computer. Before disconnecting, he told them he would bring the iPad in the morning. "Done." Aaron stood up. "Sorry about this, but I have to go for hockey practice. It'll last for an hour, then I'll be right home."

"Drop me at Grandma's while you practice."

We left, and I spent a little over an hour with my grandparents watching *I Love Lucy* reruns. As soon as we returned home, I jumped into bed.

I slept peacefully, waking with the bright morning sun shining. Aaron lay beside me. *What would I do without him?* I decided to make him breakfast in bed. I slid from the bed and headed toward the kitchen. On the way, I took a short detour and picked up the toy bear from the extra bedroom. I set it on the kitchen counter, so I wouldn't forget to bring it to work.

By the time the fried bacon and eggs were dished

up, Aaron had joined me and began making toast.

"Ah — this leisurely breakfast is a pleasure." Aaron sat back and took a sip of coffee. "Good, too."

"Thanks."

As we ate, my thoughts circled to the letter. I said, "There are only a few people who would know about the newly found letter." I ate the last bite of my fried egg.

"None of the ladies at the tea knew about it because Blanche never arrived." Aaron grabbed the last bacon strip. "So who knew?"

"Probably Inga, Maggie, and Holly. Maybe Luke. Can't think of anyone else."

"What about Ronnie? We haven't seen his mug around here lately, either. What's he been up to?" Aaron finished his meal. "Why don't you ask around?"

After cleaning up the kitchen mess, we got ready to leave. As we walked into the garage, I said, "Why hasn't Inga's store been burglarized?"

"Good point, since the article said that other area antique stores have."

Once inside the car, I said, "I hope Inga will be there early. I have this feeling it will be a very busy day."

"I can drop you off, if you'd like."

"Okay."

Aaron stopped near the curb in front of Inga's, and I climbed out clutching the stuffed bear. The lights were on in the store, so I was certain she was inside. I headed for the front door. Cupping my hands against the front window, I found it odd that she wasn't near the front of the store where I could see her. I opened the door and went in.

"Inga," I called. Without an answer, I stepped farther inside. Since there wasn't a reply to my call, I figured she was in the back where she kept her coat and personal items. "Inga," I called once again.

I walked toward the back, calling Inga's name. A chill went through my body when I found her. She lay on the floor with vintage clothes heaped on top of her. I knelt beside her and spoke her name, but there was no response. I felt for signs of life. She had a pulse, and her breathing was shallow but steady.

I dialed emergency services, and then Aaron.

"Go straight out the same door you entered," Aaron said. "Whoever did that could still be in the building."

"I can't leave Inga alone. I've moved aside the rack of vintage clothes that were on top of her. She needs medical attention."

"I'll be right there," Aaron said. "Don't move."

Was I next?

Chapter Fourteen

Aaron arrived almost immediately and found me hovering over Inga.

"Where are the police," I asked.

Aaron held his finger to his mouth as a sign to be quiet as he leaned over the prostrate woman. He softly said, "Inga. It's Aaron." No response. Aaron straightened up, and then walked to the back door while I stayed crouched near Inga. He stopped to look inside a spare closet but saw nothing untoward. Frowning, he cocked his head and whispered, "Bathroom?"

"There." I mouthed and pointed.

I smoothed my hand over her forehead and whispered, "Inga, it's me." Although I watched for any sign of recognition, none came, and my eyes filled with tears. I said, "Can you hear me? Stay with me, Inga." She seemed to nod slightly and then moved her lips. I couldn't hear very well.

Aaron returned. "The bathroom is clear."

Glancing upward to Aaron, I said, "She said, Lincoln."

"I hear the ambulance." Aaron returned. "I'll open the front door."

"I'm staying right with her." I gently ran my palm across her hair and down her cheek while I told her everything would be fine. My cell phone chirped, and I figured it must be Grandma. She had an uncanny habit of calling at the most inopportune times.

Aaron took out his cell phone. "I better get some shots of the crime scene before the medics arrive." He snapped several shots in quick succession.

"Here they come now" I told him. I pulled the Mary Lincoln dress to which she clung, from her unconscious grasp, and placed it on a nearby chair.

The medical team rushed through the store to where we were "Feel a pulse?" the head of the medical team asked me. "Yes." I tried to stay near, holding her hand, but a medic brushed mine aside.

"Let me in here, lady," he asked abruptly.

"Sure." I moved aside, but not before kissing Inga's forehead and telling her everything would be all right. I went to stand near Aaron, who was speaking with the newly arrived Erlandsen.

"What can you tell me?" Erlandsen asked me. His black eyebrows looked bushier than normal.

"She asked me to bring in my Tad Lincoln toy bear early this morning because she had a prospective buyer. The door was unlocked, and I walked into the store, calling her name. She was on the floor right over there, clutching the dress on that chair. I phoned the emergency number, and then Aaron."

"You were expected?"

"Yes. Sort of like an appointment."

"What did you touch?" Erlandsen stood poised with his pencil and pen.

"Doorknob...and the dress that covered her."

"I want the pictures sent asap." He looked at Aaron. "Already have."

"Good work."

I piped up. "One more thing, detective." He frowned at me.

"I sent an e-mail earlier to Inga that jokingly said something like, 'lock up the Lincoln antiques in the bathroom.' I didn't really expect someone to break in and attack her. It's just that there has been that rush of stolen Lincoln antiques, and it got me to thinking."

"Right." Erlandsen wrote that down. He scratched his head. "You sure have a way of drawing bodies to you, dead or alive."

"Thanks for the wonderful encouragement."

"You're welcome. That message...we'll need to see it."

"Will do. I've still got your card with your e-mail address."

"Let's walk around the store. You can point out to me which are the Lincoln antiques. Oh—also where you've walked." He urged me away from the crime scene.

"Right this way." I headed toward the front door and began walking through, just the way I had previously. Once I came to the closet, I made sure they knew Aaron had been the one who opened it. "You can check this out." At the bathroom, I stopped. "I haven't seen anything of Lincoln's here. Nothing. Not even his desk, which I planned to purchase."

A chill from the open back door caused us to look toward it. An officer had entered. "There's an old desk right outside the back door," he reported. "It'll get ruined if it's not brought indoors." When the detective didn't answer, he said, "I'm bringing it in."

"Take some pictures first."

"I have, and also of footprints."

"Good." Erlandsen pulled on a pair of plastic gloves and gradually opened the bathroom door. "Didn't know what I would find, but nothing's here."

"I'm going over to the presidential area, just to see if she hid her valuable pieces in the bathroom." I quickly walked over to the area and noticed Inga had indeed moved the Lincoln items from where they had been. A noticeable line of dust from where the pictures once hung was apparent. A few toys had been removed and replaced by other antique items of the same likeness. All looked undisturbed. She must have moved the Lincoln antiques last night as I'd suggested. "The items are safely hidden," I called, walking back to them.

"Lincoln's?"

"Yes."

"Thanks. We can take it from here." Erlandsen looked at Aaron.

"We'll be over in Liv's dollhouse store. I go to work at three," Aaron replied and placed his hand on my back. "Let's go."

"I want that desk when you're finished with it," I told them. "You'll have to talk with the owner."

"Already did... Consider it mine."

Aaron steered me outside and into the bitter cold morning air. The gray sky fit my mood. Sniffling, I reached for a tissue and blew my nose. Aaron pressed in the code, and we entered the rear of the store.

"I'm freezing." Chilled to the bone, I left my coat on, hoping to warm up. "I'm calling Grandma."

"I'll go for coffees. Be right back."

"Lock it."

"Of course." He left.

Poor Inga. I pulled out my cell phone and speed dialed Grandma, who answered immediately.

"What happened?" I pictured Grandma pulling Grandpa close to the phone to listen in to our conversation.

"Inga's been injured. She may have surprised a burglar. I found her, Grandma. The paramedics took her to the hospital. Aaron is here with me."

"How is she? You better be careful. People are dropping like flies around you."

"Yes, Grandma, I've heard that. Inga's going to be fine, it looks like she was conked on the head. The police are swarming the area."

"Go home. We'll bring over a pot of chicken soup, and you can tell me all about it, dear."

"We want you safe at home," Grandpa butted into the conversation. "Listen to your grandpa."

"Okay, Grandpa, but I have to wait for the police to finish their questioning."

"Pay attention. Go home. Tell them you're leaving. They know the way to your house by heart by now." He hung up the phone.

"Yes sir," I said to the empty line.

Aaron entered and said, "I'm taking you home."

"Grandma's coming over with a pot of soup." I sighed. "The police will want to ask me more questions, I suppose." Just then the back door opened and in walked Erlandsen. "Is it all right if we go home? It's been quite a day so far."

"Sure, but we'll be over to question you later."

I suddenly felt chilled. I didn't like the feeling. "You've called the hospital?"

"Yes, I've filled in your husband on the details. Officer Reynolds," Erlandsen added with a smile. "I think you'd better stay right with her until this gets sorted out."

Aaron's smile was Erlandsen's equal, "Will do." As soon as he left, Aaron handed over the hot beverages. "Here. Let's get out to the car." We settled inside and fastened the seatbelts.

"Can we make a quick hospital detour?"

"Nope. Inga's being taken care of. Erlandsen told me she has a concussion, and they've sent for her daughter. Nancy should be there soon. She only lives a short distance away."

"Well, that's a relief."

"She is pretty shaken up, but no broken bones, just a bump on the back of her head."

"Do they have any idea what happened?"

"Not yet." He drove down the alleyway toward the street. "Why Inga, do you suppose?"

"We've got to get this figured out fast before more people take a nasty hit." I took a sip. "She must've grabbed the dress and was able to turn so as to not fall on her face."

"Could be. Very possible."

"This all sounds fishy to me. Someone knew I

would be coming. Which reminds me — I forgot to pick up my toy bear."

"I'll let the detectives know. They can bring it with them when they come out to the house for more questioning." He reached for my hand. "It'll be fine. Inga will be fine."

Will I ever figure out what this person was after?

"This all started when Blanche arrived to play Mary Lincoln." Aaron stopped at red light.

"Right. Blanche talked about the diary, and also the Lost Speech. So we're back to that." I had another thought. "The Masonic signs must have something to do with all of this, don't you think?"

"I do." Aaron turned from Main Street and headed toward our house. "You'll feel better now."

"I just want to go to bed." A cute snowman family in a neighboring yard made me smile. Two small snow children, with a daddy snowman. The sight took my mind off the Lincoln puzzles, at least for a moment

"We'll get you settled on the couch," Aaron said, parking in the garage.

"That's right where I want to be." I felt safe being in the house. The phone rang almost immediately.

Aaron answered and said, "Yep. She's going to be here all day. We left the toy bear of hers on the front counter of Inga's store. Please bring it with you when you come." He disconnected. "See? We've already been tracked down."

"I can be in a cave and they'd find me." I continued to the living room, grabbed a small quilt to cover myself up with, and crawled onto the couch. Soon Aaron appeared with our warmed-up coffee and sat down beside me. "When do you expect them to get here?"

"Not for awhile. They've got a mess on their hands. The fingerprint guys will need to do their stuff. But they found footprints outside the back door, near where the desk was found. The snow was deep, so I'm sure they were able to make a cast of the prints."

"That's good. That should help." I drew in a deep breath. "I want to call the hospital."

"Let's wait. Inga needs her rest, and Nancy needs to get there first." Aaron made sure I was covered. "Let's give her another thirty, then call. They'll patch you through to her room if she's been admitted. Now, you would speak with only a nurse. Talking to Nancy would be better."

"You're right. Call me impatient, but I'm so worried about her." I thought for a moment and said, "Maybe in the morning, Grandma and I can both go up and see her?"

"That shouldn't be a problem." Aaron went to the window and looked out. "They're here. Marie is lugging a large pot."

"I can smell it already." I pictured a bowl of chicken soup and felt cozy.

Aaron opened the door, and Grandma and Grandpa kissed him on the cheek. "Let me take that." Aaron took the pot from Grandma and headed to the kitchen.

"Tell me all about it, Olivia," Grandma said. She

held up one end of the quilt, then sat down, placed my feet on her lap, and covered us. Grandpa sat in a chair opposite.

"I went early to see Inga at her store, and then all this happened." I proceeded to relate the story once again and finally brought Grandma up to date. "Something crazy is going on and we're trying to figure what it's all about. We think it has to do with a speech Abraham Lincoln gave a few years before running for the presidency."

"And you think those symbols are part of the puzzle?"

"I think so." Then I remembered the newly found Mary Lincoln letter and said, "Someone had to have hacked into the Lincoln House computer to get that, too. It wasn't posted on their website. Who would do that? Who could do that?"

Aaron returned from the kitchen and sat down. "This is a mystery that dates back over a hundred and fifty years. We're not exactly sure where to look next, though." He raised a brow and looked at me, then Grandma.

"I go in to work at three. It's still four hours until I report for duty. Can you stay with Liv?"

"We'll stay with her." Grandma squeezed my hand.

"Thank you." I gave my grandparents a big smile. "I've checked to see if Mister Lincoln was a Mason, but he wasn't. However, Mary's family members were. Most of the men, that is." I cleared my throat. "I also have discovered that Abe had planned to join the

Masons after he left the White House."
Did the Masons help hide the speech?

Chapter Fifteen

The detectives arrived as we ate our chicken soup, and Erlandsen placed the bear on our kitchen table.

"Thanks," I said, reaching for it. We stayed seated at the kitchen table while the detectives leaned against the counter. "I suppose you have a few questions?"

"Yep," Mergens agreed.

"Just a few," added Erlandsen. "Can we talk someplace more private?"

"Sure. Let's go to the back bedroom." I got up and led the way, knowing my grandparents would finish eating and would be sitting in the living room watching TV when the questioning was through. Grandma would also have the kitchen cleaned up, except for my half-empty bowl, which would be waiting for me on the table.

"Right in here." I steered them into the room, flipped on the light switch, and one of the detectives closed the door. "Fire away." I sat down on the bed and looked up at both.

"By the way," Mergens softly said, "just contacted the hospital. I'm happy to tell you that Inga is doing fine. She seems to be coming around. They figure by morning she'll be in good shape and ready to talk. It's possible she'll be released later in the day tomorrow. It depends on her condition."

"That's really good news. I suppose a call before visiting is in order? Is Nancy, her daughter, with her?"

"Yes. We also have a security guard posted."

"Oh. And what about the woman I found in the dumpster?" My eyes opened wider. "You think Inga might have been the next victim?"

"I knew you'd ask. It's hard to say," Mergens studied me. "This case seems to be all about the Lincolns."

"Have you thought of anything else?" Erlandsen asked, poised with pad and pencil. His eyes seemed to pierce me.

"About Inga? No." I ran my fingers through my hair. "She tried to speak, but I couldn't understand her. It's possible that she said 'Lincoln.'"

"Anything else that's struck you as funny or odd in the past few days?"

"Not really." I frowned. "Except my computer was hacked. Someone messed up my Mary Lincoln file and deleted certain messages, but you know about that."

"It's all been scanned and cleaned, hasn't it?" Erlandsen glanced at Mergens. "Won't do any good to haul it in. Still, if it happens again, we need to be told immediately. Anything else?"

"Yes, as a matter of fact." I looked at Erlandsen. "Blanche mentioned that a newly found letter of Mary Lincoln's was at the Presidential Library. I visited the website but couldn't find it, so I messaged the contact there. He replied that the letter wasn't for public view." Mergens crossed his arms and motioned for me to continue. "I mentioned the letter to Holly. You see, once when I went to see Inga, she wasn't in at the moment, so I talked to Holly a few minutes and mentioned the letter. Then I got an anonymous e-mail with the letter as an attachment."

"You think it came from her?" Mergens asked. "Very interesting."

"Who else from the block could have known about the letter?"

"You're narrowing it down, eh?" I raised a brow and studied them. "Possibly Luke and maybe, Inga. However, Holly is the only person I spoke to about it being not for public display."

"How about in email? Did you mention it to anyone in a message? Remember, someone hacked your computer and has been reading all your emails."

I hadn't thought of that. "Wow, I guess it could be anyone."

"All right, I guess that's everything," Mergens said, walking to the door. "By the way." He opened it up with Erlandsen following.

"Yes?"

"Inga's *Pennies for Our Troops* jar wasn't taken."

"Then it wasn't a robbery for money. It's back to Lincoln, though I'm not surprised."

"I'd like to take Blanche's dress for a look myself."

"Sure." I took it out and gave it to him.

I flipped off the light switch and as I entered the hallway Aaron joined me in uniform.

"Aaron," Erlandsen said. "Off to work, I take it?"

"Yep." Aaron cocking his head. "Anything new to tell?"

"Not really. We'll keep you updated."

"Right."

They opened the front door and walked out. The sudden chill sent shivers down my spine, but the warmth when the door was closed again chased the shivers away.

"Sit down, Olivia. I'll warm your soup." Grandma got up from the couch. They'd been watching an Andy Griffith rerun.

"He wanted the dress?"

"Yep. He wanted a look at it himself." I shrugged.

"I'm going, hon," Aaron said. "But keep the doors locked and shades drawn."

"I will."

"I'll call or text later." He kissed me, said "Goodbye," to Grandpa, and headed toward the door.

My grandparents stayed for another hour, passing the time by watching *I Love Lucy*. Grandma's head nodded a few times while Grandpa's eyes glazed over once or twice. I was happy to see them leave as dusk descended upon us. Now I had the needed alone time to put my thoughts together.

The events left me wondering if I shouldn't just stay home until the murder was solved. I turned on the History Channel to see what was on. I got lucky — they were showing a program about President Lincoln's rise to the White House. I had missed only the first ten minutes. When the program ended, I did a Google search for "the Lost Speech" again and found several more websites. I clicked onto each, but none of them had anything I hadn't already discovered. Maybe the speech was well and truly lost.

Did his office partner, William Herndon, keep it? Could

he have given it to Mary for safekeeping? Possible, but for what reason?

I let that thought percolate and work its way around in the recesses of my mind. Since the discovery of the Star Spangled Banner manuscript, I knew anything was possible. With this fresh thought in mind, I shut off the television and headed to bed.

As I tossed and turned, my thoughts circled to images of that tall, lanky, young man full of hopes and dreams and promise as he delivered the speech. As was customary, only men attended political speeches. Although Mary had most likely prodded and pressured him into the political arena, she saw the intelligence behind his homespun words. She was very interested in politics and could hold her own during any conversation. She was not only well-read, but she was also brilliant in her own right. The old saying, *"Behind every good man is a good woman,"* came to mind.

I also recalled Grandma's comment about bodies dropping all around me, which made me frightened at every little sound in the dark. I got up several times to look out the front window, out into the street, apprehensive about what I might find. At one point, I fixed myself a small cup of hot chocolate. Sometime during the early morning hours, Aaron crawled into bed. I curled up against his warm body and fell asleep dreaming about times long ago, and how hard it was to eke out a living. That thought was still on my mind as I woke to sunshine streaming in through the window blinds.

Aaron was still asleep. I kissed him lightly on the cheek before softly slipping out of bed, making sure the blankets covered him well. I tiptoed into the hallway, jumping into the shower. When I was dressed, I headed toward the kitchen resolved to turn over a new leaf. I wanted the perfect breakfast, including bacon that wasn't two stages past crisp. Aaron also liked his eggs sunny-side up, not cracked-yolk style. I hoped to not burn the house down.

It was striking eight o'clock when I tackled the bacon and eggs. I tried to cook exactly as I'd seen Aaron do it. Shortly after, as I sat eating my burned egg and overdone bacon, I scanned through some old recipe books I had collected over the years. At the sound of Aaron's footsteps in the hall, I closed the book and brought my dirty plate to the sink. After cracking two more eggs into the pan, I asked, "Hard night?"

"Sort of, but not really." He hugged me. "How are you doing?"

"Didn't sleep well." I yawned.

"Let me take over." He grabbed the spatula from me, but I kept a close eye on how he fried the eggs. "I checked on our store on my way home. It seemed fine. I didn't go inside but probably should have with the way things are shaping up around here." He flipped his eggs onto the plate with ease. *Men!* "I'm staying at the store with you today." He yawned. "At least until I need to leave for my shift this evening. I've already talked to Max. Someone will be there with you at all times."

"Bodyguards." I grunted. "I hate to admit it, but I feel better." I crossed my arms, shivering. "I'm worried I'll be the next victim."

"Nah, I've got your back."

"The creep doesn't stand a chance." We sat for a few minutes, giving me time to check my e-mail account since that had not been done yesterday. I found a note from the university that read:

Dear Liv,

Today, Wed, would work out great. Call me first thing when you get this message.

Call me,

Dr. Bill Williams

His telephone number was included under his name.

I reached for my phone, saying, "Dr. Williams wants me to call," and quickly dialed. Aaron gave me a thumbs-up. The phone was answered. "Doctor Williams?"

"Liv? Good to hear from you. Come over to my office at two today. I'll try to be there, but if I'm not, I'll leave a message with my secretary and she'll take care of it. You won't mind leaving the necklace with me a couple days, will you? We've a ton of course work we're preparing."

"No problem." I disconnected and told Aaron what Dr. Williams had said.

"We'll meet him together. I'm not letting you or the necklace or anything out of my sight," he said, crossing his arms.

"Fine with me. You chauffeuring me around? Couldn't be better." I smiled. "Now, let's get moving. I want to stop in to see Inga for a minute."

"Can't. Until things get sorted out, the detectives don't want anyone to go near her, except for her daughter. They're taking no chances about anything."

"I'm not a suspect, why would they prevent me from being there?"

"Just because. Rules are rules." He frowned. "Now let's git."

I headed to the bedroom and retrieved the small safe box with the necklace from the closet. I placed the box inside my bag and headed out to the kitchen. Hearing the car's engine running, I knew Aaron was waiting. I pulled on my coat and went out to the car.

"I'm sending a message to the detectives alerting them that we are taking the necklace to Doctor Williams this afternoon," I told Aaron.

"Makes sense."

My phone dinged with their reply. "They'll drop off Blanche's dress when they're finished with it."

In less than ten minutes, we were inside the store and our jackets removed. Together we strolled through the workroom and showroom, not something I cared to do alone.

"Nothing seems out of place," I said with relief.

"However," Aaron said, nodding over at the First Lady pictures, "aren't they a little crooked?"

"Maybe a little bit, but these old buildings shift and creak." I thought of a listening device, because that was how the killer learned about the hidden manuscript of the Star Spangled Banner and me almost being murdered on my wedding night. Kind of natural that I might be a little anxious.

The morning flew past. Since Aaron and I weren't very familiar with the campus layout, we left early to go to the university.

We found a parking spot and took an elevator down to the main level, walked out into the street, and headed for the closest university building. From there, it didn't take us long to find Dr. William's building and his office on the third floor.

"Thank you so much," I said to him as we entered his cluttered office. I stared at the full bookshelves of textbooks and numerous magazine piles on the floor. "We sure appreciate this."

"Liv, Aaron, good to see you two again." He motioned to the chairs. From a nearby stack of newspapers, it was apparent that the chairs had been piled with them earlier. "Have a seat."

"Nice view." Glancing out, I noted the cluster of tall buildings of academia, and tree branches swaying from the strong wind. I removed the box from my bag, and then I placed it on the desk.

"Thank you, I'm grateful you brought this." Dr. Williams held up the box. "This is a mystery, isn't it?" He opened it and held the silvered ornament between his fingers. "I'll get to it in a day or two and let you know my findings."

"If there is an acorn inside, I'd like to have it tested for age, and perhaps general area where it grew." I raised a brow. "This has me completely baffled."

"As well as the detectives in charge." Aaron frowned. "The department will certainly pay whatever reasonable costs you incur with the university."

"No trouble. It'll be a good exercise for the students." We chatted for a few more minutes, then left.

Why on earth would anyone silver an acorn?

Chapter Sixteen

Checking e-mails when we arrived back at the store, I found a message from Frances, asking me to send Blanche's dress to the Mary Todd Lincoln House. I replied:

Hi Frances, I'm more than happy to send it tomorrow. It's good to hear from you. Someone broke into my house and destroyed the hat, the police have Blanche's dress and will return it today. Please let the authorities know what's owed for damages. There's a report on file with the Minneapolis police department. Detective Mergens and Erlandsen are on the case.

Another matter has come to my attention. The newly found letter of Mrs. Lincoln's isn't shown on the Presidential Library website. Any idea why not? Also, in the published diary, there are a couple of pages of concentric puzzles. Do you know of anyone who has deciphered them or why she would have them in her diary?

If you can shed any light on these two issues, please let me know. The dress will be dropped in the mail tomorrow.

Many thanks, Liv

Owner of White House Dollhouse Store

After the message was sent, I checked for further messages. There were two questioning the Lost

Speech. One read "Lady, get a life. Who cares?" The second one read, "You seem to be an educated person. The race is on, but I'll win." That caused my heart to skip a beat. Did the mysterious hacker send it? Who were they, and what were they after? Did they send me the Mary Lincoln letter that was removed from public view? Finally, *What are the consequences of this game we are playing? Death?*

I forwarded all the messages to the detectives.

Aaron came in from shoveling and stood behind me as I logged off.

"Two more messages about the speech. One was off-color."

"Don't worry, the detectives should have them soon."

"Good."

" It's tough, you being here alone, and will be until this situation is wrapped up. There are too many crazies out there."

"Now you're the one making me nervous." What else was going to happen to my circle of friends? My grandparents needed attention, too.

"Let's close up. No one's coming in, business is slow up and down the street." Aaron massaged my shoulders. "You are really tense. Let's get you home and relaxed."

"You're right. What do you think about closing the store for a few days? Maybe like a short, mid-winter vacation?" Just then my e-mail dinged and I opened the inbox. "It's from Inga."

"Oh, yeah?" Aaron leaned over my shoulder to

read the message along with me. "Must be her daughter writing. See, she's signed her name, Nancy. So... she says we can take the desk, eh? We have to drop off a check first at the store?"

"Looks like it." I frowned. "For some reason, this makes me very puzzled. There's something about the desk that makes me uneasy, like it's trying to tell me a secret."

"You're getting spooked from all of this. We do need a vacation." Aaron rubbed my shoulders. "I'll call the precinct for information about Blanche's dress." He pulled out his cell phone and called. After disconnecting he said, "They'll bring it by right away. They had wanted one more close look at it. This case really has them stymied."

"We'll put the desk over there in the corner where the Civil War-era dollhouse is situated. I'll keep the toy bear on it, since the buyer never showed up for it. It will look quaint, and hopefully catch people's eyes as they pass the window." My eyes lit up as I thought about it. *Maybe I should invest in more presidential memorabilia to set out.* "I need to pack up my mini-dollhouses to bring in and place on a shelf. That might help draw customers in."

I thanked Nancy for the desk and told her that Aaron would soon stop with a check. Her reply came quickly and I told Aaron. "She's at the store for a few minutes, if you want to run the check over to her."

"Will do." Aaron slipped into his coat while I hurriedly wrote out Inga's check. Aaron stuffed the check into a coat pocket. "I'll get Max to help me." He sent Max a text message asking that they meet at Inga's to carry the table back, and then took off without waiting for Max's reply. Knowing my husband, if Max didn't show up, Aaron would carry the table back to my shop by himself, without breaking a sweat or mentioning it.

As I watched for the squad car bringing the dress that they'd taken from home the other night, it occurred to me that my ladies hadn't had their daily greeting. Strolling among the houses, I deliberately stopped near the Civil War house and looked at the president. "Mr. Lincoln, your old desk will soon arrive. Isn't that spectacular?" Turning to the first lady, I asked, "Mrs. Lincoln, can you please tell me what the concentric puzzles mean? Please give me a clue. I'm not good at round puzzles." After a few moments, I continued wandering among the houses, stopping to rearrange furniture or place a fallen doll upright. Soon, I was back to the computer.

I rearranged my message files, noticing a few emails had been deleted by the hacker. It was really becoming a serious problem. Next, I sent Maggie a message explaining all that had happened. Just as I hit "send," the detectives arrived with the dress.

"Thanks, guys." I took the large box.

"Anytime." They left as quickly as they came. Someone banged on the back door shortly after that. I set the dress down on the work counter and opened the door wide for Aaron and Max to carry the desk inside.

They carried it to the designated corner. The small

desk certainly looked different from what was shown on the History Channel. The tour of Lincoln's Springfield home had shown a small, short, cubby-holed desk that barely had enough room to write a letter. Pictures of Abe sitting beside it showed his legs sprawled out, crossed, and him sitting sideways, in his efforts to accommodate the desk's short structure.

Claw-foot legs, dark with age, provided support for the desk. A slanted top, when raised, revealed a comfortable writing area. Abraham Lincoln's name was engraved on the back panel. There was a long, narrow shelf with a wooden top at the rear of the desk, presumably to hold candles. Under the writing space was a long drawer where writing pencils, quills, bottles of ink, a blotter, and a pen knife would have been stored. Letter writing certainly was much more difficult back then.

I wondered if the desk might hold a clue to finding the hidden speech.

"I'm going to find a dust rag," I said, heading toward the workroom.

"Look hon," Aaron said when I returned. He was studying the brass plaque with Lincoln's name. "It's got to be original, don't you think?"

"Let me clean it a bit." I wiped it down, cleaning off a smudge under the names. That revealed the date. "It was made in 1849. That's when Lincoln returned from serving a term in congress and resumed his legal career."

"Is there a manufacturer's name?"

"Nope." I sneezed a few times. "Allergies." I

continued to run the rag over the surface of the desk, removing the dust that hid numerous scratches and scars. "I wonder if this has ever been restored?"

"Probably, but it looks like it was kept as original as possible. If Inga says it's Lincoln's desk, that's good enough for me. She's been working with antiques for years." Aaron slid his palm across the smooth wood. "It's a beautiful piece."

"Well, Inga has the documentation showing that it really did belong to Lincoln, but I also agree. It's an awesome piece of furniture regardless of who owned it."

I smiled lovingly down at it. "The stuffed bear will look cute on it. We can set him on a small doily." I finished wiping the desk, then reopened the drawer and stuck my hand farther inside and ran my palm over the surface. "Just checking for any hidden messages."

"You never give up, do you? Aaron asked with a smile. I could tell he was proud of my tenaciousness.

"Nope, not me. I wonder, do you think Lincoln wrote any important speeches on this thing?"

"Shouldn't be at all surprised." Aaron squeezed my shoulder. "Let's go home. I have to get ready for work."

"All right."

We closed up and exited through the back door, but not before letting Max know we were leaving.

After Aaron left for his evening shift, it gave me a few moments to gather up Blanche's dress for one more look at it before I mailed it back. It took me a long time to repack the enormous dress, with all its many layers, into the slim box. After sealing and addressing the box, it was time to reward myself with some television. Tonight was not a night for researching. In the morning, after I dropped the mini-dollhouses off at the store and the dress at the post office, I planned to spend some time at the university library.

I went back downstairs to get the toy bear and set it by the back door to make it handy for the morning. A bowl of hot, leftover soup sounded good, so I heated one up and brought it with me to the living room. A number of unfamiliar cars driving past the window struck me as odd since we have a quiet street, and I know everyone on the block. I pulled the curtains closed.

When showering later, I found myself worrying about the unfamiliar cars, and stopped myself. *Was I becoming paranoid?*

I vowed to stay away from the window and went straight to bed after packing up the dollhouses. *Wait! Was that a prowler?* I rolled over and told myself I was hearing things. At that moment, Aaron crawled into bed.

Morning came, cold and frosty.

Aaron was sound asleep as I climbed from the bed and quietly dressed. What I saw in the bathroom mirror was the deciding factor to wear my hair in a ponytail. I scribbled a message for Aaron before leaving home, telling him what I planned to do that day.

I dropped an old notebook and pen into my bag

and carried the package, bear and the dollhouses out to the car, placing them in the trunk.

My plan was to drive to the university after checking on the store and dropping off the packages. Snow dripped from the trees and the cars splashed mud as they drove past. It was definitely an end-of-February heat wave. The notion of soon to come spring rain and blooming flowers made me smile.

I turned down the alleyway and parked and locked the car. Farther down the alley, Suni, Luke's wife, was going into the backdoor of the café. Holding onto the bear and my bag, I glanced down and saw footprints embedded in the slushy snow leading from my back door to the café's. "Strange." I removed my boots after going inside, so as not to track across the wood floor, then went straight to the showroom.

Why was my computer humming?

I piled the dollhouse boxes on the workroom countertop to be taken care of later. I set the toy bear on the desk in the corner, and then shut down the computer. I hoped no one had hacked into my computer again.

Next on my agenda was the post office. After paying the postage, I drove to the university library.

Making tracks in slush as I walked from the parking lot, my thoughts flashed back to the slushy footprints leading to the back door of the Brew Café. *Had Suni been in my store?*

It didn't take long to locate the library's reference section. All those hours spent researching back in college had taught me how to navigate libraries with ease.

I found the right shelf, thanks to Mr. Dewey, selected four books, and carried the stack to a study carrel. I decided to visit the restroom before immersing myself in the past, but on my return, the books were topsy-turvy. Perplexed, I glanced around, but no one was near.

I opened the top book to the table of contents, found the topic, flipped to the appropriate page, and read the short entry about the Lost Speech. I shook my head. It didn't tell me anything I didn't already know. I scanned other pages in the book that referenced Lincoln's speeches, making a few notes, but not finding any new information. I did the same with the other books. Before putting the books back on the cart for re-shelving, I read through my notes but felt like ripping them up.

For the life of me, I could *not* figure out what the speech had to do with any of the clues we had found.

How on earth could Mary's notes connect to murder or the missing speech? If anything, I was more perplexed than when I started.

With my bag and notebook in hand, I hiked over to the elevator and took it to the main level. Soon, I was out the front door.

After all the snowfall, walking down the dry sidewalks was a welcome relief, but I feared that another winter storm would happen soon. A shiver went down my back and I stopped and looked behind me. *Was someone following me?* No one appeared to be taking an interest in me. I walked on, but it happened again only a block later, and I dashed into a bookstore. I stood near the storefront window and peered out. Passersby were either busy walking or chatting with a partner.

It's only my imagination. Just as I was about to leave the store, my cell phone beeped with a message. Aaron needed cough drops. My response read: ok. I finally reached the parking lot, marched straight to my car, jumped inside, and promptly locked the doors. My heart raced. I heard the crunch of footsteps directly behind my car on the frozen slush, unnerving me. I glanced around but didn't see anyone. A small car backed out from behind mine and drove past. I kept my eye on it until it left the parking lot. Another car came from the other side of the lot, and like the other, continued past me and left. Nothing was out of the ordinary. I drew a deep breath and slowly breathed out. After repeating that exercise a few times, I felt ready to leave. I put the car in reverse and backed out, then drove through the lot and to the exit.

Once out onto the street, I turned toward River Road, which took me to Washington Avenue. I crossed the bridge and drove into Minneapolis, winding my way through the area where a large number of Scandinavian immigrants had settled. Near a small store around the Seven Corners area, I parked and climbed from the car to look around. *Did that small white car follow me?* I walked into the store, purchased the cough drops, and returned to my car. I planned to soon have a cup of tea heating in the microwave in our kitchen, but a little white car image reflected in my rearview mirror. I quickly changed my mind and detoured away from home.

Circling around, I went back out onto Main Street and turned to the direction of University Avenue. I made a few quick turns and then pulled into an available parking lot to wait. In a few short minutes, the little white car drove past. After several minutes more, the white car drove by again.

Was I being followed?

Chapter Seventeen

"Honey, I'm home," I called. I dropped my boots and coat, and went to the living room with the cough drops in hand. Aaron was lying on the couch watching *Madmen* reruns. I kissed him on the cheek before making a stop in the kitchen. "Some weird things happened today," I said when I returned to the living room.

"Like what?" he asked. Aaron turned off the television and turned his attention fully to me.

"There were footprints this morning at the shop, from my store's back door over to the Brew Café's back door. I saw Suni going in but have no proof she made the tracks in the slush. Is that weird enough?" I sat beside him, pulling a coverlet up over us.

"It might be a coincidence, but there's been too many of them lately," Aaron said.

"Someone had to have followed me to the university. It gives me the creeps." I shook my head

"The detectives need a heads-up about this. They'll want it in the report." Aaron pulled out his cell phone, pressed the quick-dial button to the precinct and asked to be passed to Detective Erlandsen.

As he spoke to the detective about what happened, I checked my e-mail account and sped through the messages. A new message from Dr. Williams brightened the moment. It read:

Hi Liv,

Will be doing an analysis on the acorn found inside of the silver encasement beginning next week. I'll work it into the class syllabus. I've saved the silver, but would like to keep it and the acorn, just to show the class. Is that all right or is it part of an investigation?

Dr. Williams

I responded:

Hi Dr. Williams,

Thanks a bunch for everything.

I would like the pieces restored. The necklace belongs to the police.

You'll have to contact Detective Mergens or Erlandsen." Liv

The message was sent at the same time Aaron disconnected from his call.

"He wants us to tell him everything. Any little thing that doesn't seem right, no matter if we think it's stupid or not." Aaron brought his hand up and pulled me closer, giving me a kiss. "He isn't exactly sure of a motive for any of this. The police in Lexington, where Blanche lived, have helped as much as possible by providing names for cross-referencing. Our detectives have come up empty-handed."

"Did you tell them my thoughts on Luke and Holly?"

"Yes, and they are both high on their suspect list." He smiled down at me. "Show me what you found out today."

I pulled out my notebook and showed him the copied pages from the few known paragraphs of the speech. "Here are a few pages of the Lincoln-Douglas Debates and the beginnings of a few speeches. I searched as much as possible but found nothing more. The speech is mentioned in a few textbooks but with the same outcome. The scholars claim Lincoln threw it away."

"We don't have anything new. We're kind of back where we began, aren't we?" Aaron sat straighter, then glanced at the clock. "It's time to get ready for work."

"What about those concentric puzzles?"

"Why not try and figure them out tonight? That should keep you busy." He winked. "Just sayin…"

"You know I'm puzzle-dysfunctional." I grinned. "Almost completely, but not totally dysfunctional. I guess it's worth a try."

"Yeah, give it a shot." He stood up. "See if you can make any sense out of them."

"Okay…I'll get started on them and also do more research on the symbols. I need a better grasp on what I'm diving into." As Aaron walked down the hallway, I said, "What time will you be home?"

"Around midnight."

"I might go in to the store to rearrange a few items. I feel jittery."

"Call or text, if you do. Be careful." Aaron stopped. "I want to know what you're doing all the time, all windows covered and doors locked."

"All right. I'll be careful."

I didn't want to be home alone any longer than necessary because it made me feel anxious. The hair on the back of my neck stood on end.

I reached for the drapery drawstrings and pulled them shut. The possibility of passersby seeing me through the windows only added to my uneasiness.

After Aaron left, the quiet totally unnerved me. "That's it. I'm outta here." I slipped into a heavy flannel shirt and jeans. As I walked through the house, I switched on some other lights to make it look as if someone was indeed home. In the kitchen, I slipped into my heavy jacket, started the car with the remote key, and then sent Aaron a short message as to my whereabouts. Before marching out the door, I made sure the other doors were locked. I headed in the car toward Main Street and soon parked behind the store. It occurred to me as I stared up at Max's back window that he should have been contacted to know I would be working tonight. I texted him, knowing he would see it soon since he always kept his phone in his pocket.

As I walked to the back door, something didn't seem right. I glanced at some nearby parked cars. *Is that the white car that had followed me earlier today?* I walked over toward it, slipped out my cell phone and snapped a couple pictures of the license plate. While backing away from the car, the back door of the Brew Café opened, startling me.

"Luke, you're open," I said. "I was just going to come for a cup of coffee, on the off chance you were still there. It's hard to stay awake until Aaron gets home from work, and watching reruns is tiring. I thought some fresh air might do me good." I was rambling on like an idiot so I tried to slow myself down. "Anyway, are you?"

"You sound like you've had enough caffeine, Liv." Luke laughed at me and came closer. "I'm locking up. Suni and I did some shelf-stocking this evening."

"Tomorrow, then," I replied, slowly moving away. *His grin made me anxious.* I didn't want to turn my back toward him, so I watched as Suni appeared. "Hi. I haven't seen you in ages."

"You, too." She raced to her car and opened the door, clenched her teeth and said, "Bye. Bye." Then she ducked into the white car.

"Good night." Luke climbed into his car.

As soon as they drove away, I felt relieved and finished walking toward my store. I punched in the code numbers, opened the door, and stepped inside. With the lights flipped on, I went into the workroom and removed my coat, stomping the snow from the bottom of my shoes. The silence of the empty building was unnerving. I turned on the radio, tuned to a jazz station from Chicago, and adjusted the volume. My cell phone was void of messages, which was surprising. Why hadn't Max replied?

I pressed the call button and waited while his phone rang, but there was no answer. In a few short minutes, I was up the steps to his apartment, banging on his door at the top. Through the crack in the door it was apparent there were lights on, but no movement was detected. Since I owned the building, I had the master key and unlocked the door.

"Max," I shouted, running through the living room and down the small hallway. "Max!" Still no answer. I hustled to his bedroom, nearly tripping on the piles of clothes strewn across the floor. Max was face down on his pillow, fully dressed. "Max! Max!" I went to his side. He didn't appear to be ill. I reached down and touched his forehead, it felt cool, and then I placed my fingers beside his neck to feel for a pulse. I let out a sigh of relief when I felt a weak pulse. I quickly called the emergency number, and then called Aaron to explain the situation. After covering Max with a blanket I went to fetch him a glass of water, should he regain consciousness and was thirsty.

I had just returned to the bedroom when sirens blared down below. I went to the door and shouted down to the medics. "Up here!"

Within minutes the small apartment was flooded with medics and police. Aaron came up beside me. We stood to the side as the medics performed their tasks.

"Did you see anyone?" Erlandsen asked upon entering the room. I was seated on Max's couch.

"No, but Aaron filled you in on what happened earlier, right? I'm sending Aaron two pictures of a license plate, and he can forward them. The plates, I believe, are from a car driven by Suni, Luke's wife. I'm sure she was the driver of the white car that was following me... and there was a passenger in the car." I watched Erlandsen write it all down before pulling out my phone to send the photos. "I just witnessed

Suni drive away in it."

Erlandsen checked his phone. "Got 'em," he said. "We'll look into it."

We all sat silently and watched as the paramedics wheeled Max to the door on a gurney. The head medic looked at the detective, and said, "There's bruising across his neck."

My eyes opened wider as I looked from Max to the medic. "It's like a karate chop on his right side, under his ear."

"Thanks," Erlandsen said. "Much appreciated. Now we have a little bit to go on. He'll come around in due time."

"There doesn't appear to be any forced entry." When Mergens entered the room, he looked ready to drop.

"Maybe we should go downstairs to take a look around the store," I suggested. "I haven't walked through it yet. I had texted Max and tried calling him. The fact that there was no answer brought me upstairs."

"Still have a coffeepot?" Erlandsen cocked his head and yawned.

We hiked down the stairs and went inside the store. Aaron brewed the coffee while the detectives wandered through the showroom. I listened to them mumble. Even though I could pick out a word only once in awhile, I gathered they were just as perplexed as I. *Why would anyone want to hurt Max?*

"How in the world does this have anything to do with Max? He's completely innocent of having anything to do with the desk or houses. He should be all right, shouldn't he?" I said to Aaron as he filled the four coffee cups. "I don't understand the motive behind injuring him, do you? We need to get to the bottom of this."

"Yes, asap." He shrugged as he lifted two cups. I picked up the other two and we walked into the showroom and handed two to the detectives.

As I strolled around the room, my eyes were drawn to the desk where I had set the stuffed bear. I gasped as I saw that the bear was ripped apart. Tad's uniform was still hanging intact. I almost dropped my full cup of coffee. "*Oh no!*" My eyes opened wider. "This isn't happening." Aaron followed with the boxes and set them on the counter.

"The miniature Lincoln house is in ruins," he said.

"I can't believe this."

"Oh my God," I said. "That display was just set up. The bear was Tad's, and you already know about the desk."

"It's funny that the intruders didn't take it," Mergens said. "Let me take a look at the other items." He shook his head. "We better have it all fingerprinted."

"President Lincoln all over again, right?" I took a deep breath. "I'd just purchased that miniature dollhouse."

"What on earth is going on around here? That's what I'd like to know," Mergens said. "The Civil War has been over for how long?"

"Let's get some photos." Erlandsen scratched his

head. "Why did they leave the little uniform alone? Why not rip that all apart too?"

"Not sure." I took a deep breath. "I brought my own mini house collection in this morning, and it's untouched. They only destroyed the Lincoln dollhouse. Weird."

"It shows they know exactly what's important, and where to look." Erlandsen glanced around the room. "They have a mission, and I bet they're after that speech."

"It sure seems like it. Maybe they searched for clues and left the uniform as an incentive or warning," Mergens said.

"Something like that," Aaron said.

I went to pick up the remnants of the bear. "The rear end had an embroidered oak tree on it. The limbs almost looked like the images you see of a family tree, like when you record your ancestry. I'll take a look through the seams in the uniform, just like I did with the dresses. Who knows? Maybe we'll hit pay dirt." I took the uniform down and went to sit by the sewing machine. I focused my bright sewing light on the seam and began to slowly finger the stitching on the pant legs. It took quite awhile for me to examine every stitch. I got up to join them when finished. "Nothing that I could see."

Erlandsen wiped his forehead. "Do you have anything new to tell me about any of your discoveries?"

"No. I spent the morning in the university library and didn't find out anything different than what I already knew." I shook my head. "Someone did shift the books around in the study carrel when I left for a few minutes."

"You did learn something new," Mergens said.

"I did? What?"

"You need to keep a sharp eye out, wherever you go."

Does this mean my life span is on a short timeline?

Chapter Eighteen

A bright morning sun masked my mood, causing me to squirm further under the blankets. After last night's discoveries, Aaron had taken the remainder of his shift off.

"Let's get dressed and get out of here." Aaron flipped back the covers.

"No choice but to get up," I groaned. Reluctantly, I dressed.

Together, we walked down the hallway to the kitchen "There's a weird feeling snaking through me, like do I need the extra set of car keys?" I shook my head. "Can't figure out why." I went to the kitchen junk drawer and grabbed the extra keys, along with the memory stick. "Oh, and look at this."

"Let me see." Aaron rubbed his chin. "Where did you get it?"

"It was on the sidewalk outside the shop, the night Blanche was murdered." I placed it back into the drawer, and Aaron made sure that the house was locked before climbing into the car. "Mergens will want to hear about that memory stick." *Could it be yet another clue?*

My mind spun in circles about all the clues and how they might fit into the Lincoln Puzzle as we drove to the hospital to visit Max.

"Hey, you. You'll do anything to get out of work, won't you?"

I felt funny as we stepped inside Max's room. Max had tubes hooked into him and he looked pale. I'd never seen him look so haggard and it was awful to see him this way—the opposite of his usual vibrant self.

"I'm all right, really I am." Max looked back at me through cloudy eyes. "I feel like shit, though. One helluva headache... and my neck hurts like hell." Half-grinning, he said, "You saved my life."

"I wish there was something more that I could've done to prevent this." With his hand in mine I said, "But tell me what happened."

"Went for gas. Thought I saw a light on in the store. So I parked and checked it out. Don't remember much else." Max rubbed his neck and grimaced. "Ouch!"

"Basically all you did was enter? What'd you do, clunk your boots on the floor?" I massaged his forearm. "Who would have guessed you'd be the next victim."

"Gee, what an honor," Max said between clenched teeth. Looking at Aaron, he grumbled, "What in the hell is going on?"

"Good question," Aaron replied, plopping into a chair. "We're all mixed up."

"That's comforting." Max turned his gaze on me. "Liv, what's up?"

"Mary Lincoln is the focus. All those crazy clues that we've found must add up to something." I almost melted from Max's bloodshot eyes.

"Century and a half old mystery." Max frowned. "Go on, let's hear it."

"The toy bear is ripped in shreds. Tad Lincoln's bear...but they left his uniform alone. Go figure." I cocked my head. "Last night we carefully searched for clues, but came up empty handed. There's so much we don't understand."

"How many years has it been since the Civil War, and this speech was given how many years prior to his inauguration? It's ridiculous."

"It all seems to tie together." I honestly didn't know what to think myself. "Well, I'm tired of this nonsense." I noticed that Max had raised his right foot under the blanket.

"Don't come back unless you have something of importance to say. Geez. First it was Dolley Madison causing all sorts of shenanigans, now mysteries around Lincoln." He yanked his blanket higher.

"We'll keep you informed," Aaron told him.

We used Aaron's cell phone when we were back in the car to do a Google search to find out where the nearest Masonic Lodge was located. There was one only twenty minutes away.

The lodge was in the heart of Northeast Minneapolis, the section of town where mainly Polish, German, and Slovakian immigrants had settled. It was full of Catholic churches as well as plenty of wonderful ethnic restaurants and meat markets. Traffic rushed around us as we tried to find a parking space in a lot. Aaron finally gave up and parked on the street.

"Do you think we'll be able to enter?" I asked. "The symbols are right there, on their building, and they're just as Mary had drawn them. I feel in my bones that we're nearing some kind of revelation, don't you?"

"Yes, but what is it?" Aaron asked. "Let's get out so we can take a look around."

The large, square, red brick building looked even more ominous the closer we came to it. I hesitated in front of the door. "Should we knock?"

"Maybe it's always open, sort of like a church."

"Right." I reached for the doorknob but happily stepped aside as Aaron tried opening it. It was locked. So much for that theory. With Aaron leading, we walked around the packed down, snow-covered sidewalk to the back door but found that locked.

Aaron knocked, but after a couple minutes with no response, we turned and walked toward the car.

Once inside the car, I asked, "Now what do we do?"

"There must be pictures online showing the interior of these lodges. They are bound to be similar, as they are all part of the same organization." Aaron started the engine and began to drive away from the curb, still eyeing the building. "It's got to be several stories high."

"The staircase." My eyebrows rose in puzzlement. "Mary deliberately drew it. If only we knew why."

"Where to now?"

"Back to the store. It's time to take another look at the stuffed bear and the desk."

We drove onto Main Street and headed toward the store. Aaron spotted the frown that came to my face as we arrived in the parking lot behind the store.

"Don't worry. The police have beefed up the patrol. It's all safe." After we parked, he offered, "I'll go in first. How does that sound?"

"Good. Much better." I opened the car door to step out and the fresh air felt good on my cheeks. "Too much has happened." Aaron climbed from the car. "Thank you, baby."

Aaron opened the door and entered with me following close behind.

"Any bad guys here?" Aaron called with a smile.

In the workroom, we removed our jackets and hung them on the clothes tree.

"Let's take care of the house last." When my gaze fell on the ruined little house, I said, "This hurts. It's so unnecessary and hateful."

"I know, Liv." He placed his arm over my shoulder for a moment. "Let's do it."

"You first."

"All right. Come along."

We stood at the showroom entrance, and gazed around the room.

"Well, let's start picking up this mess."

"Right. Let's get a bag to hold all the toy bear parts." I walked over to the desk. "I want to take a closer inspection of this, too."

"Me too. All we did before was glance at it, open the drawer, and that's about it." After grabbing a plastic bag, I went over to the desk and picked up each fragment of the fragile old fabric. Each seam and the filler appeared to be like any normal stuffed animal, except the rear, which had the long-john-like trapdoor.

"Why the oak tree?" I carried the pieces over to the counter and sat down in front of the computer. While the computer went through its start-up procedures, I held up the embroidered section to the light and studied it. In my mind's eye, there was an image of Mary's chubby, short fingers pushing the needle in and out. The points of the stitched leaves were impeccable. The brown looked like a trunk. One nut hung from a branch, which was barely visible. "There's a nut on this tree." I held it up. "Come here."

Aaron got up from where he had been kneeling and came over to me. "Let me see."

I pointed to it. "The nut might be important to the investigation. We need to keep it safe. We shouldn't part with it or talk about it except between us."

"Agree, not until the meaning behind it is made clear."

"Let's remove this small bit with the tree on it and hide it when we get home." I placed the scrap inside a business envelope. "Before we go, I'm going to check my messages and send one to Inga. I haven't heard from Maggie in a while, either."

The website had ten messages, most of them pertaining to the houses. Three caught my eye.

The first read:

It's lost but not forgotten.

The second:

You're entering the waters of the unknown.

The third was cryptic and gave me the creeps. It

read:

> *Miss Olivia, Follow him to the grave, that's where you'll find it. Seek and ye shall find, but make sure you watch your back.*

"Aaron, come here. You have to read this!" I turned the monitor so he could see it better.

"I'm calling the station, don't delete it."

"I won't. They're being forwarded right now to the detectives." I logged into my personal e-mail account, where there were several messages that needed replies. Maggie had written to ask if the four of us could get together soon for dinner, and I replied positively. Inga sent a message saying she was back to work, and that Holly was working more hours to help her out. In my reply, I told her what had happened with the toy bear and about the embroidered oak tree. All relevant information pertaining to the Masonic Lodge was relayed before I sent the message. Afterward, the message went in the Mary Lincoln file. I noticed that all my messages in the file were in a different order.

"Honey? He did it again. My files are rearranged." When I didn't hear Aaron coming, I called, "Aaron!"

"I'm right here," he said. "What else?" He stood with his hands on his hips.

"The Pennies jar." I looked under the counter for it. "Have you seen the jar?"

"Nope." He shook his head.

"Me neither." I looked where it was usually stored. "Gone." I snapped my fingers. "Better call the police.

Besides the messed up files, the missing jar, there's a cryptic message in my webmail."

"What next?" Aaron said. "Let me in there. You did forward the messages to Mergens, didn't you?"

"Yes." I walked away so he could read them. I went to get the miniature dollhouses and removed each from its box. I carefully made sure they were in perfect shape before setting each dollhouse on the shelf, beginning with Dolley's White House, Abigail's, and then Jackie's. The Rose Garden looked magnificent after a bit of rearranging. "Jackie, now your Rose Garden looks as beautiful as you." After they were properly displayed, the next job was to pick up the ruined pieces of the Lincoln house. Painstakingly, I picked up each piece. A tiny table leg went into the nearby basket—ruined. The table top, the war room where the desks were lined in a row like soldiers going to battle, one by one, they all went into the trash. Lincoln's watch. His bedside table. Mary's mirror. Such a waste.

When I closed my eyes I could see Mary stitching. In and out. In and out. Snipping, and sewing the tiny family tree with the nut on the tallest branch. She glanced in the mirror, but what had she seen? Whom had she seen? Had someone tried to kill her for the speech?

Chapter Nineteen

"The image of the toy bear reappeared as my desktop background. I'm letting the detectives know," I said.

"Go ahead. Something's not right, honey."

The Lincoln desk fit into the room better when it was relocated to the side and out of the way of prospective customers. I had previously shifted the Rose Garden scene from one of the other dollhouses, now it needed some readjustments. The chinaware in a couple of the houses needed attention, so I saw to that as well. My cell phone beeped when I finished.

I read the message out loud so Aaron could hear. "They're sending someone out tomorrow to take a look at the computer. We're not to touch anything."

"They'll get to the bottom of it," Aaron said. "Let me recheck my messages."

"Then we'll lock up. I would venture to say that once they hear about the bear, the detectives will be over themselves next time they're on duty."

"You're probably right." I opened a new response from Inga. "Listen to this... it's from Inga. She wants to know if we've found a hidden compartment in the desk."

"Hidden compartment? I've looked all over it, but there's not one to be found. What's she talking about?"

"No idea." I shrugged.

"Where would it be? I've searched the desk high and low."

I logged out and shut the computer down. "Here's another thing I forgot to tell you… the computer was on yesterday morning, and I always shut down before I leave."

"Maybe the detectives are making better progress than we are." Hand in hand we walked into the workroom where we put on our jackets. "Let's go." I grabbed Tad's uniform with Aaron taking the box.

"Brrr." I shivered as the cold, late afternoon air hit my cheeks. "At least it's staying light longer… a sure sign spring's around the corner." We rushed to the car, popped open the doors, and jumped inside. My phone rang, and I answered when I saw it was Grandma.

"Grandma, we're doing fine," I reassured her. I told her about our day, but kept Inga's message to myself, as well as the discovery of the embroidered nut and the ripped-up bear. I promised to keep her informed.

"Let's work on the concentric puzzles tonight, honey," I said to Aaron after I'd ended the call. "We should also take another look at that uniform, too."

Once home, we settled in the living room. "The diary is in the back bedroom. I'll go get it." Aaron turned on the television in the meantime.

I came back and plopped down beside Aaron with the book in hand. "I forgot to make copies of the pages," I brooded. "We almost need to have one for each of us."

"We can try studying them together." Aaron reached for his cell phone. "I'm ordering a pizza. I'm starved."

I stared at the already-bookmarked pages, which led me to wonder why these few pages would be included in Mary Lincoln's diary? *She may have hidden something in plain sight.* As I studied the handwriting, it looked shaky. I thought about Mikal's explanations of certain aspects of Dolley Madison's handwriting. I recognized the letterform as Victorian in style. The boldness of the lowercase letters plus the way they started and stopped were clues that it actually was written by the same person. The upper case letters were very much the same. Before I began trying to figure the puzzle out, I decided to send Maggie a phone message. *Sure you don't want to try concentric puzzles?*

Her immediate response was: Sorry, but *no, they're impossible.*

I was on my own. I knew Aaron wouldn't be able to help much, since we hadn't made copies of the pages.

The circular pattern of the words didn't add up as I turned the first page around and around. "Hmm." I went for a sheet of paper and a pencil, then began scribbling down letters to try and make sense of it all. Nothing came to mind. On the second page I tried only looking at the lower case letters in an attempt to make words. "Pizza's here." Aaron brought it to the coffee table. "Decode anything yet? Catch anything that makes sense?"

"Nope!" I set the diary aside. "I'll get some soda."

"Figures." He bit into his slice of pepperoni pizza. "You may as well forget trying to decipher them until we get copies made."

"Thought the same thing." Different ideas rolled through my brain. "It's as if the killer is everywhere. Doesn't it feel that way to you?" I looked at Aaron. "Like we're being watched. You know?"

"I hear what you're saying. He seems to know everything about us—like he's spying on us." Aaron frowned at me. "All the more reason for me to stay close to you."

"Thank you. Really and truly, I'm scared to death." I grimaced. "But, we'll get through this, won't we? This mystery was dropped into our laps for a reason."

"Yes, but God only knows what it is." He took a sip of soda. "Or why us."

My cell phone rang. "Bill Williams here. I changed the class around. I'll have the nut, or should I say necklace, re-silvered as good as new. It should be finished by two tomorrow, if you'd like to stop by and pick it up. I'll leave the results and necklace with my secretary if I'm not in the office."

"What about your payment?"

"No problem. Call it public relations."

"Thank you so very much." I disconnected and set the phone down, told Aaron what Doctor Williams had said, and then added. "I'll call the detectives and let them know."

"Great." Aaron reached for the final slice and took a bite. "That Doc Williams is a good guy."

"Yes, this was very helpful of him. I'll ask Grandpa if he smokes cigars and buy him a couple of good ones, if so."

"August probably has a few extra lying around."

"Good idea. I think he has some Cuban cigars we could give him, now that they're legal again in the states."

I went over all the uniform seams again during the rest of the evening. It seemed as if I was searching for the world's tiniest diamond.

After watching some television, we retired for the evening and I slept peacefully, knowing the police were working to solve the strange goings on.

In the morning, Aaron leaned over and kissed me. "How'd you sleep?"

"Wonderful." I smiled at him. "I'm going to make it through this. Are you coming to the store with me today?"

"Of course."

I noticed on the way to work, that the warm, mid-February sun had melted the ice on the streets and sidewalks, making them even more slushy. As we parked in our usual space I said, "Business should be picking up with the warmer weather, don't you think?" In spite of the sun outside, it seemed chilly inside the shop, so I turned up the thermostat before removing my jacket. My task for today was sewing all the tiny, cut-out pieces lying on the table. *I'd certainly put off the work lately. I should stay one evening to sew inaugural gowns for several of the First Lady dolls, plus dress the presidents.* I was behind on everything and chastised myself for not keeping up with the task. I grabbed the feather duster and went out to the showroom.

Standing near the FD Roosevelt house, I said, "Mrs. Roosevelt, your radio addresses were superb, and so were your newspaper articles, 'My Day.'" My perusal of the shop was interrupted by a background buzz, and I realized the computer was on. Perplexed, I stared at it with my hands on my hips. I knew for certain I shut it off the day before. I left it alone, knowing the detectives would be arriving soon. At the front door, I turned the sign to *Open.*

As I dusted, the sound of the humming computer continued to bother me. Certain that the killer had tracked me with it, I was relieved to see a familiar police car parking out front. At the same time, I heard Aaron's footsteps on the hall floor.

"You're just in time for the detectives."

They slammed their car doors and were soon entering through the front door.

"Back again, eh?"

"Yes, for more complex and not-making-any-sense at-all clues," Erlandsen said, giving us a wry grin. "Why is it that I feel something else has just crept up?"

"Because something has. We shut the computer off before leaving yesterday. See? Now it's on." I nodded at the computer. "I haven't touched it."

"You two give me massive headaches," Erlandsen said, scratching his head with his pencil. "Okay." He scribbled something on his pad. "Anything else?"

"The Lincoln house was trashed," I said. "Unbelievable," Erlandsen said. "That all?"

"Nothing that's apparent except there's a memory stick in our kitchen drawer that we recently rediscovered. I found it on the sidewalk outside the night of the murder but forgot all about it."

"That might be what we need to tie the case together," Mergens stated.

"Duly noted," Erlandsen said.

"Okay. Our computer guy should be coming anytime." Mergens shifted his legs. "Let's go over it again, Liv. Start again at the top."

"Well, this has to have something to do with the Lincolns, and in particular, finding the Lost Speech." I glanced at one detective and then the other. "We have found clues that seem to all have Masonic roots. Besides that, there's the acorn necklace we found in the bottom of the hatbox—a hat that had belonged to Mary Lincoln. I'm picking up the results of the testing at two. I believe it will be revealing, but for what purpose, I haven't a clue." I ran my fingers through my hair.

"You've researched the symbols?" Erlandsen asked.

"Yes. They all leave me to think they mean 'origin.' It can't be God, per se, because that wouldn't make sense. However, what the sketch of a staircase has to do with anything has me perplexed. Any idea?" When both shook their heads, I said, "See? Beginning of what? The speech? Where it was spoken? There can't be anything there except the plaque. Is it in the old law office? If so, it would have been found by now." I suddenly remembered the message from Inga. "Inga asked in last night's message if we'd found the hidden compartment in the Lincoln desk, but neither of us found anything."

"I believe that these people are keeping tabs on you to discover the location of the speech," Mergens said, staring at me. "Everything happens around you. Not to you. And they seem to know you've been doing all this research just by hacking into your files."

"I understand all of that." I crossed my arms. Aaron placed his arm across my shoulder.

"Well, here's another thought to add to the above," Mergens said. "We believe the copy of the Mary Todd Lincoln letter you received anonymously was sent by the hacker who has been spying on your computer."

"Why would they do that?" I asked in confusion. "You meant they're helping me find the speech."

"No," said Erlandsen. "They're hoping you will figure it out and lead them to the speech."

"That can't be good," I said.

"It'll all work out." Aaron squeezed my shoulder. "Who are your leading suspects?" I asked.

"We're mainly looking at two people," Mergens said.

"I can only think of one, Luke. It's weird having such a large employee turnover."

"We're on top of it," Mergens answered without answering a thing.

Just then the police department's technical expert entered, carrying a small tool kit in his hand.

"Finally got away." He showed us his badge. "Detective Harris." He shook hands with the other two detectives.

"Mr. and Mrs. Reynolds — Aaron and Liv,"

Erlandsen made introductions.

After we'd both shaken hands with the tech, I nodded at the computer and said, "There it is."

"I'll get started and then they can fill me in," Harris said. Aaron and I went to the workroom and sat down.

"I might have an idea to catch this guy." I looked around the room. "We should set a trap for him. We can give him hints about the speech, just to see if he'll bite."

"Let's hear it," Aaron said.

"Invite Ronnie in to take pictures of the desk. Or pictures of the cavern underneath the store, which few know about. He might jump at that, since we wouldn't let him go down there after Jackie Newell's murder."

"Great idea." Aaron stared at me for a moment. "We'll have to run it past the detectives." He glanced at his phone. "I missed a call from Max. I'll call him back first."

I reached into my bag and pulled out the diary. The copier was in the corner and I made two copies of each page. When finished, I neatly placed them aside.

Just as I was about to figure out where I'd left off with the sewing, Aaron disconnected from speaking to Max. "What did he have to say? When's he going home?"

"His neck and back are still pretty sore. They want to keep him there another day since he lives alone. I offered to give him a ride home tomorrow morning."

"If needed, Max can always stay in our spare room," I said. "He heard that from me, too. I guess we're both anxious." Aaron glanced toward the doorway.

"You're not alone," I said as the sound of approaching footsteps interrupted my thoughts. "Yes?"

"Please come out here, you two." Erlandsen stood in the doorway. "You're not going to believe this."

We followed the detective into the showroom and over to where Harris sat studying what was on the computer's monitor.

"It's like this, folks," he said, keeping his eyes glued on the screen. "This guy, or gal, is a computer genius. He's set up an account with which he can forward your e-mails to an account he controls. He knows your password, everything."

"You're kidding me. Is the screensaver bear part of that hacking?" I asked.

"You're partially correct, but this is how you guys can nab him."

"And how do we do that?" I asked, giving him a perplexed look.

He answered with a mischievous smile. "Let's give him some crumbs."

The best way to catch a rat is to set out some tasty cheese in a trap!

Chapter Twenty

We locked up the store after the detectives left, but not before I brought the ladies up to speed on the recent happenings. Aaron dropped me off at the university. I dashed into the science building and headed up the stairs to the faculty offices. I wanted to personally thank Dr. Williams. It didn't take long before the office door with his name on it came into view. I knocked. The squeaky door opened exposing his office, still overflowing with papers. The floor was strewn with folders, papers, and textbooks. It looked as if someone had broken in and searched for something.

"Doctor Williams?" I whispered. "Doctor Williams?"

On tiptoe, I stepped farther inside the office, which was when I saw his arm on the floor, sticking out from behind the desk. *Did he slip from his chair?* I peered around his desk.

His lifeless body was sprawled on the floor. When I crouched down to check for signs of life, it was apparent he was dead.

I screamed.

I recalled backing out into the hallway but remembered little else after that. Campus Security surrounded the area, not allowing anyone to come or go from the floor. Somehow, I managed to grab my cell phone and fumble out a message to Aaron. He came right away and was able to get through security with his police badge. He had also contacted the other detectives, who arrived shortly after he did.

"You again?" Erlandsen shook his head at me as he advanced down the corridor.

Mergens looked perplexed. His eyebrows looked permanently arched.

"Is he really dead?" I asked. I couldn't believe this had happened. Dr. Williams was a nice man, he didn't deserve to die.

Aaron had been sitting beside me with his arm over my shoulder. "This has been an awful ordeal for Liv."

"I'm sorry," I said. "I feel like this is somehow all my fault."

"Now, why would you think that?" Erlandsen asked, leaning over and studying me.

"He called to let me know the testing was complete."

"You were here to pick up the results?" Erlandsen asked.

"Yes, to fetch the necklace also. Then, all of this happened. The secretary may have the necklace and the results, though." I stood, but my legs felt weak. "We need to know the results. They could provide a clue for solving the murder."

"We'll check with her," Erlandsen said. He shrugged. "Go on home. We'll be in touch."

With Aaron by my side, we walked to the car. Once inside, we buckled up before driving from the parking space.

"I've called Marie and August. They're on their

way to meet us at home," Aaron said.

"Good. I hope Grandma brings some more chicken soup. It'll make me feel better."

The drive home only took a few minutes.

That evening we sat quietly watching the television and enjoying the wished for soup Grandma had brought. Grandma and Grandpa kept their eyes mostly on me. When we finished our meal, Grandma carried the empty bowls into the kitchen.

The doorbell rang. Aaron got up and opened the door to let the detectives in.

"Mr. and Mrs. Ott," Mergens said as he shook their hands.

"Mr. and Mrs. Ott," Erlandsen repeated and did the same. "Liv?" He held out a large envelope. "Got something for you. The secretary at the U still had it. You can open it. Since it wasn't in the professor's office, it wasn't considered part of the crime scene."

"But, it could provide the motive," Mergens said flatly.

My fingers were shaky as I reached for the item to open it. Aaron affirmed my actions with a nod. The nut and loose chain spilled easily from the opened envelope, and I had pulled out the test results. I read them out loud, "The acorn's genetic makeup is from the Appalachian region of the United States. And guess what? It's dated from the mid-eighteen hundreds."

"You're kidding me."

"Kentucky…Tennessee, you know? It fits, doesn't it?"

"It really does in a roundabout sort of way, if we truly believe Mary Lincoln was the person who had this silvered."

My fingers felt the remnants of the silver on the table. "This is just too surreal."

"This case is not unlike the other one, now is it? When you were searching for the Star Spangled Banner manuscript?" Aaron said.

"All convoluted." I smiled up at him.

"It's just one thing after another. I might have to retire after this case," Mergens mused. "Talk about confusion?"

"Tell you what—we'll talk to the lieutenant. He's up to speed and understands how mixed up this case is. Either he, or one of us, will keep the Mary Todd Lincoln House up to date. If you do find the speech, it'll be up to the authorities to decide what to do with it. Go ahead and keep the necklace pieces where you had it."

"Right back inside our hidden safe box for now, " Aaron said.

"Good."

Just then I heard the slamming of two car doors outside the window. We looked out. Ronnie emerged from one car, and another person climbed out of a van. I recognized him as a local television reporter.

"Ahh, jeez. The reporters are here," Grandpa moaned. Mergens drew the drapes closed.

"I'll get rid of them," Mergens said, walking to the door. He stepped outside, and before long the reporters returned to their vehicles and left.

"That was quick service," I said. "Thank you."

"No problem," Mergens said. "I used to work the traffic division. I simply told those reporters they could stay if they wanted, but I was going to look their vehicles over, and if I found even the slightest problem, well, let's just say the ticket would cost them plenty."

"Let's go." Erlandsen went to the door. "If there's anything … anything at all that you remember about anything that happened, no matter how minimal it seems, be sure to call. You have our numbers."

I blew out a long breath after they left. "I wish this was finished. I feel terrible about Dr. Williams. He was such a good man and so generous to do this testing for us." I shook my head. "Why was he murdered? What was the motive?"

"That's the main point. No one knows," Aaron replied, pouring sodas. He toasted. "To getting this solved."

"To discovering the motive."

"We'll drink to Liv," Grandma said.

"No. Let's drink to Doctor Williams. He deserves it."

We clinked our glasses and sipped our drinks. I thought about how lucky I was to have such wonderful grandparents and husband. "We have to figure out the symbols," I said, shaking myself out of my daydream. "We haven't really found the true meaning of the 'G' or the staircase."

"How do you know it's not just doodling?" Grandma asked. "I've been doing some thinking about what I've read, plus all the library research."

"Yes. We also tried to peek inside the Masonic Lodge on Lowry Avenue the other day. We didn't get in, but we saw all the symbols on the walls outside." Aaron shook his head. "But, Mister Lincoln wasn't even a Mason."

"The staircase was drawn with fifteen steps. That might mean something."

"The square and compass are geometric and make up the pentacle, whatever that means.

"Let's look up the 'G.'" I reached for my iPad. "It can't just stand for God, can it? It seems as if it should have another meaning."

No one spoke as I typed *G Mason symbol* into the Google search engine. Immediately several link sites popped onto the screen. After skimming through the first two links, I found my answer.

"It means *origin*. It's what I'd said the last time." I smiled at them. "It says 'The letter G in Freemasonry stands for both the Great Architect of the Universe and Geometry... or, to be more technically correct, it stands for Geometry under the Great Architect of the Universe.'"

"I suppose that could be a clue to where he hid the Lost Speech," Aaron replied. "That could be what Mary had in mind."

"Somehow, it doesn't seem right," Grandpa said. "It's too easy."

"With her, it's hard to say." Grandma glanced out of the corner of the drapes. "Ronnie's back."

"I'll handle it." Aaron went outside. In a few

minutes, he reentered the house. "He wanted to know if the murder was part of the ongoing investigation concerning Blanche. I told him to speak to the detective."

"We really don't know if they're connected or not. Presumably, they are."

Soon after, my grandparents left and Aaron went to shower, I had time alone to think about Mary Todd Lincoln.

Mary Lincoln embroidered. She came from well-to-do-parents. She owned slaves earlier in her life. A free slave, Elizabeth Keckley worked as a seamstress for her in the White House. Images of a desperate Mrs. Lincoln with Tad clutching her skirt came to mind. Tad in his little uniform, clutching the stuffed bear. The favored doll I had as a child was still tucked away inside of my grandma's trunk for safekeeping. For all intents and purposes, Mrs. Lincoln would have kept the bear for Tad. He would inherit it upon her death, most likely. Knowing that it was treasured, she embroidered the tree with the tiny nut inside the rear flap for a reason. For Tad's eyes only to find.

The diary. Concentric puzzles. Robert, the eldest of the two remaining children, would be less likely interested in them. Tad was devoted to his mother, but he passed away before she did, leaving her alone. Did she hibernate in her sister's house during her final years because of not being able to face the world? Or were people questioning her about the Lost Speech and she became frightened?

Chapter Twenty-One

"No new developments," Aaron told me the next morning in the kitchen.

"Figures," I mumbled. "What about the jar thief?"

"Hard to trace, but several jars are missing. Maybe there's a new cat burglar in town."

"Not related, just coincidental. Right?"

"Right."

While I put on my jacket, I wondered what the day would bring. Would it be a repeat of the day before? I needed solace with more time to think about what all had happened within the last few weeks. "You ready to go?"

"Yep." Aaron rinsed his dirty juice glass in the sink. "I'm anxious to hear how Max made out last night."

"I worry about him." I yawned. "We'll be open all day, won't we?" I opened the garage door, and he followed, locking it behind us.

"Plan to. Harris will be back to see if the bait worked."

"Good," I said. "You do have the pond hockey tourney over the weekend, don't you?"

"Sure do. You're coming, aren't you?" He glanced at me and said, "It'll be good for you to come watch the games after the store closes."

"I'll be there."

Backing out, I noticed that the snowman family

from across the street was half-melted. It brightened my spirits knowing spring was around the corner. I'd be able to see the neighborhood children who had fashioned the snow family out playing with their skateboards and other warm-weather activities.

As we drove down our street, my thoughts turned again to the Lost Speech. I asked Aaron, "If not for the Mary Lincoln House and the police investigations, what would we do with it?"

"What any good American would do, give it to the Library of Congress or the Smithsonian Institute." He stopped at a red light and smiled at me. "Bet you were thinking the same thing."

"Sure was. Or else to the Presidential Library in Springfield." I waited a moment then added, "It's exactly what should happen—if we find it. We'll see that it's donated to the library."

"But it's not ours to decide, is it?" Aaron asked. I had to admit he had a point.

We crossed the Hennepin Avenue Bridge, which brought us to our alleyway. As Aaron parked, I realized how good it was to see Max's truck parked in its usual spot. Life was going to be fine. "Coffee?" Aaron asked, getting out of the car. He slammed the door shut. "Want to come with?"

"Yeah, it sounds like a good idea." With his hand in mine, we hiked down the alley and then walked around to the front of the building. "I was surprised to see Suni at the café the other day. She almost never leaves their house."

"I've heard they have the fastest connection to the

Internet in town." Aaron opened the front door of the café for us to step inside. "Hey, Luke!"

"The usual?" Luke asked. He returned our smiles, but his seemed a cold one. "You want a muffin, too?" His hand hovered over the screen of his register.

"Not today. Thanks." I rubbed my hands together to warm up. "What's this scuttlebutt going around about you two yesterday?" Luke asked as he dropped our payment into the till. One of his employees got busy fixing our beverages.

"Did someone take your penny jar?" another of Luke's employees asked in heavily accented English. "Ours is gone."

"I was wondering about what happened to Max," Luke harrumphed, interrupting his employee, and giving her a hard look before turning back to us.

"News travels fast. Hopefully nothing else will happen to me or my friends." I took a sip of my coffee. "Ever again."

"How did you hear?" Aaron raised his coffee to his lips. "Just talk," Luke said. "Of course, seeing the cops was the tip off."

Later, as we entered the back door of our own store, I glanced up the alleyway and saw Holly at the back of Inga's antique store. "Hey, Holly," I called. "How ya doing?"

Holly hurried down the alley to greet me, a big smile on her face. "Great. Taking the last of my required courses this semester, and, hopefully, I'll be finished soon. What a relief." Aaron continued indoors while she continued chatting away.

"Inga's doing well. She's back at work. She tried dropping by, but your store has been closed. Couldn't help but notice. It's too bad about Dr. Williams. He was such a nice guy and a good teacher, even if he did give me a D in his class." She turned a little pink while balling her fist. "He shouldn't have done that ... I didn't deserve it. I'd studied so hard." Holly burst into tears, so I motioned for her to come over for a hug. "I wish I hadn't said all those mean things to him."

"What did you say?" I tried to look her square in the eye, but she looked away. "Fess up."

"Well, all right." She glanced around before whispering, "Unfortunately, I told him that if the D messed up my GPA, he'd be dead. Dead as in doornail. Of course, it was said in the heat of the moment. But now the investigators will probably question me again."

"Shush, now. If you're innocent, you have nothing to worry about." I held her hands and stared into her eyes. "The authorities have their hands full with gathering evidence. Don't worry, it'll all be clear in a few days' time."

"I hope." She sniffled and wiped her nose with the back of her hand. "It's time for me to get to work."

"I'll check in later." I gave her a hug. "Keep your chin up."

"Okay."

As she rushed toward the antique store, I wondered how a pretty young girl could get so broken up over a low grade. When I entered our store, my ears perked up to loud voices in the workroom.

"Guess what?" I announced, interrupting Max and Aaron's conversation before even setting down my coffee and pulling off my jacket. "Holly had Dr. Williams for a teacher. You won't believe this, but when he gave her a D in his class, she yelled at him and threatened to kill him if it affected her GPA." Aaron's eyes opened wider and so did Max's.

"Holy cow. Unbelievable," Aaron said, drawing out his cell phone. "I'm calling the detectives."

"Oh, Aaron, do you have to?"

"Sorry, hon, but rules are rules."

"Now what?" Max asked, watching Aaron press in a few buttons on his phone.

"Probably more questioning." I collapsed into a chair. "Think about it, though. It makes sense. The Lost Speech could easily be worth a small fortune on the open market, plus it would cover Holly's college tuition, and then some, for a number of years."

"But, Holly has never said anything about being so strapped for cash, has she?" Max asked.

"Not that I've heard or am aware of. However, I've been thinking about that missing speech. There's got to be any number of folks itching to get their hands on it... for a number of reasons."

"My thoughts, completely." Aaron looked at us as he disconnected and stuffed the phone inside of his pocket. "You're not going to believe this, but the young woman you found in the dumpster has vanished."

"Oh dear God. You're kidding." I sat straighter. "How did that happen?"

"She recovered from her ordeal and then was whisked away by federal immigration agents. Our detectives can't get within ten miles of her. They're probably holding her as a material witness. Happens all the time," Aaron explained. He gave me an encouraging smile. "Don't worry. The tech guy will be here shortly. We're right here with you, too."

"Exactly. I'm sticking like glue to you, Liv," Max stated, cocking his head. "Ouch. Not that I'd be of much good with a sore neck and all."

"Didn't they give you any pain killers?"

"Yes, but it sure seems like the last pill is wearing off. When I take one it puts me out almost immediately." Max got up and said, "Nightie-night. I'll be back when I wake."

After he left, I went to the window.

"Harris just stepped out of his car," I told Aaron.

Harris bounded through the front door of the store. "Good morning. Have you checked your e-mail accounts yet?" he asked after greeting Aaron and me.

"No. We've been waiting for you. There's been too much happening lately. Gosh, when will you guys nail this down? Can't you just take the computer in to examine it and figure out who is doing all this?" I glared at him. "There's been two murders, and something has to be done!"

"First, we're not sure if the guy who's messing around with the computer is the killer, but we do believe it's connected. In that case, we have to keep it looking as natural and normal as possible. If anyone should happen to come into the store, I'm just another

IT guy. Got that?"

"Sure." I watched him sit in front of the computer. "We think we know what he's after."

"I've read the notes," Harris answered. "It's something about President Lincoln and an important speech." He logged into the account and his eyes lit up. "Yep. Our boy was on the move last night, but he's smart." Harris shook his head. "He detected my

little paw prints, and he's switched his attack vector. I'll start a port scan, should find him soon."

I glanced at Aaron, who only shrugged "beats me!" at Harris' cyber-talk. We watch Harris type in a series of cryptic commands.

When he stopped to flex his fingers, I figured it was safe to interrupt the master at work. "Are you getting anywhere?"

Harris shook his head, but his gaze never left the computer monitor. "I'm getting nowhere fast. The hacker has forwarded all of your relevant messages using a remote-control Trojan virus installed on a zombie PC somewhere in the Ukraine. That means this guy needs to be handled with extra special care." He pulled his cell phone out of his pocket and punched in a few numbers. He spoke for a just a couple minutes before disconnecting. "Mergens and Erlandsen will be here soon. We need to talk about this."

"Yikes!" I said. "This doesn't sound good." Aaron placed his arm over my shoulder. "Let's all go and sit in the workroom."

"Right now, the most important thing is to not give

away that we're on to him. We're going to walk softly and carry a big stick, as Teddy Roosevelt once said," Detective Harris said.

"A strong cup of coffee sounds good right about now, it would calm my nerves," I said. "I'd go to Luke's, but I'm scared to leave the store by myself."

"I could go for it, since we're out of coffee grounds, but don't want to leave you," Aaron said, placing his arm over my shoulder. "Don't worry, I'm with her. Get a cup for us all." Detective Harris gave Aaron a stern look. "Make sure you say nothing.

Nothing…to anyone."

"Right. I'm a cop, remember?" Aaron squeezed my shoulder before releasing his hand and walking away.

"Liv? While we're waiting, why not give me a tour of your dollhouses? Maybe you can talk me into buying one for my wife," Harris said. He strolled over toward the displays. "Where's the TR house? Teddy's my favorite."

"Right over here." My anxiety ebbed while I explained about the Roosevelt family. "Did you know this? TR, his brother, Elliot, and his wife, Edith, watched from a window as President Lincoln's body traveled through in New York City on its way to Illinois."

"Interesting."

Aaron came back through the back door, and we heard the slamming of car doors. "The detectives have arrived, so we're all here," he announced. "Let's lock the doors. I'll get the back."

"I'll get the front," I said as the detectives came in.

242

"Erlandsen and Mergens, here. Work room?"

"Yes, go on in. We have some coffee waiting for you. I'm going to lock the front door." I turned the *Open* sign around, locked the door, and followed the detectives into the workroom. Aaron rearranged the chairs. I noted that a chair was left for me, with Aaron perched right beside it. I sat.

"This speech... what's this thing worth, in your estimation, if found?" Harris asked.

"Could be millions," I said.

"Boy, that would pay our mortgage and our neighbors' too, plus set us up for life," Aaron replied. "Money is the motive. Has to be."

"He'd have to sell it on the black market," Harris said, sipping his cup of steaming coffee. "That's why this guy is elusive and leaves soft footprints."

"I'll have to speak with the department people to figure out how to proceed, but we have to leave bread crumbs for him." Erlandsen looked at Harris. "Any suggestions?"

"Throughout all of this, there haven't been any clues, have there?"

"Few. Very few. Frankly, not worth much."

"Has anyone found one of these things?" Harris pulled a memory stick from his pocket and held it up. "It can be plugged into any computer and download all its files in minutes."

"That may be why our home was invaded. We have seen one of those. It's in our drawer. I picked it up from the ground outside our shop shortly after Blanche was murdered. It's so small — well— it almost looked like a key. It was in my pocket for a few days before I dropped it in a kitchen drawer. Oh, my gosh."

"Now that we know the computer is involved, we need that memory stick," Erlandsen said.

"What next? What comes after this memory stick?"

"We're going to come up with a plan that will pull the hacker out of hiding." Mergens scratched his chin again. Maybe he was past due for a shave. "I want to take a look around your store, especially that desk."

"Do what you need to do." I took another sip of coffee. "What can Aaron and I do? How can we help?"

"You two go home and look for that memory stick. We'll stop by later and pick it up," Mergens instructed. "Don't worry, we'll lock up."

"I'll shut down the computer, just as you normally would," Harris stated.

Within a few minutes, Aaron and I had finished our coffee and were heading for home.

Aaron easily found the memory stick and tried plugging it into my laptop.

A skull and crossbow lit up the screen. The caption in bold letters read:

Death to all.

Chapter Twenty-two

The minutes ticked by as we nervously waited for the detectives to arrive. "I'm scared half to death." We sat in the living room with the TV on low.

"I'm going to make sure the house is secure," Aaron said. "You stay right here."

"Not on your life." I stood. "I'm going with you. Let's check the bedroom and the acorn, first."

"Okay, good place as any to begin."

As we stepped inside our bedroom, it seemed chilly. "It's locked," Aaron said after checking the window.

The hidden box holding the necklace and results of our investigation was still locked. Even then, we were careful and opened it to ensure everything was in place.

"On to the other rooms," Aaron said.

We checked every room in the house. When we returned to the living room, at last, I plopped onto the couch, gathered the crocheted afghan and flung it over myself. I glanced at Aaron.

"Honey, I'm calling your grandparents. You'd feel better." He cuddled beside me. "I'm keeping you close."

"Thank you. The detectives should soon be here," I said. I listened as he talked to Grandma on the telephone.

"Honey, they are on their way over here. Don't

worry." Glancing out the front window, he said, "They're here."

"Who, my grandparents? That's not possible."

"The detectives. Harris just drove in, too. I'll let them in," Aaron said. "You look like you could use some rest."

"This case just keeps rolling out of control, doesn't it?" I asked as they all entered.

"It'll be wrapped up soon," Mergens said.

"The pieces are slowly coming together," Erlandsen said.

"Yes, but too slow for my taste."

"Here." Aaron handed the memory stick over.

"Just what I needed." Harris held it up for inspection before sliding it into a bag. He pushed it into his pocket. "Thanks."

"I hate to admit it, but we slid it into our laptop," Aaron said. "I knew better, but this case has me stymied and my wife scared half to death."

"You over stepped, Reynolds. What did you find?" Harris asked.

"A skull with words that read, 'death to all'." "You didn't open it, did you?"

"No. It was immediately ejected."

"It points to our man," Harris said. "You better not have screwed things up, or I'll have you reported," he warned.

"Understood," Aaron said, and then clamped his jaw tight.

"Maybe this belonged to the killer, so hopefully we can tie up the loose strings. You never know." Harris stared at Aaron then looked at me. "I'll keep you all posted." We watched as he let himself out the door.

"Mind if we sit? It's been a long day," Erlandsen asked.

"Go ahead," I said.

"We examined the desk completely," Mergens said as he leaned back in his chair. "We tipped it upside down and were just about ready to give up our search for a hidden slot when we accidentally found it. It was right under our noses, but we didn't see it." He tapped his nose. "Right under our noses."

"Which is where, exactly?" I asked.

"The upper right corner twists off and exposes a small shelf.

"Was there anything there?" I was bursting with excitement.

How could he be so blasé about it?

"Nope, clean as a whistle."

Oh, that was why. Darn!

"I suppose the desk's former owners didn't realize the value of it at the time," Erlandsen said. "Interesting, eh? Lincoln could have hidden the speech in there, couldn't he?" He massaged his chin. "Unbelievable, isn't it?"

"I'd do anything to get this over with and settled," I said. "Let's take a walk around the outside and check things out before we leave," Mergens suggested to Erlandsen. "Just to be on the safe side."

I watched as Aaron and the detectives zipped up their coats. I stayed on the couch as the detectives headed out the door. Better they than me.

"Go ahead," I said. "No one's going to come in now, not with the house full of police,"

"I'll be back in five," Aaron called.

As they walked out, I reached for the remote and had barely turned on the TV when car doors slammed nearby. I looked out and saw our neighbors parked and climbing from their cars. It wasn't much longer before the back door opened.

"Grand Central Station," I grumbled ungraciously. Getting up, I joined the men in the kitchen and sat down at the table. "Have you heard anything from Harris yet?"

"No. We're leaving now."

Like a revolving door, the two detectives left, and my grandparents arrived shortly after. They carried another huge pot of chicken soup along with a fragrant loaf of homemade bread, right out of the oven. Grandpa also brought in a chocolate cake that I wanted to instantly devour.

"The cake looks delish!"

"It's Mary Lincoln's cake. Six eggs in it," Grandpa said. "I ought to know—I cracked 'em myself to help your grandmother out. Only the best for our granddaughter, you know."

"Ahh…you're so sweet." I gave him a big hug; then gave another to Grandma as she set the pot on the stove and turned on the burner. I figured that standing and stirring the pot would keep her out of the conversation that was about to happen. But no such luck.

We hiked back into the living room.

"Don't worry." I tried to make her feel better. "The police are all over this." In an effort to focus and calm my own anxiety, I changed the subject. "What about Max?"

"He's doing fine. We think we have narrowed down the motive and what the person, or persons, were after. It's almost as bad as the search for the Star Spangled Banner manuscript."

Grandma gasped and covered her mouth.

"Yep. This time it's the search for Abraham Lincoln's Lost Speech."

"Just as suspected." Grandpa slapped his knee with his right hand.

"Let's read the scientific results from the acorn necklace." I retrieved the necklace and the result information. "Let's go through this completely before we decide on our next move."

"We're all ears."

"An oak tree dated from the mid-1800's, in the area around the Appalachians, like maybe central or southern Kentucky." I held the nut and rolled it around with my fingertips. "Unbelievable." I frowned. "I've got to discover the speech, so Doctor William's death won't be in vain."

"Let's locate some old maps for Springfield, Lexington, and…what town was he born in?" I glanced at Aaron, who shook his head.

"Look it up," he said. "There must be maps somewhere in this town that are large enough to show the location of his birthplace in Kentucky, as well as these other places. We'll try to connect the dots by using the pentacle points."

"What is the center?" I asked.

"How about if August and I try to locate the maps?" Aaron asked.

"Nope. Grandma and Grandpa can check the bookstores. We're going to tackle these concentric puzzle pages."

"Marie?" Grandpa stood, holding his hand out to Grandma. "Looks like we have our work cut out for us. Let's go. Finally, we have a way to help our little girl."

"Yes. We won't return until we find the maps. We'll certainly try to find them for Springfield and Lexington—plus one of Lincoln's birthplace. Look it up quick, will you?"

"Sure." I grabbed my iPad and searched Lincoln's birthplace. "A cabin near Hodgenville, Kentucky." I hesitated and said, "Go to the library first and search for the old maps on a computer. You can then ask to have them printed."

As they went out the door, I was happy there was a way they could help. Knowing they'd return with the maps in hand, I turned my attention back to the puzzles. We needed silence and time to think without interruption, exactly my motive for sending them to the library.

"Let's get started." I got up and found the puzzles, then sat back down. "Here's your copies." I handed a set to Aaron.

Again, I started by writing all the letters down in order on a separate sheet of paper, in an effort to try to make sense of them. I tried copying every other letter, every third, and so on, but it always ended the same, with a jumble of letters without any apparent meaning. Next, I tried doing the same in reverse, but that didn't work, either.

"These are tough to decipher." Aaron frowned, and his shoulders slumped.

"They're impossible." A different tactic was in order. "Let's paper punch them and attach some fasteners. Then, they'll turn like a wheel." I stood. "Sounds good, doesn't it?" I started for the kitchen.

"That's a great idea. Even Einstein couldn't make heads or tails out of this."

I returned to the living room, setting the small box between us containing office supplies, including the paper punch and scissors. "Let's hope we don't need more copies of these pages before we figure this godforsaken thing out." I cut out the three pages, lined them up, punched out the center and put in the little brass paper fastener. The task made for an easy turn of the wheel. "This will go much better now." I smiled confidently.

"Why do you suppose some letters are capitalized while others are not?" Aaron frowned.

"I don't know. This is hard because nothing is sequential." I turned the pages on the fastener, around and around, lining up letters, but that wasn't the key either. I was about ready to fling the whole thing across the room in frustration when another thought came to mind. I tried placing the clip through the first letters, rather than turning the pages and trying to fit the letters. "This is ridiculous!"

"Exactly." Aaron turned his pages, frowning.

"One more thought." I placed the pin in another location and wrote down only the capital letters. Suddenly the words began falling into place. "How could I be so stupid?" I dropped the puzzle onto the table. "Look." I quickly transcribed the correct letters and stared at the page. "It reads: *Father's birthplace*. But is that the location of the speech? Or the center of what has all happened?"

"How could she have transferred the manuscript to Hodgenville? She never went there after leaving the White House. The president never returned. Once he left, he was gone."

"We know that this mystery is centered around the Masons. All of the clues are symbols really." I stared out the window. "I'm not sure where to go next, are you?"

"No, but let's be sure to put the acorn, plus the test results, in a safe place." Aaron frowned. "I don't feel safe having anything like this in the house anymore."

"Banks still open?"

"Another hour before they close. It's already getting late."

"Quick, take the necklace, results, and what I've written to the bank safety box."

Alone, I stared out of the window and watched him drive away.

Death to all?

"Well, mister or sister or whoever you are—you haven't won yet! I'm going to beat you at your game!"

Chapter Twenty-three

My grandparents returned with the maps in a short length of time.

"I sure hope these help." Grandpa handed me the copied maps.

"The librarian was a sweet little old lady who helped us out." Grandma's eyes twinkled. "Actually, I think I'm older than she is."

"It's just that her hair was grayer and she walked slower than your grandmother." Grandpa chuckled. "Let's get busy."

"Okay. This part of the equation needs figuring out." I grabbed the rolled up maps in one hand, the puzzle with my other hand, and set them all down on the kitchen table. Grandpa unrolled the maps. *Would the center of the pentacle be Hodgenville?*

I considered the Mary Todd Lincoln House. *Was anyone in Mary's family a Mason?* That could be a viable explanation as to how the document could have been placed in Hodgenville.

I laid out the maps and drew circles around Springfield, Lexington, Bloomington, and Hodgenville. As an afterthought, I drew one around Washington D.C., just in case it would fit the parameters of the pentacle. With a ruler in hand, I set about drawing lines from point to point. Unfortunately, the points were uneven, which made for a lopsided pentacle. That blew that idea, it was time to come up with another. My mind jumped back to the puzzle… his father's birthplace. *Could it possibly be that easy?*

By now, Aaron had returned from the bank. He joined Grandma and Grandpa as I poured over the drawn lines.

"Hmm… Doesn't line up," Grandpa said and tugged an earlobe.

"Not at all."

"Honey? We need to do more research, don't you think?"

"Probably. First off, we're going to find out more about Mary's family and whether any of her relatives were in the Masons. Once that's determined, it'll be easier for me to believe that the speech could be located in Hodgenville. It's too bad the store computer isn't hooked up here. We do have a router that it could connect to. It's easier than trying to type this stuff in with the iPad or this little laptop."

"Should August and I to go over to the store and get it?" Aaron asked.

"We should find out from Harris if we can bring the computer from the store. I think the hacker would know if we were using a different computer. If we're using something from home and are trying to track him from here, he'd know it. In the end, it's best if we get the store computer. Would you call Harris to make sure I'm on the right track?"

"Right on it," Aaron said, taking out his phone. He went to the kitchen for privacy. Upon his return, he said, "Yes. The hacker would know the difference. He wants us to keep using the same computer, so the footprints are the same." Putting his phone back in his pocket, he said, "I'll go and pick it up."

"That would be terrific." I plunked back into the chair and Grandma did the same.

"We'll get 'em." Looking at August, he said, "Let's go for it. I'll drive."

They put on their coats and overshoes and took off. Less than an hour later they returned, and Aaron set up the computer.

"Now, let's see who all in Mary's family were Masons. I bet her dad was." I logged into my Google account, found my bookmarked pages, and pressed on the website for the Masons.

First I searched "Abraham Lincoln as a Mason." Not one link appeared. The next idea was to search for Masons in his administration. It generated a list of several names, including the Secretary of War from both terms, the Secretary of the Interior, Navy Secretary, and Vice President, Andrew Johnson.

"He was surrounded by Masons in his cabinet. He could have joined after his presidency. He probably didn't have time to think about it, what with the war and all." I read further and found that Lincoln was a close friend of the Commissioner of Public Buildings: Benjamin Brown French, who was Grand Master of all the Knights Templar in the U.S at the time. "The list is endless. It's far-reaching." Further digging led me to information about Mary's family, where I stopped. "I'm right! Mary's father was a Mason, and so were her brothers, uncles, and cousins." I clicked out of the website and sat back. "I bet Mary did hide the speech."

"I agree one-hundred percent," Grandma said, yawning. "I'm with Liv. We are going to leave now, but we'll call you in the morning." She leaned over and gave me a kiss. "It'll turn out just fine. Keep your chin up."

"I will. Thank you again. You're both great." I stood and gave her a hug before going into the living room to hug Grandpa. "Careful driving."

"Of course."

From the window, I watched until their taillights were no longer in view, and then I plunked down on the chair. I jumped up again. "Before doing all of this research, let's figure out this map. Maybe we can tell if she meant Hodgenville, Springfield, or Lexington?"

"But she didn't want anything to do with Lexington nor the house where she grew up," Aaron said.

"True, but that house deserves to be on our list, simply because it's her birthplace. She may have meant it, instead."

Aaron readjusted the maps. Side by side, we studied them. My lines were drawn already, and I saw clearly that the pentacle didn't ring true.

"Only three points of the pentacle meet. Here's a question. Back then, roads between towns were either non-existent or terrible for travel. How did the speech get there?"

"Her family. She wouldn't have mailed it, that's for certain," Aaron said.

"Especially with the war on. Sending something to

the southern states would be difficult, if not impossible," I agreed. "Maybe after the war? Or before it began?"

"Maybe family members, visits, after the assassination." Aaron shrugged. "Don't have an answer, but it's worth researching."

"You're right."

I sat back down, and searched the town of Hodgenville, Kentucky. Many sites came up, but the link to the Hodgenville Chamber of Commerce seemed most logical. Next, I clicked on the local businesses and to my surprise, an image of the Hodgenville Masonic Lodge popped into view.

"Take a look," I said.

"We're heading in the right direction, honey. I swear, we'll find it."

"Let's hope."

Upon further reading, I found that the lodge had been in existence since the mid-1800's, which furthered my curiosity. The link for the log cabin mentioned that the Burr Oak, a towering, ancient tree, had been a forest landmark for settlers moving West. *Was it still standing?* The manner in which Mary hid clues proved that she was clever. *Would she have hidden it in the tree?* The acorn necklace would finally make sense. The website didn't say anything more about the tree, so I made a mental note to call and ask about it. I bookmarked the website before continuing to read. Dignitaries and foreign travelers still visited the birthplace, the log cabin, and to look for the burr oak. Past presidents, such as Teddy Roosevelt and John F.

Kennedy, also had visited the historical home of Abraham Lincoln. I clicked out of the website and logged out.

"Did Harris say anything about shutting the computer down?" I asked.

"He said to leave it running."

"Okay." I logged out but didn't power down. I yawned and stood up to stretch. "No wonder I'm tired, it's already eleven."

"It's been a long day," Aaron said. "Don't forget that I have the hockey tourney in the morning. Fortunately, we don't play until nine."

"Yikes! I'd forgotten all about it."

"Max will take care of the store, don't worry, you won't have to go in. It's already set it up with Maggie. She will meet you at Lake Nokomis," Aaron said.

"What would I do without you?"

Aaron shut the lights off, and with his arm around me, we walked into the bedroom.

I couldn't sleep. The blankets were twisted around, making a mess off the bed. Aaron growled at me a couple of times for hogging all the covers. Finally, I got up and went to the kitchen for a drink of warm milk to calm me down and help me sleep.

The glow from the computer monitor flooded the floor like a sheet. I held my breath as I approached the kitchen door. The bright light lit my way. It ought to have been dark as the night.

I inched back to the bedroom.

"Aaron." I nudged him and yanked back the blankets. "Get up." When he opened his eyes, I put my finger to my lips, motioning him to be quiet. I finger waved him to follow but waited as he grabbed his gun.

We crept quietly down the hallway. The monitor still cast an eerie light in the darkened kitchen.

At the doorway, Aaron nudged me aside. With his gun in position, Aaron entered the room.

"Come in," Aaron said. "We need to call Harris." I entered behind him.

Aaron gazed at the screen and watched the cursor move back and forth across it.

"Let's make it a three-way call," I said. *Sneaky little monster.*

Aaron made the call. "Okay, go ahead," he said. "Liv is also on the line."

"Press the ESC button on the computer's keyboard," Harris told us.

I pressed the button. "Okay." "Now what?" Aaron said.

"Watch the screen," Harris said. We watched the hacker remotely deleting all of the items he'd forwarded earlier from the sent folder.

Aaron said. "He's deleting his sent files. All were Lincoln-related. I guess he's cleaning up after himself, so we won't spot him." We kept our eyes glued on the monitor. "Okay. He just shut it down and restarted it."

"Open an Internet browser. If we find what IP address he's using, we can trace it and get a better handle on his location," Harris stated.

"I'm ready," I said. Following his instructions, I opened in a set of internal log files.

Aaron read off a series of numbers to Harris. "This will catch him?" Aaron asked when he finished.

"It's possible," he replied. "By-the-way, that memory stick had copies of email messages, and they are very pertinent to this case. Now I've got to get busy, catch you later. Make certain there's someone monitoring that computer twenty-four seven. I may stop by in the morning to check on it." He hung up.

"Okay." I disconnected. "Now what do we do, since the game starts at nine? Someone has to be here."

"Bummer luck," Aaron said.

"I'm fine. You go when you need to, and I'll follow as soon as Harris gives me the all clear." I took his arm. "Let's hit the sack. Should we leave it on like this?"

"You bet."

"If we're lucky, the hacker won't realize we are watching him. Now we know how he does everything," I said as we walked to the room.

"And we can hopefully trace the hacker. Harris is a real whiz at this and should be able to track him down," Aaron said.

"Let's try sending an email. One that will scare him out of hiding. Next time we'll know when he's sneaking into the computer. This time, it was a chance to discover him at work," I said. "That's how we'll be able to pull him out of his lair."

"We'll talk with the detectives tomorrow."

"I'm still bothered. I'm going to sit with the maps. You go on to bed, if you'd like."

"I'm staying right by your side."

In the kitchen, I said, "We have drawn out the

pentacle. Where the heck is the center of it? The 'G' stands for the beginning. The pentacle has to mean the same." I erased the pencil lines before I drew lines from Hodgenville. "Look, now. They're all kind of connected in an odd way."

"She knew the Masons were trustworthy, given her family connections. The Masonic building is still in use." Furrowing my brow, I thought for a moment. "I'm calling to find out about the Burr Oak tree in the morning as well as the lodge."

"This is still crazy," Aaron said. "But, the nut didn't fall far from the tree."

"When will the hacker strike again? And, is the hacker the killer?"

Chapter Twenty-four

"Honey, I'm leaving," Aaron whispered, standing over me. "Time to get up."

"Oh my goodness, I didn't realize the time," I said. He kissed me, and then moved to the door. "I'll come as soon as possible. Text me."

"Of course. I left the bagels out and cream cheese. Coffee's made," Aaron said, then continued on his way.

"Good luck!" I jumped from the bed and dressed, sliding into a long sleeved shirt and jeans plus knee-hi length socks. I grabbed a sweatshirt and found a heavier pair of socks to have ready for later.

In the kitchen, I'd just finished my meal when there was a knock on the door. I swiped my mouth with the nearest napkin before going to open the front door.

"Good morning," I cheerfully greeted Detectives Erlandsen and Mergens with Harris shuffling in right behind them. "Coffee?" I filled mugs for all and refreshed mine.

"Let's sit at the kitchen table and discuss all of this first. We need to be brought up to speed, especially after last night," Erlandsen stated. He reached for his notebook, and so did Mergens. "Right from the top, Liv."

"We stayed out here in the kitchen almost all night. As you can see, the monitor is still on. I would've known if the killer had logged back in." I glanced at each of them. "How do we know we have the right person?"

"Right here." Harris shoved a stapled stack of pages toward me. "This says it all." He cleared his throat. "Read through it, and then we'll discuss it."

"Okay." I reached for the few pages and began reading. My mouth dropped open as I read each message:

Chun-money coming soon.

Impersonator shouldn't have fought back. Her fault she's dead. Speech saved for not-too-bright Tad. Positive.

Ripped bear. Family tree on rear end? Don't understand.

Masonic symbols? Pentacle? Birth of Jesus? No. Can't be. G? God? I don't understand. Must follow Liv. Only way to find speech.

Speech worth much. Lost Speech? Plenty money to do what's necessary. I looked for a hidden compartment, but couldn't find one.

"The messages explain it all, don't they? This has to be the killer, but who?" I slid the sheets back across the table to the detective. "The motive is loud and clear, just like what we thought. Money and greed."

"Now the question is how to flush him out." Mergens subconsciously reached up to his cigarettes but quickly dropped his hand. "Any suggestions?"

"I'm putting a different tracer on the computer."

Harris scooted over to it and began clicking. "We'll get him, don't worry."

"I would hope so," Erlandsen said. "He needs to be caught."

"We should send out some kind of message like, 'I might know where it's located. I've got a bit more research to do; then I'll know'." My mind was filled with ideas. "We can send the message to the Mary Todd Lincoln House. That would make it seem more official," I added. "Also, there's the Presidential Library."

"That's a great idea, but we do have to discuss all of this with our lieutenant," Mergens said, taking notes. "If we can send the decoy messages today, we'll be able to monitor the hacker's response tonight."

"Fine by me." I glanced at them. "So we know it's the right man. Let's trick him into believing we truly have found the speech."

"How? We don't know what was said," Erlandsen asked. "It's easy," Mergens said. "All we need is a handwriting expert to write the first transcribed lines out on some old-looking paper. When it's ready, we'll place it in the hidden pocket of the desk."

"Hmm. The culprit's already searched through the desk, though," I said, scratching my scalp. "However, we didn't find the hidden compartment right away, either. It had been painted over with stain, and Aaron had to pry it open. We could barely see the seam in the boards."

"So?" Mergens said. "It'll work. I'm positive."

"We'll get back to you." Erlandsen looked at me.

"This is dangerous, so please be careful."

"I'm going to Lake Nokomis to watch Aaron play pond hockey. I'll probably stop in the store on my way home."

"Good luck to Aaron's team," Mergens said.

"Ditto," Erlandsen said.

Both detectives stood and walked to the doorway. "We'll be in touch."

I looked back to Harris, frowning. "Ready?"

"Almost done." Harris made a few notes in his notebook and pressed a couple keys. "Liv? Come here." I stood behind him, and he said, "Use this username and password. Make sure you enter them exactly as shown. If all goes as planned and you catch the hacker at work when you're online, call me immediately. It's programmed to play, *Three Blind Mice,* really loud, when he logs back in."

"Sounds good," I replied, giving him a wry grin. "Can you write down the username and password, just to make sure we key it in correctly? "

"Will do." Harris did as requested and ripped the sheet from his notepad. "I'll leave it right here." He placed it on the table.

"Thanks bunches."

"Oh, and by the way, don't check your e-mail accounts until I tell you to."

"I can do a search though, can't I?"

"That'll work. But keep it simple and on target. Let's not do anything different from what you've already begun."

Harris stood up and I walked him to the door.

The little tune that he'd installed was fitting. Like blind mice, we were all heading into uncharted waters. I sent a text to Aaron. He responded that the game was running late because the first team started later than scheduled. It gave me about ten extra minutes.

I sat at the computer and did a Google search for Lincoln's birthplace again and waited as the screen filled with a list of sites. I pressed a link to the Sinking Spring Farm, where the famed log cabin was located. Then I scanned several of the sites for mention of the Burr Oak. If Mary had visited the town, she would've stayed near the birthplace since there were so many Southerners in the area. Continuing with the theory that "if there's a will, there's a way," she would've found a way to hide the speech on the main property. The Burr Oak tree or a niche in one of the cabin logs were the two main theories I held to.

The reconstructed cabin looked as the original had. A memorial building surrounded it like an envelope. Since the logs weren't original, I decided to forget the cabin.

Not much was written about the Burr Oak, except that it served as a landmark for folks going west. Travelers found fresh, clean water to drink because of a nearby, flowing spring. But that didn't answer my questions. Contact information was readily available, so I jotted the phone number down to call later. Aaron texted to tell me the plows had to push new snow from the rink. His team was being moved to the "little" beach.

After acknowledging the message, I told him my plans to make a call to Kentucky to further investigate the Burr Oak tree.

I keyed the Kentucky phone number into my cell phone and waited for a park ranger to answer. "Hello. I'm curious about the famous Burr Oak. Is it still standing?"

"No. It had to be cut down a few years ago because it had become a safety hazard. We kept it standing for as long as possible. Dirty shame, isn't it?"

"Yes, as a matter of fact." I frowned. "Thank you. By the way, can you tell me if the Masonic Lodge there is the same building that was standing during the Civil War days?"

"Not positive about that, but I think it is. It's an old building, but they've remodeled it."

"How?" I prayed that none of the interior walls had been altered.

"Updated plumbing. Wiring. That sort of thing."

My heart leapt. "It was gutted?" I asked. "Oh, no. Just the basic repair jobs."

"Thanks. Thanks bunches," I said before disconnecting. *I'm almost to the end.* A two-year-old couldn't be any happier with a new toy. "That's it! That's the place! If it's to be found, that's where the speech is—I'm sure of it!" I said out loud.

My thoughts jumped to the evidence as I chased for the sweatshirt and heavy socks. While putting them on along with heavier outerwear, the memory stick came to mind. We couldn't connect this person to Max's unwarranted attack, nor to the break-in at

Inga's. That person was a monster.

And how did the woman end up in the dumpster?

I grabbed my keys and headed into the garage. The door lifted open, and I backed out into the street. Immediately, the kid next door pummeled the car with snowballs. I put the car in park, climbed out, snatched up snow, packed it good and hard, then sailed it over to him—hitting him square in his back. Before he had time to retaliate, I jumped into the car and continued on my way.

Since Lake Nokomis, in South Minneapolis, was where I took swimming lessons as a child, I wanted to take a memory lane drive. I passed over the Hennepin Avenue Bridge and kept going until reaching Washington Avenue. The road turned, but I followed the signs for Cedar Avenue. Upon reaching the Minnehaha Parkway, I followed it until turning toward the little beach. Cars lined the parkway and up into the neighborhood. I ended up parking near an ice cream shop on Twenty-Eighth Avenue. I texted Maggie to find out where she was. She responded that they had just started playing and she'd meet me where we used to hang out. I sent: *ok.*

It took a few minutes, but we finally located each other. Fortunately, Aaron's team had been on the ice for just a few minutes. The temperatures were climbing, and the local thermometer told me we were in a heatwave—it was sixteen degrees, warm for our Januarys.

"Look at them! How can they move with all that equipment and skate on this ice? It's rough," I said.

"I'm glad you thought of lawn chairs."

"No problem. Now we can try to wrap ourselves up with this blanket. Our guys have enough padding," Maggie said, watching them skate. "A little wobbly." She put the blankets across our laps.

"We've got ourselves two jocks." There was a vendor nearby. "I'm going for hot chocolate," I said. "Want a cup?"

"Sure."

"Be right back."

I purchased two cups of cocoa. We covered ourselves up again and enjoyed watching and cheering.

"We'll have to rent a sailboat next summer again, like we did last year. That was a fun day," I said.

"Yes, only let's get a larger one—it makes for a bigger party," Maggie said.

"I agree. We only fit four people, and ten is a good number. Maybe we should get a pontoon up north for a weekend?"

"Sounds like a plan," Maggie said.

"Hey!" I saw Aaron raise his stick to us. Tim was right beside him and did the same.

The game ended in a shoot-out with Aaron's team losing. At the end, we made arrangements through texting to meet them at Matt's Bar for a Juicy Lucy burger.

Maggie and I sat opposite in a booth at the bar. Soon the men of the team charged through the doorway. Aaron and Tim were in the lead. Aaron had saved ten goals, and Tim made the only point for the team.

"Whoo-hoo!" I shouted.

"Whooey!" Maggie called.

The other women piped up also. When the burgers arrived, the men joined us.

"You looked good out there, honey," I said.

"Thank you," Tim replied, winking. "Oops! You meant that ugly guy beside you."

"You're incorrigible," Maggie said, nudging him.

"I'm going back to watch the games, but I would guess that you ladies are frozen?" Aaron asked.

"Cold and kind of a headache," Maggie said. She rubbed her temples.

"Frozen solid comes to mind. I'll just meet you at home," I said. "You enjoy yourself."

Maggie and I stayed for a short while, but when the guys left to watch the games, we left for our cars.

"Take care of yourself," I said, giving Maggie a hug.

"Will do," she said and climbed into her car.

I did the same and followed her out into the traffic, but where she turned toward our old school, I kept on the main road. It was always nice to drive past our high school, Theodore Roosevelt, but this time, I drove past the Swedish Institute and thought about how beautiful it was during the holiday season all lit up like a Christmas tree. The reminiscing brought my thoughts full circle. The murder of Blanche and Dr. Williams, and all that Mary Lincoln lived through, was a tragedy. I was happy to reach home. I parked, and went inside. Once the heavy clothing was shed, I started thumbing through recipe books. The garage door reopened, and soon Aaron entered.

"Honey, how come you didn't stay?" I asked.

"I didn't want you home alone," Aaron said. "What are you doing?"

"I've had enough of worrying. I'm going to look up some recipes." *Maybe researching Mary Lincoln recipes will take my mind off the case for awhile.*

"You? Digging up recipes? What is this world coming to?" Aaron playfully knocked the side of his head. "Tell me it isn't true? Tell me I'm not hallucinating."

"Hush. I'm onto something. Now be nice," I chided. "I just thought, well, what the heck. I'll see what I can find." There was one food site that featured her infamous cake. Mary Lincoln was known to cook like a master chef all day and invite crowds of people over for dinner. She would prepare several different meats, and no one seemed to care about watching calories in those days. Mary baked plenty of cakes and desserts, and for Mister Lincoln's morning snack, cornbread. While Mary was considered a Southerner, and Abraham, a symbol of the North, both were gracious hosts, and dinner with the Lincoln's was a coveted invitation.

"Hmm," I moaned, a little disgruntled because there wasn't a particular recipe that struck my fancy. I decided to make a grocery list, adding baking apples for a Civil War recipe called Brown Betty, a forerunner to apple crisp. When the shopping list was completed, I looked over at Aaron. "I think we've got it all set and know where to go. We just have to wait until we nab the killer."

"We really should stay home and wait for the detectives."

"I know. It makes me nervous to wait. I'm going in to the store tomorrow. It's making me buggy staying home."

"Well, we'll see what we come up with to keep you busy tomorrow." Aaron reached for my grocery list. "Let's run to the grocery store to get this stuff. We'll be back in a flash."

"Sure."

Upon our return, I put together the ingredients to concoct the Brown Betty. It took time to bake, but it was delicious. We smiled at each other, tiptoeing around the predominant thoughts that circled our minds.

Eventually Aaron received a message stating Erlandsen and Mergens would soon be dropping by. Just as he clicked out of the message, they appeared at the door.

"We came up with a usable message to use as a decoy," Erlandsen said, wiping his feet.

"You're going to like it," Mergens added, doing the same with his shoes. "May we?"

"Sure."

Aaron and I followed them into the kitchen. Erlandsen sat down on the stool in front of the computer and pulled his cell phone out of his pocket. "I'm calling Harris so he can give me the directions."

I stood directly behind Erlandsen and watched as

he followed the directions Harris gave him. After opening the mailbox, he typed in the e-mail addresses for the Presidential Library and the Mary Todd Lincoln House. In the subject line, he entered: Lost Speech location found. The message read:

Dear All,

Through plenty of research, I have finally figured out the whereabouts of the Lost Speech that Mr. Lincoln gave in Bloomington, Il, May 29, 1856.

Isn't that...

"What?" I asked when he cocked his head at me.

"Would you say, marvelous or wonderful? What word would you use?

"Wonderful."

He finished the message by typing in *wonderful* before he added,

Will be in touch. "Is your signature saved in here?"

"Yes, that and my website link are already in place."

"Okay." I watched as he hit *send*. "Tonight, stay nearby and give us a jingle when he logs on, will you?"

"Will do," I answered. "Both you and Harris?"

"Yes." The detectives looked at each other and nodded. "We've got our handwriting expert copying the lines from the speech that are known onto a sheet of paper, which he's prepared to look really old and yellowed. We'll sneak it into the desk sometime tomorrow, if this guy doesn't bite tonight."

"I really think this message is going to flush him out," I said. "I'm glad you guys are as confident as I feel."

"Let's see, it's six now." Erlandsen rubbed his chin. "We'll call you about ten to check in."

"Is the volume turned up high?" Mergens asked. "It should be loud enough to wake them."

"Right." Erlandsen made certain it was. "All set."

With Aaron right beside me, we followed them to the front door where they both said, "We hope this works."

If it doesn't, guess who might be next?

Chapter Twenty-five

The remainder of the evening seemed to drag on and on, never ending. Grandpa and Grandma came over for a short while, and we finished the Brown Betty. Grandma even congratulated me on my baking. It was the only high point of the evening.

Aaron and I camped out in the kitchen in a makeshift recliner we devised by plumping up pillows and spreading blankets across the kitchen chairs. Eventually we managed to become semi-comfortable as we dozed off, each with one eye open to keep tabs on the monitor.

Just as I started drifting off again, the short song blared and woke us. We jumped up, stumbling over the chairs and knocking one over.

"I'm calling the station." Aaron fumbled sleepily with his phone.

"Give it to me." I grabbed his phone, found the contact number, and speed-dialed Harris. He answered on the third ring.

I simply said, "Got it."

"Good. Put us on speaker so Aaron can also hear."

I hit the speaker button. The computer's cursor seemed to have its own mind, maneuvering around the screen, reorganizing the messages, making copies and deleting my incoming e-mails. When the hacker logged out, Aaron asked, "Now what?"

"We wait. The tracer should lead us to him. Hold

on," I said. I could almost hear Harris's heart beating over the phone as we waited to see if our plan had worked. "Nope, but don't worry. I've got plenty of tricks up my sleeve."

"Doggonit! It should've worked. This makes me mad!" I said.

"We'll get 'em. Usually, these guys aren't this smart," Harris said.

"We're taking the computer in to the store in the morning. Liv has work to do and it was only Max on Saturday," Aaron said.

"I'll come by later this morning or early this afternoon to work on it. Until then, don't do anything besides check your usual accounts," Harris said.

"We'll meet at the store," Liv said, "in the afternoon, since tomorrow is Sunday."

Aaron disconnected. "Let's go back to the real bed before my back breaks. It's killing me." I started gathering the pillows and Aaron put the chairs back in place.

We crawled into bed and somehow managed to get in a few hours of sleep. I felt miserable in the morning with the lack of sleep, but my heart raced, exhilarated and confident the whole, convoluted puzzle would soon be solved. Convincing myself was the hard part.

Yawning, I crawled from the warm sheets and headed for the shower. The sun bleached through the draperies as I shuffled through the living room into the kitchen. I couldn't wait for the snow to melt and splash onto our deck. Thoughts of blooming daffodils, tulips, roses, and a flood of colors that would emerge from the plentiful spring rain we'd soon get, made me smile. The end of snow and cold for a few months sounded like heaven.

Hearing Aaron whistling as he walked down the hallway toward the kitchen, I quickly loaded the toaster and poured us each a glass of orange juice.

"Time to get started. I'm ready to face the day, how about you?"

"My sergeant called. I have to go in for a suspect interview in a short while. It shouldn't take too long."

"Shoot."

"It won't take me long, I promise." He kissed me. "Can't be helped."

"Well, all right," I said. "The toast is up." I buttered the slices, handing one to Aaron.

"Let's get moving and carry the computer out," Aaron said. "I'll take the tower, you carry the monitor."

We ate quickly and then tackled our task. Shortly, we had it loaded into the car, and we were on the road.

As we parked and began carrying our cargo into the store, Max greeted us at the door and held it open for us. It didn't take long to get the computer connected.

"I'll bring you down a coffee before I take off," Aaron said.

"Thanks." Looking at Max, I said, "It's great to be back. How are you feeling?"

"Still a little stiff, but not bad." Max shrugged in his boyish way. "I'm gonna have to run to my sister's, but then I'll be back. It shouldn't take more than an hour. She's putting up bookshelves and needs help. You won't be alone for long. I'll probably beat Aaron back here."

"I've got plenty to do."

"I'd say! You have to solve the puzzle. No one else has a clue as to what's going on, right?" He grinned. "I won't be long."

"Right."

Max had no sooner left when Aaron entered with the full coffee cups. I took mine from him and said, "Thanks."

"What? No Max?"

"Had to run a quick errand."

"Busy guy." Aaron shook his head. "I'll call if there's a delay." He kissed me, and then left. Sipping my coffee, I paced the showroom floor. After double-checking the backdoor lock, I walked to the show room. Staring at the front door, I knew it must be unlocked in order for my store to be open. It had been only a couple days since the store was closed, but it seemed longer. I was pacing—something I hadn't done since my parents were killed in the car crash when I was a kid. I opened the door front door and flipped the *Closed* sign to *Open*. With that step behind me, I felt slightly better.

Strolling around the houses, I reacquainted myself to the ladies by telling them about the recent happenings. Rearranging furniture in the various dollhouse rooms, and doing a little bit of dusting, kept me busy. The First Lady photos hung crooked, so I adjusted them. The Penny Dolls on the shelf also needed attention. When finished with all that, my attention turned to the Lincoln desk. As I approached it, a surge of cool air come into the room. *Isn't the door locked?* I called, "Hello?" *My mind is playing tricks. Did I just hear the lock from the backdoor turn?*

I listened intensely. Hearing only silence, I leaned over the desk. The floorboards creaked. My nerves tingled.

Peering closely under the desk, I carefully ran my fingers over the wood, hoping to find the hidden pocket, and that was precisely the moment when the radio came on.

"Aaron?" I softly whispered. "Is that you?" My bag with my cell phone was in the workroom. I didn't know what to do. *Should I run for the front door? Where is my hammer? What else can I grab as a weapon?* Keeping low, I began inching my way toward the front door.

From the corner of my eye, I saw movement. Hurrying, I tried to make it to the door and out before whoever it was could get to me but was too late.

"Gotcha." His whiskers burned against my cheek. The man's breath felt hot against my face as he pulled me closer.

I screamed.

"Not the right thing to do." One arm held my arm across my chest, pulling me to his while the other poked a pointed object into my lower back.

"Where's the speech?"

"What speech?" Wiggling, I tried to pull away, but he squeezed my arm tighter. "You're hurting me."

Struggling only made it worse.

He jabbed the object into my back, and pain shot down my leg. He fastened his grip tighter.

"My lips are sealed."

Yanking my hair, he growled, "Tell me now or you'll pay dearly."

He poked me again. This time I felt blood running down my back.

"You're making all this up, aren't you? You don't even know where the speech is, do ya?" I shook my head and kicked. "You're not going anywhere."

I wiggled toward the cup of hot coffee, but he realized what I was planning and squeezed me tighter. My neck was bent over his shoulder. I tried to drive my heels into his leg or higher into his abdomen, when the point of the knife dug deeper.

I screamed from pain. A warm stream of blood trickled down my back. It must've scared my attacker because he pulled the knife back, but at same time he tightened his fist around my throat. *The last thing I remembered was thinking his shoes looked weird.*

When I awoke in the hospital bed, Aaron was holding my hand. The doctor had come and gone, and I learned that I had been stabbed.

"Just as I thought," I whispered. "I'm so tired."

"It's the meds, hon. You're all taped up. Nothing too bad…you only need to be careful while you are healing. The knife didn't go too deep, so it missed all vital organs."

"That's a relief." I tried to sit, but it hurt. "I should've been safe. I was so scared when he attacked.

He kept asking for the speech." I glanced at the water pitcher on the bedside table. "I'm thirsty."

"Okay." Aaron filled a glass with fresh water and held it to my lips. "The detectives are right outside, and you need to speak to them whenever you feel you are up to it."

"I'm ready."

Aaron fluffed my pillows and handed me a mirror so I could rearrange my unruly hair. He also handed me my makeup case he had pulled out of my bag. I applied a coat of lipstick and gave myself a brief touch-up, then handed the items back to him.

"Ready?" He leaned over and gave me a kiss. "Yep."

"You're a trooper, Liv."

The two detectives entered the room. Their expressions were grim, but their demeanor was calm. *They were used to this.*

"You ready?" Mergens asked.

"Sure, but begin by telling me how I got here. I haven't been told the complete story yet. I gather, the medical staff's been busy trying to get me to wake up."

"Max returned from his errand and found you bleeding on the floor."

"We've questioned everyone but you, Liv." Erlandsen pulled out his pad, and Mergens took out a small recording device. "May we?"

"Sure. Go ahead." I waited while they got ready to record. "From the top?" When they nodded, I began relaying all that I remembered. My heartbeat increased as I neared the part where I was looking underneath the desk and heard the floor creak and the door closing. "I also remember one thing in particular that's rather perplexing, actually."

"And, what's that?"

"Shoes. The attacker's shoes were weird looking…like sandals or flip-flops, but they looked like they were made of wood." I yawned. "Sorry, I'm getting sleepy again."

"Okay, we'll check into that clue. Can you remember anything else?" Mergens asked, studying me closely.

"I smelled coffee, but it may have been mine…especially since I was trying to reach my coffee cup to throw it at him."

"You sure your attacker was a male?"

"Yes. There wasn't anything petite about those shoes or his whiskers."

"We've dusted and made imprints, which match with the other break-in. Too bad the murder scene outside the store was all messed up by the time we got there."

"Now what?" I asked, glancing from one detective to the other. "I want to know. I'm part of the deal, you know."

"Don't worry about this, we've got it under control." Mergens turned off the recorder and slid it into his jacket pocket.

"What's the plan?" I hoped my persistence would urge them to open up and tell me what the next step would be. "Still going with the speech as the motive?"

"It's the only motive we can come up with. We'll keep you informed," Erlandsen said. "Good day." He nodded toward me and looked at Mergens.

"Thanks again. You've been very helpful," Mergens said.

"Anytime." I kept my growl to myself as I watched them walk out of the room. "Meanies!"

"They've got their jobs to do." Aaron tried to reassure me. "They don't tell what they're going to do...then it wouldn't be a secret."

"Oh, be quiet." I closed my eyes and pictured Lincoln's speech lying hidden in the desk. "I hope no one else is coming by."

"Me, too." Aaron stood. "I'm going to the lounge for something to drink. I'll be right back. Want me to get you a nurse so they can bring you juice or something?"

"Please." After he walked out, I decided it was time for me to get up and move around. I knew I should wait for someone to come and help me up, but something urged me onward. My first order of business was the bathroom. I'd have to pull the intravenous contraption along with me, since it was still connected to my arm. Slowly, I brought my legs over the side of the bed and stopped to rest. After a few moments, I pushed myself upward with my palms and was grateful that the bathroom was only a couple feet away. Once inside, I debated whether to close the door for privacy or not. I closed it. Just as I sat down on the toilet, I heard a creak. It sounded like someone walking across the old flooring, but...the shoes. Walking in those wooden shoes made a distinctly different sound. Quickly, I pressed the call button alongside of the toilet.

After I pressed the lock button, the person on the other side of the door jiggled the knob. "Help!" I screamed. From my confinement in the small hospital bathroom, I heard the banging of furniture, probably the cart. "Help!" I called again.

After a few moments, I heard pounding on the door.

"Honey? It's safe. You can open the door now." I could almost hear Aaron's heart beating. "The coast is clear."

"Positive?" I waited a moment to catch my breath and steady my nerves. I also wanted to hear his voice once again. "Promise?"

"Yes. You're safe."

"Someone just tried to come after me!" The lock button popped out as I opened the door. "Whew. I'm out of wind and energy." I looked past Aaron to see the two detectives' coats piled up at the end of the bed.

"Be right outside."

The nurse pushed in front of Aaron, and she helped me stand and take care of myself. "Ready?"

"I feel awfully weak after all that," I said. "Did they catch him?" "Not yet," Aaron said.

"It's understandable that you're tired." The nurse helped me walk the few feet to the bed where I immediately crawled in between the covers.

"Get some sleep. Ignore them," she whispered and made me comfortable.

"I'll try."

Later, after answering several more of the detectives' questions, I realized the creaking was actually the sound of the shoes on the polished floor. The detectives wouldn't tell me their next move, but I gathered they intended to continue with the plan to post the forged message about the hidden speech. Harris contacted Aaron, and they discussed what to type into the subsequent decoy e-mails. *Would the murderer still take the bait, since now he must realize he was a wanted man? No one could be that stupid. But most criminals were just that – stupid.*

The doctor also gave me a quick check and deemed me fit, but he still wanted to keep me in the hospital overnight for observation. I was happy to stay. The detectives had my room guarded by a uniformed officer.

Grandma and Grandpa came for an evening visit. They wanted me to come back to their house until the case was solved, but I turned them down. Max phoned instead of visiting in person, which gave us time to talk for a few minutes.

Aaron reached for the iPad at the chosen time to send the decoy email. He typed in the message he and Harris had drafted. Before sending it to the chosen few individuals, he let me read it.

Dearest Taddie,

Remember playing hide-and-go-seek near your father when he was busy writing speeches?

Your loving mother.

Home is where the Heart is.

I liked this cryptic message and said as much. "It says it all.

Now we just have to wait and see."

"It'll work, Liv. It has to. The shoes alone, the messages—at least the retrieved ones, don't add up to a motive or lead to the killer."

"Hopefully, catching him in the act will."

"Harris told me how to have, *Three Blind Mice,* set up to play if the killer checks the e-mail tonight.

"Let's hope."

After the message was sent, I slept.

The drugs knocked me out for a very long time. The nurses woke me only to feed me more meds and check my vital signs. A cot was brought in for Aaron.

Sometime during the night, Aaron nudged me awake. I heard the nursery rhyme playing, and we watched the cursor fly around the screen. A nurse came into the room and stood with one hand on her hip with the other pointing at us. When she turned and left, the guard entered.

"He bit," I whispered.

"Let's hope we got him this time." Aaron smiled at me.

The guard stood at the foot of the bed and pulled out his cell phone. After a minute, he disconnected. "The suspect is under surveillance." After a few short minutes, he answered his phone,

and whispered a few words into it. He slipped it back into his pocket. "Got them."

"Who?"

"Your neighborhood coffee maker, Luke, and his wife, Suni."

"That figures. Why?"

"Money and greed." He shook his head. "I'm leaving. Since the attacker has been caught, I think you're safe and in good hands now." He headed for the door, then stopped to turn around. "I'm sure the detectives will fill you in when they have more of the story."

"Thanks."

We watched the door quietly close.

"It's over, Liv. Sleep. We'll go home tomorrow." Aaron kissed my forehead as I fell right to sleep.

Chapter Twenty-six

Two weeks later…

After touring Bloomington and Springfield, Illinois, and Lexington, Kentucky, we continued our journey. We checked into the Lincoln Motel, near Hodgenville, President Lincoln's birthplace.

When we got to our room, I logged into the website and read the history of the area. There were few slave holders in LaRue County. Most of the citizens had ancestors from Revolutionary War days, so they had fought for preservation of the Union. The region was developed by hard-working farmers who cleared the land and tilled the soil with their own sweat and grit. The town was made up of a general store, post office, newspaper office, an ice plant, a diner, and two banks. The courthouse was on Main Street, but it had burned and been rebuilt. The Masonic Lodge sat in the far corner of town. It was possible that if I stuck around this town long enough, I would hear personal stories of Lincoln told around campfires.

Photos of the old buildings on the website were available to study. The comparison of the way it looked today must have been almost identical to how it looked in Lincoln's day.

"Let's mosey around the town square first."

"Nah." Aaron shook his head. "Let's unpack and get settled before we go out to take a look around."

"We should contact Frances right after we locate the speech, if we find it, that is."

"We will," Aaron said. "The detectives have taken care of contacting the FBI."

I opened my small briefcase filled with the gathered information on Masonic symbols and meanings. I pulled the acorn out of a small pouch and put it in my pocket. "Let's take another look at these symbols. Between the two of us, we should be able to remember the meanings of the key symbols."

"Right, like the letter G, the pillar, pentacle, and the staircase."

After we had spent a while getting reacquainted with all of the information, I stood up and stretched. I gave Aaron a long hug.

"Whatever happens, happens. Right?" I said. "Right. Let's go."

The square was filled with people, all shapes and sizes. A festival was in progress, and square dance music filled the air. The rich seasonings of barbecued ribs and chicken smelled delicious. My stomach growled. Dancers dressed in period clothes took turns recruiting people from the audience for impromptu square dance lessons. Abraham Lincoln's statue overlooked the merrymakers like a great-grandpa who was dying to jump in and sashay the good-looking girls around. I could almost see the twinkle in his bronze eyes when I glanced at the statue.

"The music is fun, isn't it?" Aaron stated. "It sure is."

We stopped into the local diner for a bite to eat.

"I'm still shocked about Luke." I bit into my sandwich, adding, "Why would he risk losing everything for a speech that most people don't even think exists? We don't know for sure, ourselves. Plus his business seemed to be doing well."

"He and his wife were greedy," said Aaron. "They found there were people willing to pay a great deal of money if Luke would provide a fake job for people smuggled in from their home country. Luke would hire them for only as long as it took them to receive a green card. They weren't really employees, they were more like indentured servants."

"At least the young woman's story has a happy ending," said Aaron.

"Yes. Who would have thought she jumped in, trying to commit suicide? And all because her parents had sent her from Cambodia, away from a boy they didn't want courting her. Straight out of Romeo and Juliet."

"She's going back, isn't she?"

"Yes, and we can thank her for all the evidence the immigration service has on Luke and Suni. Imagine, Suni had hacked her way into our computer, and she could read everything I wrote on it—and of course, I wrote everything on it. Talk about gall."

"Well." Aaron smiled. "She did you one good turn. She hacked into the library's website and got you a copy of the Mary Lincoln letter."

"Only because she and Luke were using us to find the Lost Speech."

We spent the next few minutes quietly eating our

food and reflecting on our adventure.

I wiped my mouth with a paper napkin. "If we do find it, do you think the agents will show themselves?"

"Yes, someone is probably shadowing us."

"Good. I don't want any more nasty things to happen." I nervously glanced around me. "I suspect they'll appear when we've found it."

"Most likely." Aaron gave me a reassuring smile.

We finished eating, then headed for the Masonic Lodge. "Got the necklace?"

"Of course." I reached into my pocket for reassurance. "Can you believe we're here?"

"Let's do it."

We began briskly walking toward the lodge, noting that the dancers were entering and exiting the building at regular intervals. "Going in there might be harder than expected." I took a deep breath.

"Just say that we're dancers. They're all busy and won't take much notice."

I was thrilled as we walked up the few steps of the Masonic Lodge. My thoughts were of President Lincoln's father, Tom, and of Mary, and all of their ancestors that had been Masons. I opened a side door and stepped back to let two dancers exit.

When we reached the center of the main hall, I gasped, squeezing Aaron's hand tightly. Straight across from us, on the main wall, was a large portrait of George Washington. Beside it was a pentacle with the letter G in the center. Of course! George Washington had been the first Masonic Grand Master in the United States. A two-story balcony looked down on the main floor where seats lined the sides.

"This reminds me of a church. Look at the Bible sitting center stage."

"Let's hurry." Aaron stood beside me as we gazed around the room. "Where do we begin? There are steps everywhere."

"The Grand Master's staircase is where?" I studied the room.

Neither of us heard the approaching footsteps, causing us both to jump at the sound of someone's voice.

"You two wondering where to dress?" a young man asked.

"Yes, but first we were wondering where the restrooms are."

"Down those stairs, to the left." Quickly he walked away.

"That was close." I tried to relax by slowly counting to ten.

"Here's the plan. You go look on that side for something out of the ordinary, which means that I'll start on this side. We'll meet in the middle." I nodded to the right.

"This flight leads up past that throne, and you have a set of stairs that does the same on the opposite side."

"Duck if a bystander should happen in and see us. They may start asking questions."

We each went our separate ways, carefully studying the markings on each of the risers. I still couldn't prevent my mind from going back to one of the first seen toe smudges. There was something about the imprint of the dirt and how it had adhered to the wood, making it appear almost like an etched imprint. Continuing along the balcony risers, I looked across and saw that Aaron was equal in his inspection. Coming together, we decided to continue to opposite sides, in case one of us missed something on the way down. I almost mentioned the riser with the imprint but decided to wait and see if Aaron noticed something different about it.

When finished, we sat on the top stairs of where we'd started. "Well?" I asked. "See anything?"

"No, not really. One riser looked a little odd." Aaron shrugged. "I know which one, too. Follow me." I climbed down two steps. "Look at that." Leaning over, I touched the smudge mark.

"Look how it's kind of an etched-in picture."

"I see what you're saying. Let's get a damp towel and try wiping it clean."

"I'm staying here." As Aaron left, I studied the drawing. "Clearly someone had etched in a drawing." The step creaked, sending shivers up and down my spine. Just then Aaron returned with a damp paper towel, and I reached for it.

"What do you see?" Aaron knelt beside me.

"I'm not sure." I studied it.

"It says something, doesn't it?"

"Nope. Acorn picture." I pulled the acorn out of my pocket and, holding it tight, I held it up next to the etched-in acorn. "Interesting," I whispered. I brought it flush against the wood. "It's the same size." Gently, I pushed on the etching and the upper step popped up. "You're kidding? It's for real." The opening revealed a small metal cylinder.

Just then a dozen dancers entered the main hall, voices filled the air, and laughter bubbled out. Someone put in a CD and bluegrass music drowned their voices.

"Take it. I'm letting the authorities know," Aaron said, slipping out his phone.

"You bet." I grabbed it before Aaron slammed the riser back down. "Let's get out of here."

"I'm hurrying." My heart pounded as we ran out the main door, heading toward a distant picnic area. "Where are they?"

"The FBI and National Park Service are waiting for us. They want us away from the spectators."

Wind rustled through the trees, whipping up dust from the side of the road as we hurried toward a picnic table. Birds flew overhead as squirrels dashed in front of them.

"I'm nervous." I saw two park rangers draw near plus two men dressed in suits. "So much for staying undercover."

"True," Aaron said.

I read the rangers' names off their uniforms—Samantha and Ryan.

All six of us studied the tin cylinder as I turned it around slowly. "This is fairly heavy, but I can feel something moving inside it. It's definitely old. It looks like it had been sealed with beeswax and a round cork, but most of the cork is missing."

"Be careful with it," Samantha said. "It belongs to the town."

"Actually, it belongs to the lodge," an agent stated.

"I bet that's the Mason's representative," I said, nodding at the approaching man.

"I want to see your badges," Aaron said.

"Agent Brown," he stated, displaying his badge.

"Agent Winters," the other stated, doing the same.

"Here! Here!" the man called. "I'm the Grand Master of this lodge and must be involved in this charade."

"It's not a charade," I said. "Your name?"

"Grand Master Hanks," he stated. "Let me take over."

"Sorry, sir."

I started to hand it over, but Agent Brown reached out and said, "We're all present. No one knows what's in there for sure. She's been on this trail for some time. Let her finish, then we'll decide what to do with the find."

"All right. We'll let the lawyers take it from there," Grand Master Hanks said.

"Sounds good," Agent Brown said. "Liv — go for it!"

"Great! I'm finally getting to the bottom of this." I stood, pulling and tugging at the cork as I held the cylinder tight against my body. At last it loosened up. "It's off!" Slightly tipping the tube, the skeleton of a mouse landed in my palm along with shredded paper. "Oh yuck!" Screaming, I dropped it while the wind took the shredded paper, scattering it far away. I could barely breathe as I scrambled to pick up the remnants of the paper. I took a couple of deep breaths to try and calm down. Aaron chased after the pieces, but the wind whipped stronger, blowing the shreds all over. "That stupid mouse must've chewed through the honey and cork, and ate the paper. Lost to a mouse. No one will ever believe this." Collapsing on the picnic bench, I grabbed the largest scrap of paper and began to read: *Mr. Chairman and Gentlemen: I was over at, I say, that while I was at Danville Court, some of our friends of anti-Nebraska got together in Springfield.*

"The rest is shredded. Lost to history," I whispered as Aaron sank beside me. "Lost to the ages."

"But never forgotten." Aaron handed a few snippets of paper over. "Now what?"

"We'll take what we have for display purposes in the museum," Samantha said.

"Nope, it goes to the federal government to decide," Agent Brown said.

"Maybe someone can piece these shreds together and make something out of it."

"I doubt it," I said as we gathered all the pieces while the wind scattered the remnants. "Shoot." I stared at the mouse skeleton. "The *Lost Speech* is firmly and finally lost for all generations, but the outcome will never be forgotten." I brushed a tear from my eye before looking to the mess in my lap. I held up the largest piece to read aloud, "*We are here to stand firmly for a principle.*"

"Look." I picked up a two-inch round circle of hair.

"What is this?"

"Let me see." Agent Winters held it up toward the sun. "It's hair."

"What? Let me see." I took it from him. "There's two different colors braided together. It's like a ring."

"Infinity. Mary and Abraham," Aaron replied. "It's possible."

"Yep. I think this should be given to the Lincoln museum," Ranger Ryan said.

"For now, I'll take it. Let the big guys figure it out," Agent Brown said, taking the paper and hair. He placed it into a plastic bag."

Within a few minutes, they'd walked away, leaving us alone. "What time is it?" I asked.

"Hmm." There was a glimmer in Aaron's eye. "I'm sure it's five o'clock somewhere."

"You betcha." I took his hand.

THE END

A Review of the Lost Speech:

Abraham Lincoln gave the speech in Major's Hall, Bloomington, Illinois, May 29, 1856, and the building was razed in 1959. Forty news reporters were present at the speech. They were so captivated by Lincoln's words, they stopped transcribing after Lincoln had spoken for about fifteen minutes. The reporters "threw their pens and papers away" and "lived only in the inspiration of the hour," as reported by William Herndon, Lincoln's law partner. Over a thousand people were present. The audience was so mesmerized they kept moving closer and closer to Lincoln, crowding him. Many stated that flames of fire danced from the top of his head.

Below is the reported transcription of the speech:

"Mr. Chairman and Gentlemen:

I was over at — I say, that while I was at Danville Court, some of our friends of anti-Nebraska got together in Springfield and elected me as one delegate to represent old Sangamon with them in this convention, and I am here certainly as a sympathizer in this movement and by virtue of that meeting and selection. But we can hardly be called delegates strictly, inasmuch as, properly speaking, we represent nobody but ourselves.

I think it altogether fair to say that we have no anti-Nebraska party in Sangamon, although there is a good deal of anti-Nebraska feeling there; but I say for myself, and I think I may speak also for my colleagues, that we who are here fully approve of the platform and of all that has been done, and even if we are not regularly delegates, it will be right for me to answer your call to speak. I suppose we truly stand for the public sentiment of Sangamon of the great question of the repeal, although we do not yet represent many numbers who have taken distinct position on the question.

"We are in a trying time — it ranges above mere party — and this movement — to call a halt and turn our steps backward needs all the help and good counsels it can get; for unless popular opinion makes itself very strongly felt, and change is made in our present course, blood will flow on account of Nebraska, and brother's hand will be raised against brother!"

The rest of the speech is forever lost to history.

About Barbara Schlichting

Barbara Schlichting was born and raised in Minneapolis and graduated from Theodore Roosevelt High School in 1970. She and her husband moved their family to Bemidji, Minnesota, in 1979. She attended Bemidji State University where she earned her undergraduate and graduate degrees in elementary education and special education. Ms. Schlichting has been married for forty-seven years and has two grown sons who have blessed her with five grandchildren and three great grandsons.

References

TEAM OF RIVALS
by Doris Kearns Goodwin

MARY TODD LINCOLN: A Biography
by Jean H. Baker

LINCOLN: The Presidential Archives
by Chuck Wills

ABRAHAM LINCOLN: From Skeptic to Prophet
by Wayne C. Temple

SPANGLED TO DEATH

A White House Dollhouse Mystery
By Barbara Schlichting

Chapter One

I felt slightly giddy when I dug my key out to unlock the back door of my White House Dollhouse store. The First Ladies were my passion and my shop's specialty. Emails arrived inquiring about various First Ladies, their personal quirks and characters—even questions asking how many affairs their husbands had while in office. I loved answering the questions. *It's bittersweet. What if a time comes that I can't answer the question?*

After stepping inside of the workroom, I flipped on the light and proceeded to remove my coat and cap and place my bag filled with store stuff upon an open spot on the counter. I clicked on the coffee machine, turned up the thermostat, and headed out into the store.

The store was located on a city block in downtown Minneapolis. It was across from the main shopping area on the other side of the Mississippi River near St. Anthony Falls. There were plenty of old eating establishments that dated to the early part of the twentieth century. The old Pillsbury Flour Mill was nearby as well as the Stone Arch Bridge. The street that ran down the front of the store was cobblestone — thus the rumbling of cars and trucks messing with my wall hangings and sometimes screwing up the electrical wiring. On the corner was Inga's Antiques. She has known me since I was a little girl and was friends with my grandma. The other side of Inga's was an old eating and drinking establishment, Dumpy Grumpy, dating back to 1930. The Dumpy Grumpy used to be a speakeasy and from its basement, the buildings on the block were all adjoined. The basement was where Al Capone and John Dillinger plus the rest of the gangsters used to hangout when in Minneapolis. Between Inga and The Dumpy Grumpy was Mikal who read handwriting and on the other side of me was a small coffee shop, Swizzle Stick. Each business presided in an individual brick building, a brownstone, but were connected underground in a city block.

With plenty of time before the store opened, I checked the window display of our newest addition, the infamous rose garden. First Lady Jacqueline Kennedy had had it restored and updated to the beautiful flowers we all see from time to time on the news or in person. The brisk November wind blew outside, rattling the windows. I shivered and thought of a good hot cup of coffee.

I circled to the wall where the shelf of my Penny dolls was. Every so often, a heavy truck rumbled past and one of the dolls would move slightly. Next in line, was the First Ladies pictures that are hung. Sometimes they shifted because of heavy traffic.

"Why are you crooked, Barbara?" I stopped to straighten the first Mrs. Bush. "Don't worry, ladies, I'll return shortly to properly coif your hair. Mrs. Carter, I hope last night was worth it. All that Billy Beer." *Something isn't right. Mrs. Carter has never been this tipsy.* "Don't worry, ladies, you're back to looking good."

Grandma embroidered a replica of the sampler she has displayed at home, so it can be hung on the wall near the First Ladies pictures. We believe the sampler was originally embroidered by Dolley Madison. It has a border of strawberries but in one corner there is a flag, which I thought was odd since it was the only flag. The embroidered center had birthdates and the marriage date of Dolley and President Madison. Grandma was a direct descendant of Dolley, which means so am I.

I winked while moving on toward the dollhouses.

I glanced over at the clock above the cash register and computer and saw there was plenty of time before a dollhouse buyer from New York City, Jackie from New York, planned to stop and view the houses. I always started my morning rounds with the Madison White House and the two miniature dolls, Dolley and James.

"Good morning, Dolley! Did you sleep well? You're still my favorite," I said, certain she loved the attention. I fell in love with Dolley early on, before learning we were kin. My mother loved her too. I'd crawl into bed, and Mommy would tell me the story about how Dolley had saved the White House. The best was for my birthday when Mommy offered Dolley Madison cakes to all the guests along with my cake and ice cream.

"Ladies, listen up!" With my hands on my hips, I glanced around the room. "You have to all be good today because we have a special visitor. Be on your best behavior. That goes for the men, too. Mr. Clinton? Mr. Kennedy? No chasing the female staff around the Oval Office. Got that? Good." I waited a beat. "Then we're set for the day. This person is going to propel the store into the national spotlight so be good." I gave them the evil eye.

I made sure I dressed up in a new pink dress to match Dolley's inaugural gown. After two months showing interest in several White House dollhouses for her store's toy department, Jackie Newell was coming to get a firsthand look. When I searched for her, I found her store located near Central Park. When combing through the store's website, I realized she had stores around the world—England, Scotland, Ireland, and Canada. For me, it meant the possibility of international recognition and sales. She was scheduled to arrive within the hour, which left me with just enough time to spruce up the showroom and ensure that my 1814 White House dollhouse arrangement was in perfect shape. This was my chance to make the big time.

"There, there, now Dolley," I said. I straightened her up because she'd tipped slightly. "Mr. Prez? You need to be on your best behavior today. No chasing

Dolley around the house with my perspective buyer coming soon! No pinching her bum." I wagged my finger at him.

"Mrs. Lincoln? You're looking marvelous today, per usual. How's the headache after that awful carriage ride? It was an attempt on your life, wasn't it?" I'd had an awful headache after the car accident that killed my parents when I was eleven. I thought the pounding inside of my head would never quit. Now it was an ache in my heart, still—twenty years later.

After making a circle around the final few dollhouses, I went to the workroom once again to retrieve a hot cup of coffee. I poured my cup full before having a seat near the workbench. My employee Max usually sat at this spot and carved the dolls' heads. Now was my chance to take a closer look at the heads. He'd labeled each one by number on a notepad with a sticky note beside each head. The Madison heads were slightly askew on the stand, which didn't seem right since Max always left the doll heads upright so he could get a hard look at them as he entered the room. It helped him notice distinctive flaws in the carving.

I wanted to recount the number of dolls in the cabinet, to make sure my inventory book was in order. It showed six of each Madison dolls. The clothes for each was the same count. When I counted the dolls, there were six of each Madison dolls, six Dolley inaugural dresses but only five of James Madison's outfits. *What's going on? I must've miscounted the last time.* I recounted the number of historical dollhouses sold and dolls from the inventory, which added up correctly. I definitely was short Mr. Madison's outfit. *How could that be? Who would want that little outfit, especially without the doll?*

I texted Max,

> *Do you recall how many James Madison outfits we should have? I thought six. Me.*

I wasn't sure when he'd respond because he worked other places besides for me. He could be sound asleep, also.

Max texted,

> *Should be six.*

Max's response perplexed me even more. Something was not right.

My neighbor, Mikal was not only a handwriting expert, he was also part psychic. I wondered if he could make some sense of this mishap. I also wondered if he'd seen anyone lurking about. I had thirty minutes until Jackie was expected, so I went next door to ask him about it.

"Liv, what's wrong? You look perplexed. Are you locked out?" Mikal walked toward me with a client following. "Another mouse?" He grinned and glanced at his client. "Stephanie, my neighbor, Liv."

"I don't have time for this stupidity." The short, stocky client peeked out from behind Mikal, narrowed her eyes and crossed her arms over her flat chest. "Listen, missy. I was in the middle of a reading. It was just getting good! I found out about my husband's little girlie friend with the big boobs. Now this!" She threw her arms in the air. "My reading is botched. I want a refund."

"You haven't paid." Mikal glared at her.

"I won't either." She marched away but not before giving me the finger.

"Hey! Loser! Don't blame me for your stupid husband!" Just because I'd evicted a live-in mouse family from my shop a few weeks ago didn't mean it was back. "I think someone has been in my shop. Have you seen anyone lurking about?" I pulled my cell phone from my pocket, called Aaron and left a message.

"Sit down, right here and explain," Mikal said.

"The inventory says I should have six Mr. Madison outfits, but I only have five. I've added everything up correctly. It's odd. Do you get anything psychic about this?"

"I haven't seen anyone lurking nor do I feel a sense of doom. Aren't you expecting an important client from New York City?"

"Yes. She owns a chain of department stores across the country and Canada." Just then, Aaron returned the call. "Aaron, someone has been in the store and stolen an outfit but not the doll." I sank into the given chair. "The outfit was for a James Madison doll."

"That doesn't make sense. I'm going to mention it to the detective. Are you in the store?"

"No, I'm at Mikal's. I'm going back now. I wondered if he'd seen any weird looking person lurking around."

"I'll stop by before I begin my rounds. It should be pretty soon." Aaron disconnected.

"I'm going back." I headed for the door. "I'm not sure if there was a break-in. Minnesota Nice had been by recently and checked the code pad, and that was in working order. Maybe earlier, I hadn't counted correctly? It's always possible that an outfit was sold without the doll."

"That's true, but it doesn't make any sense," Mikal said. "Do you want me to walk you back and look around?"

"No, but thanks. Max should be coming down soon. I'll send you a text if anything else catches my attention."

"Okay. I can be there in a jiffy."

"I've got to get back to the store." I had to protect the ladies. The First Ladies had already been through so much in their lives, and now it was up to me to make sure nothing else happened to them. Mommy always said they were special, like being the Nation's Mother. In addition to hosting foreign dignitaries and formal dinners, the First Ladies made sure the President looked out for our interests.

I texted my best friend, Maggie, as I walked out the door. My feet crunched in the snow, and I started to shiver.

Max Johnson worked part-time for me and rented the apartment above the shop.

He should be around here someplace, but who knows? Max often gambled away his money. I was always getting cryptic messages from parts unknown, asking how to reach him, presumably to remove body parts. A reassuring chuckle from behind made me grin. Max's voice boomed from above. "Livvie! Now what? Another mouse in the house?"

My headache suddenly grew to the size of Texas. I glanced upward and   massaged my temples.

"Come down to the workroom. I want to talk to you about a missing item." Max

may have seen someone during the night or an unknown car in the lot.

Aaron's squad car drove up and parked.

The cold sliced through me. Aaron's presence was slightly warming.

Aaron and his partner, Tim Dahl, climbed from the car.

"Once I'd told the detective about the missing item, he said he'd be by and ask questions," Aaron said as he walked over toward me.

"Why?" I asked. "I'm not positive I'm missing anything."

"Hold on. I want to hear what's happening," Max called, walking down the outside steps. He gave me a puzzled look but stood near me. "What's missing?"

"An outfit for the James Madison doll. It makes no sense. Did you happen to sell one outfit? Usually, if someone needs more doll clothes, they'll purchase a set. You know, one for both the Mr. and Mrs."

"I don't recall selling it. You might want to question Dorrie."

"I will when she arrives. There isn't much time

until Jackie Newell of New York stops by."

"That's right." Max took a moment and said, "I forgot to put on a decent shirt. I'll be right back." He left for his apartment to change clothes.

I noticed two plainclothes officers approaching, one older with gray hair, the other younger and blond.

"We'll take over. There's been a rash of burglaries in the area, centering around patriotic memorabilia," the detective stated, showing his badge. "Detective Mergens. Ms. Anderson? Olivia Anderson?"

"Aaron is my neighbor and I had told him about it. I'm Olivia, Liv, Anderson."

"Detective Erlandsen," the other officer said, showing his badge. "We're curious about this possible theft."

"Let's go inside for some privacy," Detective Mergens said.

"I'll follow." My phone buzzed, and I read Maggie's message. *Stay safe. Keep me updated.*

Quickly I sent her an emoji of "ok."

"How does the showroom look?" Mergens asked.

"Great, actually. This morning is very important to me." I stuck my hands in my pockets and went back to the front window. "Jackie Newell from New York is due here in less than an hour. She owns a chain of department stores that are located all over the country and in Canada and beyond. She's very well known and her houses are highly praised." I smiled. "I hope her interest in the houses will spike sales."

"Never heard of her, but I don't play dolls," Mergens said. He rolled his eyes.

"You use a key for entrance," Erlandsen said. "How many people have a key?"

"For sure Max and my other employee, Dorrie, plus my grandparents. The temp office that sends the cleaning ladies has it. That's about it."

"Let's jot down names," Mergens said.

"Do you have items of much value?" Erlandsen asked.

"Plenty. Look around the room. I have my Penny dolls and First Lady photos, and they sell for several hundred dollars, at least." I nodded at them, placing my hands on my hips. We stood by the glass counter in front of the register and computer. I swung my attention back to the officer's question. "Max carves doll heads in the workroom or his apartment at night. He sets his own hours. I tell him what style of house I need and which First Lady. The pieces need to be glued and, in some instances, stapled together. They're fragile, but sturdy. He fills in when needed."

"You trust him?" Mergens asked.

"Yes. He has a key. He lives here. I've known him for years." I crossed my arms.

"I see." Mergens wrote down information. "Was he home?"

"I don't know."

"Where do you live?"

"With my grandparents, Marie and August Ott." I scratched my head. "Dorrie takes care of customers when I'm too busy sewing the gowns."

"Any cause for alarm?" He studied me. "You know. Anything unusual. Pattern change such as misplacing a key?"

"We want this Dorrie's info," Erlandsen said.

"I can't think of anything unusual at the moment." I shook my head. "I keep my purse in the workroom, and it's usually hung on the clothes tree." I looked up Dorrie's contact information from the list beside the computer. "Here's her info. Can we hustle here? I'm expecting my very important client pretty soon."

"One more question." Erlandsen held up a finger. "Anyone you might have a beef with?"

"I can't think of anyone." I frowned, massaging my chin. "Unless this has something to do with Max. He gambles and often loses." I thought a moment. "Why are you guys so concerned over a small item that I'm not sure was stolen?"

"The burglar is after something in particular," Erlandsen stated, glancing up at me over the edge of his notepad.

"That alone raises our curiosity. And presidential? I can see artwork by a famous artist or antique books," Mergens said. "Well, we'll be in touch if something comes from the investigation."

"Make sure the doors are locked when you leave," Erlandsen said.

"I will."

They closed their notepads and left.

I glanced in the tiny restroom mirror, fluffed up my knotted, curly red hair and dabbed on some red lipstick. *Hopefully, I look presentable for Jackie Newell's arrival.* The back door opened just as I stepped from the bathroom.

"Hey, babe." Aaron walked toward me. "I don't really know much more than you do right now. Tim and I are leaving on our rounds."

"Thank you." The front bell jingled.

"I'll call you later." Aaron tweaked my chin and left.

I tried to calm my nerves.

He walked to his patrol car and drove away. I noticed a familiar car parked out back and realized it belonged to an old schoolmate, Ronnie Berg. He earned his living by taking pictures of local stories and writing news articles for the local paper. I cringed. At the same time, my girlfriend Maggie drove into the lot and parked. She climbed from the car with a box in hand.

"I have something for you," Maggie called.

"Hey you! Come on in."

"Here," Maggie said.

"Thanks," I said. She handed me a box of chocolates. "Can you stay?"

"No, I'm late for work. Hope this helps," Maggie said. She gave me a big hug.

"You always know what I need to calm me down. I'm a nervous wreck waiting for her." I slipped off the box cover and we both removed a candy, popping it in our mouths.

"Call me," Maggie said.

I locked the back door after she walked out, then turned to go out to the show room.

I removed another candy before setting the box under the counter near the register. A car door slammed nearby. I stuffed the candy in my mouth and went to the front window.

A long, black limousine was parked in front of the store. Jackie Newell and a thirty-ish woman climbed out, followed by a big, burly man wearing aviator sunglasses and a black suit. I figured him as a bodyguard or escort.

"You can do this," I told myself, gulping. Opening the front door, I willed my racing heart to slow down. "Good morning."

Both women stood about the same height. Ms. Newell wore a ritzy black dress coat and the younger woman was dressed in a tastefully simple navy suit. Ms. Newell's hair was black with purple highlights. Her practiced smile shone as she walked toward the store, the other woman following two paces behind. The bodyguard had his eyes glued on the passersby. *Why does she need a bodyguard?*

"Ms. Newell, I hope you'll like the store." I pretended to be calm as my fast beating heart slowed to a normal pace. I jutted my hand out. "Olivia Anderson, but you can call me Liv."

"Jackie. So nice to meet you." She shook my hand before glancing around the room. "Very nice. Yes, indeed. Love your pictures of the First Ladies. Who's your fave?"

"Dolley, of course."

The woman beside Jackie cleared her throat.

"My secretary, Wanda Brown. She's invaluable. Don't know what I'd do without her. She's the person who caught your website when researching dollhouses. Your website is fabulous the way that the houses are depicted and the dolls. Your web maven is very good." Jackie gave a winning smile.

"Thank you," I said. "I'll tell her that." *I'm the web maven. I'll pat my back later, after she leaves.*

"I always hire a bodyguard when I'm traveling to help with baggage. I'm going on a buying spree during this trip."

Calm my pumping heart. Yes! Maybe a dozen or more houses purchased by her highness.

Wanda held out her hand. "Nice to meet you." Her eyes shifted around the room. "Nice store you have."

"Thank you."

Jackie's eyes lingered on the heritage-style White House.

"I see you have Dolley Madison as the First Lady in this house." Jackie tucked her small pouch under her arm before reaching into the house. "May I?" She picked up the six-inch doll and began examining it. "Tell me about the gown. It's gorgeous. I see it's layered with crinolines and even has a pantaloon."

"I sew the clothing with as much authenticity as possible." I smiled. "The dress Mrs. Madison is wearing is representative of what she wore for the inaugural ball. It's made of buff-colored velvet with ropes of pearls and a fashionable turban with Bird of Paradise flowers. She was the first to have an inaugural ball. Leave it to Dolley."

I spoke with confidence. I'd studied the First Ladies in college, read the history books as well as the gossipy ones. I could have entertained Jackie all day with my grasp on White House minutiae, but I wasn't sure if she was an enthusiast like me.

"Very informative." Jackie's eyes lit up as she gave the doll a closer inspection. "I hear you're a descendant of Dolley Madison."

"Yes I am, as a matter-of-fact. How did you know?"

"I'm related to her, also." Jackie grinned.

"How fun! She was amazing."

"I agree."

"The sampler on the wall," I nodded toward it, "is a replica of my grandma's who inherited it from Dolley. Should I say, we presume it had once been Dolley's and embroidered by her." We walked toward the wall-hanging. "It's identical, strawberries down the side and their wedding date in the center."

"Very interesting." Jackie peered closer at it. "May I take a picture?"

"Sure." Before I could say "boo," she'd taken at least five of the sampler and several of the store.

She meandered back to the heritage house where the Madison dolls perched. "It's beautiful." She carefully picked up the President doll, then set the piece back in its original position. "Ever hear of the 'family secret'?" She removed a magnifying glass from her purse and leaned over to peer closely at the interior walls.

"A 'family secret'? No. Never heard of it," I said, startled.

"Are you certain?" Jackie eyed me suspiciously.

"Yes." I nodded. *What is she talking about?*

"Most interesting." She looked me square in the eye.

Is she trying to figure out if I'm telling the truth?

"How long have you known you're a descendant?" I asked.

"Last year. I've done plenty of research into it. There's definitely a family secret," she said. "Back to business." Ms. Newell straightened up. "Are the wall decorations identical to how Dolley decorated?"

"What do you mean?" I asked, raising a brow. "Of course they are. The interior is decorated as shown in the pictures from the White House Historical Association."

"Gorgeous." Wanda leaned closer to Jackie. She held up china from the Madison house.

The bell jingled. The bodyguard entered and stood in front of the door. He crossed his arms. "Problem solved."

"Stone, good." Wanda nodded.

What is he talking about? Problem solved? These people from New York seemed to talk in riddles, or else I was losing it. *This conversation is giving me the jitters.* I glanced out the window and noticed the chauffeur behind the steering wheel. I didn't have any idea of their identities. When Wanda cleared her throat, it jerked me back to attention.

"She's concerned about historical accuracy." Wanda looked me in the eye. "She's interested in all things Dolley, plus Mr. Madison."

"No family rumor or secret heard of, eh?" Jackie stood and dropped the magnifier into her little purse.

She glanced at me once again. "Sure?"

"Positive."

"Is every adornment on the clothing accurately portrayed on both Mr. and Mrs. Madison?" Jackie asked.

"She wants to know if this is exactly what was worn during the inaugural ball?" Wanda clarified.

"Yes. Dolley's dress. Everything on it is accurate as well as his, but his is purchased. Men's clothing are very tough to sew." *What is with the tag-team between the two? It's making me nutsy.*

"I'm interested in a family secret, but if you don't know of one—" Jackie said.

"I don't." I shook my head. *What is with her? What secret?* I had to change the subject to get back in control. "All the dollhouses are made by hand. I have two employees, one who carves the dolls' heads and my showroom assistant who helps arrange the interior settings." *Isn't she going to purchase a few houses?*

Jackie held up President Madison and scrutinized his cufflinks. I blinked. This woman confused me.

"Mr. Madison's cufflinks are missing from the Madison Museum. You know? Montpelier? The Madison Estate. It's part of the secret, my dear." She cocked her brow and stared right through me. "They need finding."

"I don't know what you're talking about," I said, running my fingers through my hair. "I know the du Ponts purchased the estate some years after it was sold by Dolley. I have no knowledge of cufflinks."

"Excuse me," Wanda interrupted. "You have

thirty minutes until your next appointment." Wanda looked at me. There was something in her eyes, but I wasn't sure what. Curiosity? "We're booked at the Twin City Hotel. It makes getting around easy. Only a couple blocks from here."

"May I take Mr. and Mrs. Madison with me today for further scrutiny? I'll place my order on Wednesday and then return them. Day after tomorrow." Jackie opened her little pouch and dropped the dolls inside before I could say, "Boo."

"Wait a second, here. Those dolls cost me. I need a credit card number." I was beginning to think she was a magician, the way she made those dolls disappear.

"We'll pay upon our return."

"When will that be?"

"In a couple of days."

"Let's make an appointment? Ten tomorrow morning?"

"It'll be either tomorrow morning or the following. Matter of fact, let's make it for two days from now at ten o'clock."

"Sure, but I want payment now, not later." Confused, I started to take care of the paper work. "How many houses do you think you'll purchase? I'd like to know so they'll be ready."

"Maybe two historicals. Not sure. I'll pay for the dolls upon my return, I said." To Wanda, she said, "Time to leave."

At the window, I watched Jackie with her purse tucked tight under her arm like a million dollar bank vault. First Jackie, then Wanda climbed into the car.

The bodyguard held the door open, shutting it behind.

What is the deal about cufflinks? Family secret? Nothing makes sense. Is she going to purchase houses or not? Are we really related? What about the dolls? Will I get paid?

I turned around and plunked down by the front desk.